# ANGEL OF DEATH

## ROB JONES

*For the real Tom, full of courage and adventure*

*"Whoever fights monsters should see to it that in the process he does not become a monster. And if you gaze long enough into an abyss, the abyss will gaze back into you."*

**—Friedrich Nietzsche**

# PROLOGUE

*River Avon, Wiltshire, 1997*

The river ran fast and cool on a warm summer evening. When Julia Crawshaw closed her eyes, the world was no more than the sound of bubbling, rushing water and the shrill calling of a kingfisher perched low on a buckthorn branch. She felt the cold flow of the river on her legs and lowered her hand until her fingers traced through the surface. Somewhere in a thick clump of reeds, an egret croaked. It was easy to imagine she was somewhere more exotic.

"Having fun?"

The words pulled her from her dreams. She opened her eyes to see the small group stepping off the bank and wading across the river towards her, orange sun in their hair. She had seen them earlier walking in the fields and hoped they hadn't seen her. Then, they had been laughing, but now their faces grew more serious.

"Waiting for someone?" one of them asked.

"As a matter of fact, yes."

"I can't believe I've never been here before," another of them said dreamily. "It's so beautiful."

The one at the back joined them in the water, tracing a finger through a thin tapestry of duckweeds floating on the surface. "Yes, it is."

"But it's getting late," Julia said, taking a step towards the bank. "And I'm waiting for someone. I'm worried that he isn't here yet."

"He'll be here," another said gently. "He told you to wait for him, remember?"

"How do you know that?" she asked.

"We just do," she said with a shrug. "Lucky we ran into you, really."

The others laughed as the moving water bubbled and frothed against her thighs. "It's just fate."

Fate.

The word that had fallen so easily from her lips echoed in her head for a few moments and made her realise how happy she had been just thinking about him, but now they drew in closer, forming a semi-circle around her. When they raised their arms and touched her, she gasped and tried to step away from them.

"What are you doing?" She shrugged off the arm and took a step back in the water. She felt her calves brush against a tangle of reedmace and willow roots in the muddy bank behind her. "Why have you come here?"

Laughter. "You know why we're here. You've been very naughty."

She frowned, and took another step away from them. "What are you talking about?"

The young man got closer still. "You know what we're talking about, bitch."

She was shocked by the word. In the soft dreamy light of the summer's evening it sounded odd and out of place. "I don't know what you mean."

They were surrounding her even more closely now, and glancing over their shoulders. Checking to see if they were all alone out here on the river.

And they were.

She tried to crane her neck and see if he had come, but there was no sign of him.

The others exchanged a glance. In that moment, she saw their intention. It burned in their eyes like black coals. They wanted to kill her.

Especially him.

"Get away from me."

In one fluid move, the man pushed her backwards in the water while another's ankle hooked her feet out from under her. She crashed through the surface of the river and felt the cold water rush over her eyes and into her ears. She darted her arms out to balance herself and try and push herself back to the surface when she saw the man's face, distorted by the water's eerie refraction.

Muffled laughing up in the world above the water, but she was straining against the force of his hands all over her now, pushing her deeper and keeping her under the surface. The water rushed downstream, colder now against her skin, and she desperately needed more air. She felt the urge to breathe and pushed her feet and hands down into the sediment in an attempt to force her way out of the water, but he was too strong, and his hands were on her head and back holding her down.

As the adrenaline pumped through her system, her eyes bulged with fear as instinct eventually drove her to draw in more air. She found only the numbing water of the river. Gasping with terror as the fresh water rushed into her mouth and down her throat, she coughed and heaved but it flowed inside her without mercy. Deep into her throat and lungs like frozen fingers forcing their way to her heart.

She felt his hands all over her, rougher now as he held her down with all his might.

*My God, he's going to kill me!*

She tried to fight him off, but she was too weak now. His strength was just too much for her. Her clothes were waterlogged and weighing her down. She saw her hands in the silt. Felt the reeds coiling around her ankles like serpents. The water inside her lungs burned like acid as she started sensing a series of intense flashbacks of her life.

Her childhood, playing in the garden with her father.

Teenagers smoking and drinking cider in the park.

Her first day at college.

She felt like she had been under the water for hours, even an eternity, but then the pain subsided and she knew it was over.

She accepted it and ended the struggle.

As her body drifted with the ebb and flow of the ancient river, the egret sang out again, its low hoarse call filling the evening air. Beyond, to the west, the setting sun was caught in the wings of countless blue fritillaries flying above a wildflower meadow and all was still once again.

# CHAPTER 1

*Saturday, 9ᵗʰ March 2019*

The man watched her as she stepped out of her car and headed towards The Crowne Inn in the rainy night. Sitting in his car, he sank down into the seat and studied her as she walked past the parked cars on her way to the warmth of the pub.

Seeing her face after so many years struck him harder than he had expected. She had aged well enough, all things considered, but there was still a coldness about her eyes. He listened to her heels clipping along the tarmac and knew this was his best chance.

He opened his car door and climbed out. The noise startled her and she turned and watched him as he made his way across the car park towards her. The top half of her face was shaded from the car park lights by the black umbrella, but he saw her mouth open slightly as she gasped. Hands behind his back, he moved through the shadows and returned her stare with an emotionless gaze.

She narrowed her eyes, hardly unable to believe what they were telling her. "You!"

"I'm surprised you recognise me," he said, hands still behind his back.

She took a step back, dragging her heel through a puddle forming in front of the door.

"I didn't know you were back," she said hesitantly.

The low, deep roar of music drifted out of the pub, muffled by its old, thick walls.

"No," he said. "I don't suppose you did."

They both heard a loud peel of laughter coming from inside the safety of the warm building. So near and yet so far, he thought, fighting a wave of rage he felt rising from deep inside him. Taking a slow breath, he kept his eyes fixed on her pale, frightened face. "Aren't you going to ask me in for a drink?"

She paled and took another step back. "I don't think that would be a very good idea, do you?"

He shrugged and moved closer to her.

"I'm here to meet friends," she said. "They're expecting me."

The man tried to resist the impulse, but despite his best efforts a grim, devilish smile appeared on his lips. "They'll have to wait."

She narrowed her eyes. "What do you mean?"

He said nothing, looking over her shoulder. He stared at the pub, paying particular attention to see if anyone was at any of the windows.

They weren't, and when he moved next it was like a bolt of lightning. Lunging forward, he pulled his arms out from behind his back and she saw he had a white cloth in one of his hands. She turned to run but he was on her in a heartbeat, smacking the umbrella out of her hand and grabbing her around the throat.

A choked scream flew from her lips like a startled bird but it was quickly silenced by the cloth which he clamped down over her mouth and nose. Gripping her hard around the back of her head with his other arm, she was forced to breathe in through the damp, foul linen. He knew it took much longer to render someone unconscious with chloroform than in the films, so he dragged her back into the shadows of the hedge away from the pub as she struggled and squirmed in his iron grip.

Three or four minutes later she fell limp in his arms.

As he hoisted her up onto his shoulder, he whispered into her ear, *Amor Fati… love your fate.*

With the unconscious woman over his shoulders in a fireman's lift, he stepped out of the lit car park and into the fields beyond. He knew where he was going and he made good time getting there. No more than three minutes after knocking her out he had reached his destination.

He watched a shred of moonlight from a break in the clouds ripple on the surface of the ancient rocks as he walked along the waterlogged ditch. Lingering in the night like some stalking beast waiting for its prey, he felt her move on his shoulder. She was coming around again, slowly at first and moaning like a wounded animal.

"What happened?" she asked.

"You know what happened," he growled.

"Where am I? Where have you brought me?"

"Say goodbye to the world."

On hearing the words, she gasped again and he felt her body tense with fear.

"Oh *God…*" she moaned. "Please!"

When he spoke, it almost sounded like he was sorry. "What happened before must happen again."

He sloped his shoulder so she slid off into the grass and then with his leather-gloved hand gripping her throat, he forced her head back against the wet ground and held her there while he scanned the area to make sure they were alone. Without warning she reached out and clawed at his face, missing him by inches. He slapped her down but she lashed out again with her hands, desperately trying to stall for time as she screamed for help.

He cursed under his breath, dodging her punches as he grabbed hold of her and turned her over, pushing her face down into the muddy, waterlogged ground and stifling her screams. Kicking and flailing her arms, there was nothing she could do to overpower him, and after a storm of mumbled, hoarse screams and brown foamy bubbles, she eventually fell still and silent.

He had purified her. She had finally met her fate.

Releasing his grip, the dead body slumped down on the earth like a paper doll. The moonlight reflected on the back of her neck while he checked the coast was still clear. Grabbing her by the ankles, he hauled her body up out of the ditch and onto the field. He glanced over his shoulder and saw where he needed to take her. As he dragged the dead body across the filthy, muddy field, he looked down at her cold, silent face with contempt.

"Yeah," he growled, low and angry. "I'm back, all right."

# CHAPTER 2

*Sunday, 10<sup>th</sup> March*

J ust after sunrise, Alison Mayfield stepped over the
damp, wooden stile and crouched down in the gloom
to let her dog off the lead. The dog felt the lead unclip
from his collar and was off like a shot, running along his
usual path down the east side of the field. Nose down in
the dewy grass and tail wagging in the air as he went, he
was soon almost out of sight, but he was safe. The road
was well behind them and there were no rivers anywhere
near.

She followed his steps, her boots pushing down into
the muddy ground as she made her way down the field.
She thanked heaven that the rain had finally stopped but
one look at the gunmetal grey sky and she knew the next
wave couldn't be far away. Shivering, she tucked her head
down into her scarf and thrust her hands into her jacket
pockets. Whenever spring finally arrived it wouldn't be a
day too soon.

Tracking her dog for a moment to make sure he was
keeping to his usual routine, she stopped and turned to
face the rising sun. It had momentarily broken through a
slit in the clouds and was just creeping over the tree line
on the far side of the field. The long, pale shadows cast

from the trees and hedges stretched across the grass towards the ancient stones encircling the village.

She had seen them so many times before but they never ceased to amaze her. The sheer age of the things was enough to make her stop and think about the world and her life. Who stood here, all those thousands of years ago and positioned them in this perfect circle? Some morning sunlight flashed on their smooth, flat surfaces, almost dazzling her before the sun was swallowed back up by the clouds.

Looking to her right, she watched the twilight receding along the Kennett Valley, and further along she saw the famous outline of Silbury Hill. The mysterious silhouette was the largest manmade mound in Europe, standing nearly one hundred and thirty feet high and built out of the chalk landscape over four thousand years ago.

She yawned and wished she was at home with her hands wrapped around a warm mug of freshly ground coffee. As she prepared to call George, she saw he had left his routine walk and was running over to the outer concentric ring of stones.

She stepped forward and raised her voice. "Get away from there!"

The old dog ignored her.

She swore under her breath and put her head against the wind as she walked to go and get him, but when she drew nearer she saw something that made her pull up short and gasp.

Legs.

Instinctively, she widened her eyes and craned her neck forward for a better view. She was definitely looking at a pair of legs. Judging by the shoes she guessed it was a woman, but the clothes looked soaking wet. Surely whoever it was hadn't slept out here all night in weather like this?

Closer now, and George was running his nose all over what she now realised in full horror was the dead body of a middle-aged woman. Cold, white flesh and glassy, dead eyes that must once have been the colour of Burmese sapphires stared through her and filled her with terror. She staggered back, barely able to summon the strength to call George away. The idea of him sniffing the corpse disgusted her and she raised a trembling hand to her mouth to stop herself throwing up.

The woman had been dead for several hours – she was sure of that – and her body was laid out at the base of the ancient stone. Her face was divided by long black streaks of lank, wet hair but there was no sign of any blood. When she saw the bruises on her neck, she felt another wave of nausea rise deep inside her.

Grabbing George's collar, she pulled him roughly away from the body and secured him to the lead before turning and making her way back to the car. Her mind raced with what she had just seen and what she had to do about it. This, she told herself, was the sort of thing that only happened to other people.

But now it had happened to her.

*

Detective Chief Inspector Tom Jacob took a sip of his first coffee of the day and leaned closer to his laptop screen, tweaking the volume control to raise Sophie's voice a few notches. She smiled into the camera before taking a sip of coffee herself and leaning her elbows on the desk either side of her own laptop. The window behind her was streaked with rain and that meant Salisbury was suffering much the same weather as he was further north in the county.

"Looking forward to the conference?" he asked.

She gave a reluctant nod. "Yes, but I'd rather spend the week with you."

He knew how she felt. Over the last few weeks they had spent more time together, enjoying each other's company and both feeling a little bit like teenagers all over again. When she'd told him she was going away to Exeter for a week-long criminal psychology conference he was surprised by how it had made him feel.

"Good chance to network though, right?"

"I suppose. Theo's going to be there, and Kit Bailey, too."

He gave a mock gasp. "Not *the* Kit Bailey?"

"Sod off, Jacob," she said, hiding her smile behind the coffee cup. "As a matter of fact, yes, *the* Kit Bailey, and he usually attracts a good crowd when he gives lectures." She paused a beat as she sipped her drink. "What about you? Any more fallout from my involvement in Grovely?"

The corner of his mouth turned up into a smirk. She was referring to Operation Grovely, the now famous murder case he had solved between last Christmas and New Year's Eve. "The Chief Constable let me off with a verbal warning," he said. "But only if I promised to be a good boy."

"Be serious."

"Fine. It was a long internal enquiry, as you know, and I just found out yesterday. I'm all good. I suppose you're the first to know."

"I'm sure Marcus Kent was the first to know," she said with a grin. "How's he taking it?"

Jacob shrugged. "I don't know and I don't care... but I'm sure it's with the utmost professionalism."

She laughed. "He can't be all that bad."

"So they say."

Jacob had more coffee and realised again just how relaxed he was whenever he talked to her. He didn't know how she did it and he quietly hoped it was some psychological device she was deploying to disarm him. Whatever it was, he didn't mind it one little bit. The past few weeks had been some of the best times he'd had since the fire which had burned his house down and killed his fiancée. And yet he was still reluctant to get any closer.

And he knew why.

When Jess was snatched from him that night, he vowed he would never get close to anyone else for as long as he lived. It was impulsive and rash but he'd meant it. But that was then and this was now and things were changing. Sophie had reached down into the darkness and offered him a hand. The only thing that stopped him taking hold of it was the terrible fear that something just as terrible might one day happen to her.

When his phone rang he was startled from his thoughts. He sighed and looked down at the screen.

When she saw his face, she feared the worst. "What is it?"

"It's the station," he said flatly. "They need me at work right now."

"Did they say why?"

He scratched the side of his head, finished reading the message and slipped his phone back into his pocket.

"Someone's found a body."

\*

Detective Sergeant Anna Mazurek pulled off Beckhampton Road and into Avebury. Turning off her music, she parked up on the side of the road between a marked police car and the CSI van. She stared up into a dark grey sky and mumbled a curse, grabbing the folding umbrella in the glove box before emerging into the cold, rainy day. Opening her umbrella and locking her car, she now saw Jacob's vintage powder-blue convertible Alvis parked up at the head of the line. First here, she thought.

She walked along the road and approached the small wooden gate which led onto the field containing the world-famous sarsen standing stones. Uniformed constables had already sealed the crime scene off from any passers-by with police barrier tape, and as she opened the five-bar gate and turned into the site, she saw a blue and white forensics tent out on the eastern edge of the ancient stones. Taking a deep breath, she walked across the muddy field in silence and gave the SIO a casual wave, which he ignored.

As she drew closer, she saw the stones up close for the first time. She had grown up in the county but had never visited the site before. Less than a mile north of Silbury Hill, Avebury stone circle was one of the most important pre-historic sites in Europe, dating back nearly five thousand years. Situated on chalkland in the Upper Kennet Valley, the Neolithic henge consisted of three stone circles running around the village of Avebury, including the largest megalithic stone circle anywhere on earth.

"And they'll still be here in five thousand years' time, too," she muttered to herself. "When we're all long gone."

Wind and rain blasted across the field as she made her way over to Jacob. He was standing beside the CSI tent inside the eastern edge of the outer circle of stones and frowning deeply. He was wearing his usual black peacoat and dark trousers but disposable forensic covers were slipped over the top of his leather Oxford shoes.

"Morning, guv."

He turned and nodded. "Anna."

"How long have you been here?"

"Not long. Arrived a few minutes ago." He handed her a pair of the disposable shoes. "Put these on."

She slipped them over the top of her shoes. "Still, you made good time, boss. Considering what you're driving."

"You may mock now, but when she's done up you'll beg for a ride with the top down."

"How little you know me. Anything from CSI yet?"

He shook his head. "Come on. Let's get started."

She followed him inside the tent and saw Mia Francis and two other CSI officers forming a circle around the body of a dead woman, each of them busy at work.

Mia raised an eyebrow as she glanced at her watch and gave her a polite smile. "Good morning, Sergeant. How nice of you to join us."

"I'm with you on the morning part," Anna said, glancing down at the body. "But can we leave the good part out?"

The dead woman was sprawled on the wet grass in the lee of one of the largest sarsens on the site. Her head was to the west, pointing to the road. Mia handed each of them a pair of blue forensic gloves.

Anna shuddered. "She looks like she's sleeping."

"She's not," Mia said bluntly. "Sorry about that."

"What's the story, Mia?" Jacob asked.

"She fought like a tiger to stay alive but cause of death is tricky. The bruises indicate strangulation, but the mud around her mouth might point to drowning."

Anna and Jacob exchanged a glance.

"What makes you say that?" Anna asked. "I can see the neck bruises and mud, but how do you know she fought so hard?"

"I divined it from tea leaves on my break. Oh, that's right – I haven't had a break yet."

Anna said nothing but stared at her.

Mia blinked first. "First, she has several broken nails and second she has mud and grass in her mouth from where he must have forced her to the ground, either to stop her escaping or to stifle her screams. Third, if you walk those very precious shoes of yours a short way down into the ditch over there you'll find clear evidence of a struggle, and then more evidence that a body was dragged from that location, over the bank and into this field, although the traces *do* run out and get lost in the grass after a few yards. She could have been killed either in the ditch or up here. Hard to say at the moment."

Jacob suppressed a smile. "Thank you, Mia. That was very comprehensive."

Anna gave her a sarcastic smile. "So if she was drowned in the ditch, why drag her all the way up here?"

"I've got an even better question than that," Mia said, holding up a crude wooden crucifix with some letters carved onto its horizontal board. "What the hell is this, and why was it stuffed in her hand?"

When he stared at the strange object, Jacob felt his heart quicken. His copper's nose smelt trouble and he didn't like it one bit. "Let me see that, please."

He took the cross and turned it in his hand. Staring at the letters he saw they had been cut into the wood with a sharp blade, probably a Stanley knife.

"Boss?"

He handed it to Anna and she slowly read the words. "Angelus mortis venturus est. What does that mean?"

Jacob sighed. "The Angel of Death is coming." He frowned and narrowed his eyes as he stared once again at the cross. "So what the hell is it doing in her hand?"

Mia pursed her lips and put her hands on her hips. "It's got to be a statement."

"A statement of what?" Anna asked.

Jacob fixed his eyes on her. "Hopefully not on future intent."

"You can say that again," Mia said. "You do realise the sarsen she was dumped under is called the Devil's Chair?"

Jacob and Anna shared another glance. "I did not realise that," he said.

"Just throwing that in there," Mia said. "Between that and the cross something tells me this isn't your average murder. Anyway, we'll know much more when Richard's post-mortem report is in."

"Ah yes, Dr Lyon," Jacob said. "And how is our new Home Office pathologist fitting in?"

"Very well, by all accounts," Mia said. "He hasn't murdered anyone yet so that's an improvement on the last hire, wouldn't you say?"

Jacob gave her a look and put his hand in his pockets. "Thank you, Mia. Any ID on her?"

"A damaged phone waterlogged by the night's rainfall. That will have to go to the computer forensics people but also a wallet, so I'm guessing robbery is not a motive."

"I guessed that when I saw the cross," Jacob said. "I'm presuming there was ID in the wallet?"

Mia nodded. "Photo ID of a driving licence that matches the dead woman's face and some credit cards. The deceased is a Dr Sarah Bennett, thirty-nine years old. Married, no kids. Address is in Marlborough."

"Medical doctor?"

"No way of telling from a driver's licence."

"No, of course." Jacob clenched his jaw and looked down at the corpse. "Who found her?"

"A Mrs Mayfield. She's given all her details to PC Cook. If you want to see her, she's with him now but she's in a hell of a state."

He shook his head. "Not now. We have her statement and details so we'll wait till she's got over the shock." He looked back down at the body. "Time of death?"

"I'd say she's been dead around ten to twelve hours, putting the time of death between nine o'clock to eleven o'clock last night."

"Can you be more specific?"

"Only about your dress sense, Jacob. That tie is terrible."

"Thanks," he said, his mind wandering. "I need some air."

Jacob and Anna left the CSI tent and stepped out into the field. A cold breeze whipped across the valley and scratched at their faces.

"How the hell did she get up here?" Anna asked.

Jacob took off his forensic gloves and turned in a circle, scanning the entire area from the Devil's Chair. He saw the signs of a struggle Mia had described, down in the ditch to the south of the outer circle, and further along the ditch to the west, beyond a little dovecot was the sleepy village of Avebury. Smoke drifted out of chimneys and somewhere he heard a dog barking. On the road leaving the village to the south he followed another column of smoke twirling out of the red brick chimney of an old pub, one of two he could see from the circle.

"Mia said somewhere between nine and eleven last night, right?"

Anna nodded. "That's right."

"Not much going on in a village of this size at that time of night…"

"Except the pubs?"

"Right."

"Want to talk to them now?"

"Not yet. Next of kin first." He looked at his watch. "And I'd better brief Kent first."

"I know how much you must be looking forward to that."

The heavens opened as they walked across the site away from the busy crime scene. No umbrella but with his collar up, Jacob broke away from Anna and headed for the shelter of his car. He watched Anna pull away and head back to HQ and then fired up the vintage car. Taking one more glance at the CSI tent beside the wind-swept sarsen, he revved the engine and pulled out into the road.

"All right," he muttered. "Let's play cat and mouse again."

# CHAPTER 3

Avoiding their boss, whose booming voice they had heard in a nearby office, Jacob and Anna made their way stealthily through the Devizes HQ of Wiltshire CID to their office on the west side of the building. The sound of hard work drifted through the open door as they continued along the corridor, passing a number of open-plan workspaces. Phones rang, computers bleeped and photocopiers hummed. She made it to safety first, but it was too late for him.

"Not so fast, Jacob!"

He cursed quietly under his breath and turned to be greeted by the square, tanned face of Marcus Kent. "I want a word with you, now."

Anna looked over her shoulder and caught Jacob's eye before silently mouthing *good luck* to him.

He sighed and followed Kent back down the corridor to his office.

"Close the door, please."

As Jacob clicked the door shut, Kent relaxed into his leather swivel chair and fixed his dark brown eyes on him. He had risen to the rank of Detective Chief Superintendent with dazzling efficiency and speed but mostly on the back of extensive networking and highly developed political skills. And yet he was an astute judge of character and had demonstrated bravery in the face of danger as a young uniformed policeman, above and beyond the call of duty. Knowing where you stood with him was a problem many at the station had, not least Jacob.

"I trust you were going to brief me about this body found up Avebury?"

"You've already heard, sir?"

Kent's jaw flexed. "Of course I've already heard. If a junior admin assistant down in the archives breaks wind, I know about it before he does."

Jacob squashed his sigh. It was shaping up to be one of those days. "Yes sir."

Kent leaned forward, cocking his head slightly. "Well?"

"We had a call earlier this morning relating to the discovery of a dead body up at the Avebury stone circle. I drove there straight from home and by the time I arrived Mia Francis and some of her CSI team had already arrived and set up a forensics tent. Shortly after my arrival, DS Mazurek arrived and we began a preliminary examination of the site."

"Victim's details?"

"Dr Sarah Bennett, identified by her driver's licence. DC Holloway is looking into her background as we speak but we don't know much more at this stage."

Kent drew in a long, weary breath before raising his chin stoically. "It's up to us to catch whoever did this, Jacob. And when I say us, I mean you."

"Yes, sir. I'm speaking with the pathologist later today and then I'll brief the team."

Kent nodded. "And I presume you've not hired any private investigators, doctors, anthropologists or archaeologists behind my back to help this time like you did in Operation Grovely?"

"No, sir."

It was clear Kent was referring to Sophie Anderson, the criminal psychologist Jacob had asked to help on the now-notorious Witch-Hunt Murders back in December last year. The Chief Superintendent had specifically ordered him not to bring her into the case and was enraged when he found out about Jacob deliberately disobeying him and doing precisely that. He had worked hard to have him sacked and when that failed he tried to have him demoted to detective constable, but the Chief Constable had been highly impressed with the way Jacob had resolved the case. He had let him off with a formal written warning, much to Kent's enduring disappointment.

"That's something, at least," Kent said. "With luck you'll get this cleared up before it gets out of hand and then we can get…" he paused, noting the expression on Jacob's face. "What?"

"I'm not sure this is going to be a straight-forward case, sir."

Kent snorted and shook his head. "Seems since you turned up there's no such thing as a straight-forward murder anymore. What makes you say this?"

"We think the killer left an object on the body after the murder."

Kent's eyes widened. Leaving an object behind with the victim of a murder could mean personation, or a signature. This could take the form of an object left behind, posing the corpse in a particular way or mutilating it and both men now knew this was more likely to be the work of a serial killer. With a heavy heart, he lowered his voice to a respectful, concerned tone. "What object?"

"A wooden crucifix, and a homemade one at that. It was stuffed into her hand and he'd wrapped her fingers around it."

"Maybe it was hers?"

"No."

"Why not?"

Jacob paused, watching his boss's hope fade away. "It had a sentence carved into it in Latin."

He sighed. "Oh, God."

"It said, the Angel of Death is Coming."

Kent winced. "The last thing we want is more people being murdered in some arcane ritual by another bloody lunatic. We had more than enough of that during Operation Grovely."

"But there could be any number of explanations for it, sir," Jacob said, trying to calm his boss. "We're too early in the investigation to draw any solid deductions yet."

Kent ruffled some papers on his desk and stuffed them into his in-tray. "Who is the next of kin?"

"Husband is a man named Matthew Bennett. Works as a magistrate in the Reading area. They have no kids and her parents retired to Bournemouth from Calne years ago."

Kent fell silent as he ran some unspoken thought through his mind. "Nasty stuff. Spoken to anyone in the village?"

Jacob shook his head. "Not until the next of kin's been informed."

"Quite right, quite right." Kent sucked his teeth. "Who found the body?"

"A Mrs Alison Mayfield. She gave an initial statement to PC Cook and spoke with DC Innes on the telephone a few moments ago. Found the body while walking her dog. We're satisfied there's no funny business in that direction."

"Good." A long pause. "This isn't the work of an opportunist, is it?"

"Too early to tell, sir, but because of the calling card my instinct is no."

"Christ almighty, Jacob." Kent's eyes grew sharp with concern. "We'd better hope this is some sort of personal vendetta and this is the end of it. We really do not need another nutcase killing people left, right and centre after all we went through back at Christmas. The press have only just left us alone."

"Yes, sir."

A long silence. "You think the Avebury site is important?" he asked nervously.

Jacob knew what he was getting at, and he too had speculated if they were dealing with another killer who was choosing sacred sites for his murders, but he wasn't convinced. "I think the crucifix is of more significance, sir. It also looks like the victim might have been laid out east to west deliberately because of the odd angle she was left at in front of the Devil's Chair. Old Christian burials were usually laid out that way."

He considered Jacob's words. "The Devil's Chair?"

"It's the name of the sarsen where the killer dumped the body, sir. Clearly she was meant to be discovered, as was the cross, but whether it's a message to us or to someone else out there, we don't know."

"Yet."

"Yet, sir. It's not a busy place. Nowhere near as popular with tourists as Stonehenge, but it's certainly not the sort of place you would leave a body if you were trying to hide the crime. To me, the whole thing is obviously a statement, and that means we're dealing with a dangerous and calculating individual."

Kent drummed his fingers on the desk. "One prepared to take big risks."

Jacob nodded but said nothing.

"What's your plan?"

Sensing the end of the meeting, Jacob uncrossed his long legs. "We've a meeting with the pathologist and then a drive over to the husband."

"I don't envy you that."

"No."

Kent looked at his watch. "When is the PM due?"

"He's working on the post-mortem as we speak, sir."

"Fast work. I'm impressed."

"Richard and I go back a long way, sir. I asked him to prioritise this one because I didn't like what I saw up at Avebury and I think we're in for some trouble. He says two hours, three at the most and he started work half an hour ago."

"Good." Kent was thinking again. "Listen, after what happened with the bloody witches up in the woods, I want things kept under much tighter control this time, understood?"

"Yes, sir."

"And don't think I haven't still got my eye on you, either. You can thank the CC for the leniency of your punishment following your disgraceful behaviour during Grovely. If it was up to me I'd have thrown you out of the force."

"Thank you, sir."

Kent's jaw clenched. "And this time, I'll be watching you like a hawk. One screw up, one indiscretion, just one foot out of place and you're gone – got it?"

Jacob nodded. "I've got it, sir. Loud and clear."

"The Chief Constable never tires of regaling me with your skills, Jacob." He leaned forward and gave a dry, crocodile smile full of teeth. "Looks like now's the time to shine."

"Thank you, sir. I'll do my best."

\*

After any amount of time spent with Marcus Kent, Jacob always felt the urge to go to the pub and sink a few of his favourite beers. Instead, he went back to his office and spent a couple of hours preparing how he wanted to organise the case, and allocating various jobs to different members of his team.

Looking at the clock when he had finished, he decided to forgo the beer and grab a cup of coffee from the canteen instead. When he arrived he saw Anna paying for a large cooked all-day breakfast. He joined her at the till and for a moment, he wavered. Scrambled eggs, smoked bacon, grilled tomatoes and crunchy toast — it all looked so good.

After a few seconds of deliberation, he settled for the coffee and the two of them walked over to a free table by a rain-lashed window in the corner of the large room.

Anna picked up her cutlery and frowned at the expression on her boss's face. "Why are you staring at my food like that?"

Startled, he looked away and sipped at his coffee. "Like what?"

"Like a madman who hasn't eaten for a month."

He winced. "Is it that obvious?"

She nodded, and mercilessly ate a forkful of the delicious food. "Uh-huh."

"What?"

A sly grin spread on her face. "You're not on a sodding diet are you?"

Jacob was a tall man, and fit. He had looked after himself but there was always room for improvement. "Do I look like I need a diet? No gut down here."

She leaned around the edge of the table and checked out his stomach. "True, but it's not exactly washboard material, is it?"

He opened his mouth to speak, but before he found the words, she spoke again.

"Oh my *god*." She lowered her voice. "This wouldn't be about a certain criminal psychologist by any chance, would it?"

He found himself looking around the canteen to see who else had heard what she just said. Lacing his fingers together he lifted his elbows to the table and rested his chin smugly on his hands. "Whatever are you talking about, Sergeant Mazurek?"

Another smirk. "I knew it."

He lifted his cup and took a drink. "I'm just trying to keep myself in shape for…"

"For a man of your advancing years?"

He cocked his head and gave her a wry smile. "I'm not that much older than you, so less of the cheek. I was going to say, keep myself in shape for the job."

She laughed, and raised a hand to her mouth. "Right."
"What?"

"Pull the other one, guv."

He knew the game was up. Hiding behind his coffee cup for a few moments, he set it down and blew out a short breath of surrender. "All right, but she's a bit younger than me and to say she keeps herself fit is an understatement, don't you think?"

Before she answered, a uniformed constable put his head around the door and scanned the room until he heard Anna's cheerful laugh and saw them sitting in the corner. Walking over, he lingered at the side of their table for a moment before speaking.

"What is it, Smith?" Jacob asked.

"Message from the desk sergeant, sir."

"Don't tell me," Anna said with a sigh. "He wants my breakfast, too?"

Smith looked confused. "Er, no Sarge."

"Then what is it?" she asked, enjoying watching Jacob hiding his smile.

"The pathologist has been on the phone. Apparently he's finished the post-mortem on the body found this morning in Avebury."

Jacob raised his eyebrows. "When I said I wanted it prioritised, I didn't expect it this fast."

Anna finished the last piece of toast and set her knife and fork down on the plate. "New guy's quick off the mark, I'll give him that."

"And he's the best in the business," Jacob said. "Trust me."

"That good, eh? Sounds perfect."

Jacob hesitated. "Nobody's perfect, Anna."

"What does that mean?"

The tall detective smiled as he got up and pulled his jacket from the back of the chair. "You'll find out."

# CHAPTER 4

J acob waited for Anna to finish her customary pre-post-mortem cigarette outside the Great Western Hospital in Swindon before their meeting with the new Home Office pathologist. To everyone's shock, the previous man had turned out to be the ringleader in an archaic druid cult and the killer of multiple victims around the county. Operation Grovely was brought to a sudden close when an armed response team shot him dead at Stonehenge, but it had left the team apprehensive and wary.

Jacob knew the new man from his Oxford days, but now, sheltering in an area specially reserved for smokers, he watched the rain tumbling out of the sky and wondered exactly what his sergeant was going to make of him.

"What's he like then?" Anna asked.

Jacob's face turned into a frown. "Well, it's hard to say. He's not a psychopathic killer with a druid fixation, if that's what you're worried about."

"It's not," she said with a roll of her eyes. "But that's an improvement on the last one."

She crushed the cigarette butt out on the bin and flicked it inside, blowing the last cloud of smoke out through her lips into the damp air. "Shall we?"

"I thought you'd never ask."

They followed a series of sterile corridors through the enormous hospital, neither in much of a mood to say anything to the other. They had both seen more than their fair share of corpses on autopsy gurneys over the years, and many in a damn-sight worse condition than this one, but each time was the same gut-wrenching experience.

"It's just up here." Jacob turned to her. "OK?"

She gave a shallow nod of her head, hand still playing with her lighter. He knew her well enough to know this was what she always did when she was anxious. "Let's just get it over with. Then I can get outside and have another fag."

"If I smoked, I'd join you."

Turning into another corridor, they took a few short flights of stairs down to the next level and approached a set of metal double doors, each with its own small circular window at head-height. Jacob leaned forward, pushed one of them open and gave her a sympathetic smile. "Here we go again."

When they stepped inside the mortuary, they found Dr Richard Lyon hovering over a stainless steel gurney beneath a glaring white light. A short, round man with receding silver hair shaved down to his scalp, Richard was a friendly face in a horrible place, especially after the Spargo killings of Operation Grovely. Jacob watched as he moved around the well-lit room, reminding him a little of a slow-motion bumble bee as he made his way from gurney to shelf and back again with a classical tune on the radio behind him.

Seeing them, the pathologist turned and presented them with an honest, broad smile.

"Ah, DCI Jacob."

"Richard."

"And you must be DS Mazurek?"

"Anna."

"Anna it is."

Richard gave her a warm smile and waved a bloody nitrile glove cheerily in the air. "I won't shake hands."

"No," she said. "I think that's for the best. Jacob tells me you two go way back?"

Richard nodded. "We know each other from Oxford when we worked for Thames Valley Police. We've chatted over many a corpse, wouldn't you say, Jacob?"

"I wouldn't put it quite like that, but yes, we go back a few years."

Richard laughed. "It's good to see you again. It must have been at least a year! How's tricks?"

"So, so. You?"

He huffed. "This time last week I was at La Scala listening to a wonderful production of *La Forza del Destino*," he said with a sad sigh. "Now I'm up to my arse in blood and guts and drowned corpses and I don't really think that's very fair."

"No, Richard."

"When I retire, I might move to Italy, you know."

"You've been saying that since the first day I met you."

Richard stopped in his tracks, a bloody scalpel in his hand and a freshly furrowed brow. "Have I really?"

Jacob nodded. "True story."

"Hmm," Richard said. "Sorry to hear about my predecessor, by the way."

Jacob and Anna exchanged a look. "Thanks."

"Fancy the killer being under your nose the whole time and you not catching him."

"Thanks again." Jacob gave him a look. "And thanks for getting the PM processed so fast."

He shrugged. "Speedy autopsies are all the rage these days, or minimally invasive targeted coronary angiography as some might put it."

"Some, but not you," Jacob said with a smile.

"Not I, sir. Not I. Still, whatever you call them it comes down to the same thing. A simple injection of contrast into the deceased via a minor incision in the neck and then a full CT scan. We can usually deduce the cause of death in eight out of ten cases."

"How does that work, exactly?" Anna asked.

Richard's eyebrows lifted an inch. "I knew you were a woman of taste and intelligence the moment I saw you."

"You never told me your old friend was such a charmer, Jacob."

Jacob rolled his eyes. "I must have forgotten."

Richard tutted and winked at Anna. "The answer to your question is simple. Using this method we're able to utilise two types of contrast along with catheterisation and special imaging to highlight the deceased's heart vessels and from that we can extrapolate the cause of death. And that's the basic outline of a minimally invasive targeted coronary angiography."

"I think you mean a speedy autopsy?" Anna said.

"I like her, Jacob. I like her a lot. More than I like you, in fact."

Ignoring him, Jacob looked down at the body. "But you've done more than a contrast scan?"

He nodded. "Yes, in this case I used a computer-guided coaxial cutting needle biopsy to take a sample of various internal tissues to analyse bacterioplankton PCR."

"PCR?" Jacob asked.

"Polymerase chain reaction. The regular method for diagnosing drowning is a standard diatom test but this can sometimes give us false-negative results depending on the quantity of diatom cells in certain water. For this reason I used the PCR method to be on the safe side."

Anna looked at Jacob. "Is he still talking in English?"

Jacob smiled. "I'm none the wiser, either. Let's start from the beginning."

Richard smiled. "A sound idea. This woman had been dead between eight to ten hours before her discovery, putting the time of her death somewhere around eleven pm last night. The tests I have run confirmed that she was drowned, most likely by being held down in shallow, muddy water."

"Which was our speculation."

"Yes, and it gets more interesting. As you know, resources constraints usually mean a toxicology report can take days, but being the charming and persuasive chap I am, I managed to get it fast-tracked and the results are clear – there's evidence of chloroform inhalation."

"Chloroform?" Anna asked.

"It's an organic compound, a liquid."

"I know what it is, Richard," she said.

"Of course," he mumbled. "Sorry. Anyway, as you'll therefore know, it's a very powerful anaesthetic whether ingested or inhaled. In this case, we found traces of it in the lungs, so it was inhaled, through mainly the nose. I would say it probably rendered her at least partially unconscious in less than five minutes."

"And she'd have been struggling throughout those minutes," Jacob said.

Anna twisted her mouth. "So it was administered somewhere out of the way."

"How long would she have been unconscious?" asked Jacob.

"Depends on the quantity. Going by what I found here, I would say no longer than ten minutes.

"Anything else?" Jacob asked.

Richard leaned over the body and pointed a pair of metal callipers at the back of her neck. "You can see here clear evidence of substantial bruising on the neck and also slightly less so on the throat. In my view she was gripped by the neck and held under water from behind. It was an extremely violent death."

Jacob imagined the scene Richard had just described and sighed. "Any prints?"

"No," he said shortly. "Our killer was wearing gloves when he drowned her and the atelectasis, or alveolar collapse indicates freshwater drowning, which again confirms your theory about the waterlogged ditch. I can be sure of this because fresh water is hypotonic, which means it has a lower concentration of various solutes in it than seawater. This means that it is quickly absorbed into the victim's blood plasma causing a rapid dilution of electrolytes and ultimately hypervolaemia."

"Hyper what?" Anna asked.

"It means the blood has too much fluid in it. Because seawater is hypertonic its effect on the plasma is different, ultimately inducing hypovolaemia."

Jacob said, "Too little fluid in the blood?"

"You should have been a doctor, old friend."

Jacob looked down at the dead body and winced. "No, I think we'll keep things as they are, Richard."

"If you say so," he boomed. "Bottom line is this means she was drugged with chloroform and then died by violent drowning in a muddy, freshwater puddle. The traces of mud we found inside her match those in the ditch. So I can say she was killed at the site, but she might have been drugged with the chloroform anywhere."

"Not anywhere," Anna said, turning to Richard. "You said she was knocked out for ten minutes."

"Yes."

Jacob shook his head. "No, she might have been knocked out, dumped in the boot of a car or in the back of a van and then dragged out on the site conscious and murdered."

The three of them fell silent. Jacob snapped his notebook shut. "OK, thanks Richard."

"You're more than welcome," he said.

Jacob turned to Anna. "Looks like we've got a lot to do, starting with talking to the next of kin."

\*

Back in the headquarters building, Detective Constable Laura Innes glanced at her watch and swore under her breath. She had been on the exercise bike for thirty minutes now and her pace was slowing faster than usual. As the newest member of Jacob's team she wanted to do everything she could not only to fit in but to be the best, and that meant keeping up her fitness levels.

She turned off her iPod and stopped cycling. Heart beating hard in her chest, she climbed off the bike and grabbed a towel, dabbing the sweat from her forehead as she slowly made her way over to the showers. She'd been called into work because of the Avebury murder, but it was a Sunday morning and she was the only one in the station's fitness suite.

She turned on the shower and steam billowed up into the room as she took off her exercise clothes and wrapped a large bath towel around her naked body. She exercised most mornings but today the call to respond had come so early she had still been in bed when she took it. Arriving at work, she'd taken a few moments out while the boss was over in Swindon for the post-mortem briefing. She knew when he got back, it would be all hands to the pumps.

Stepping inside the shower now, she tried to relax but her mind was buzzing with work. A young woman had been murdered and dumped out in the open for all to see, and it was her job to find out who had done it, and why. What sort of mind would think of doing such a thing? What sort of person was capable of killing so violently? There were rumours that the killer had left a signature, and they all knew what that meant.

She closed her eyes and rinsed the shampoo out of her hair. She felt it running down her face and neck and the warm water felt good on her body. For a moment, she felt the tension melt away from her shoulders and could almost imagine herself somewhere other than work. At home maybe, in her Marlborough flat. No, that was no good. That fantasy brought with it images of Vincent Goddard, her with-luck-soon-to-be-ex boyfriend. No, she had to go further away. Perhaps she was in the marble wet room of a ski lodge in Verbier, or maybe she was standing in a beach shower on Koh Samui.

*Clunk.*

A noise out in the changing rooms.

It was silly, she knew, but suddenly she felt vulnerable. She was standing in the fitness suite of Wiltshire Police's HQ, probably the safest place in the county, and yet she felt strangely at risk, and she knew why. All she had to do was think about the dead woman found at the stone circle and she had her answer. She spent her working life surrounded by threats, violence, burglaries, stabbings, frauds, assaults and even murders. Sometimes she had to work hard to shake her fear off and keep some perspective. Easy enough, some said, but keeping your humanity and empathy at the same time, and not becoming too cynical, was a much harder task.

She turned off the shower and stepped out. Drying herself off, she checked the time on her phone and realised Jacob would be back before too long. She got dressed, picked up her things and headed for the door. Humming a tune to herself, she stepped out of the changing rooms and gasped when she turned the corner.

Marcus Kent was standing in the doorway. He was wearing a tracksuit and had a towel casually draped over his shoulder.

"Sir!"

"Ah, another fitness freak."

She took a step back from the towering presence. "Important to keep fit, sir."

He gave an absent-minded nod and walked past her towards the gym. "How are you fitting in with your new team?"

"Very well, I think."

"You got a good result with the Grovely murders. Well done."

"Thanks, sir."

"I read the report with interest. You went above and beyond the call of duty when you were lost in that blizzard."

"I was just doing my job."

He twisted his lips as if tasting her words. "I'm sure it was more than that. I always had a lot of faith in you from the moment you joined the CID. I think you'll go far."

"Thank you, sir." She knew Kent was a creep but it was still good to hear praise from such a senior officer.

Out of nowhere, he said, "I was thinking about our little arrangement."

*I wasn't aware we had an arrangement*, she thought.

He cleared his throat and leaned in a little closer towards her. She smelt his expensive aftershave wash over her. "I mean, concerning DCI Jacob."

She felt the blood rush to her cheeks. A few weeks ago, during the Witch-Hunt murders, he had approached her and asked her to spy on Jacob for him, to report any wrong-doing, however small and insignificant. She didn't know exactly why, but he wanted the DCI out of the station. He had told her in no uncertain terms her compliance would mean a smoother journey up through the ranks, and heaven knows Jacob had bent enough rules to give Kent plenty of ammunition to get rid of him.

And yet she had seen another side of Jacob while working with him on the case. He had been kind, and funny and taken time out to help her whenever she needed it. More importantly, she had found out from another officer that he had suffered a terrible tragedy when his fiancée had burnt to death in a house fire a little over a year ago. Word around the station was he had been diagnosed with post-traumatic stress disorder.

From what she had seen during the case, he had handled himself with confidence and skill and brought the investigation to a successful conclusion. Not only that, his diligence and determination had ensured they were able to hand solid evidence to the CPS in the case against the surviving members of Ethan Spargo's Sacred Grove, including the former police inspector Miranda Dunn. Nothing she had seen suggested to her that he was on the verge of a nervous breakdown.

"I don't have anything to report, sir."

"No?"

"Only what you already know – the hiring of Dr Anderson."

"Ah, yes. That woman."

*That woman* referred to Dr Sophie Anderson, a civilian criminal psychologist Jacob had brought into the case against Kent's express orders. It had been impossible to hide her role in the case, and everyone at the station knew Jacob had been reprimanded for bringing her in. But it was obvious he had no idea of the other maverick shortcuts he had taken during Operation Grovely, including stealing police property and handing it over to Sophie and ordering an illegal search of private property without a properly obtained warrant.

"I trust that was his only infraction?"

"Yes, sir," she said.

He nodded pensively. "You wouldn't lie to me, would you DC Innes?"

"Of course not, sir."

"Good, good. As I say, if you want to get on around here you need to know which wheel to oil, and that's me, not Jacob."

"Yes, sir."

She watched him walk across the gym on his way to one of the treadmills. "You're my eyes and ears, Laura. Don't let me down."

"No, sir."

She sighed as she picked up her bag and left the gym. Talk about being caught between the devil and the deep blue sea.

# CHAPTER 5

As Jacob watched Matthew Bennett react to the news of his wife's death, he was reminded with devastating clarity no matter how many times he did this, it never got any easier. Sitting on the end of a tasteful fabric corner sofa in the front room of his Marlborough home, the well-built man's eyes hollowed as he took in the crushing words.

"We had a massive row last night," he said, searching the hardwood floorboards for some kind of sanctuary, some kind of solace. As his eyes filled with tears, he fought hard to keep them from flowing down his cheeks, even now desperately trying to retain his dignity. Now, raising those red eyes to the detectives sitting opposite him, he said, "The last thing I ever told her to do was drop dead."

Jacob caught Anna's eye and knew she was thinking the same as he was.

"I'm so sorry, Mr Bennett," Jacob said quietly, knowing the scarce value of any words he could utter at a time like this. "I understand how hard this must be for you."

On the arm of the sofa was a packet of French cigarettes, and now the broken man tapped his fingers on its smooth cardboard surface as he stared into the middle distance somewhere over Jacob's shoulder. He gave a bitter laugh and pulled a cigarette out of the packet. "Do you really? I've just been told my wife is dead."

Anna glanced at her boss but looked away as she fumbled for her notebook and a pen.

"As matter of fact I do understand," Jacob said gently. "I understand only too well."

"I'm sorry," Matthew said. "That was presumptuous of me. You're only doing your job and I don't know the first thing about you. I apologise."

"There's really no need, sir."

Anna moved forward in her seat, pen tip hovering over a fresh sheet of paper in her police pocketbook. "Is there anyone we can call to be with you?"

He shook his head. "No, not at all. My family are all up in Cumbria and Sarah's parents are down in Bournemouth. It's just the two of us here… *it was*, I should say…" the words trailed away into the faintest of whispers as he lifted the cigarette to his dry lips and lit it with trembling hands.

"A friend, perhaps?" Anna said.

A moment passed and he spoke again, this time with a strong, level voice. "I'll be fine."

"Was Sarah from around here?"

He nodded once. "She grew up in villages around Marlborough."

Jacob had also taken his notebook out and now clicked his pen ready to write. "Do you know if your wife had any reason to be in Avebury or the vicinity?"

"That's where the row comes in."

Jacob made a note, underlining the word *row*. "What were you arguing about?"

He had gone quiet again, sinking back into the soft chair as he sought the empty comfort of the familiar. He dragged on the cigarette and stared up at the ceiling. "Oh, God."

"Your argument, Mr Bennett," Jacob repeated. "What was it about?"

"Same old nonsense, as always," he mumbled. "She thought I was spending too much time on my work in the evenings and I said it's better than having my face stuck to my mobile phone morning, noon and night. It took off from there. She was like that, was Sarah. Very strong-headed. Very clever but childishly stubborn." He turned now, red eyes burying deep into Anna's soul. "How can it be that I'll never see her again?"

Jacob cleared his throat. "If you could go over the events of last night with us, it would help us to build a picture of the hours leading up to the crime. I know this is difficult, but it will help us a great deal."

Absent-mindedly, he smoked more of the cigarette and nodded. "Yes, of course. She returned from work in Oxford at the normal time, just after seven."

"Does she usually work on a Saturday?" Jacob asked.

"Not normally, no, but it's nearly the end of term and she was trying to get things squared off so we could go away."

"And what was her work?"

"She was an academic at All Souls College. She researched and taught Latin and the classics."

Jacob caught Anna's eye, then turned back to Matthew Bennett. "Go on."

"We spoke for a bit, just about this and that, and then we decided we were both too tired to cook. I'd only just got back from a public disorder trial in Reading that had taken a lot longer than I'd expected so we ordered some food – just a takeaway from a local Indian restaurant here in town. After dinner is when I told her I might do some more work and that's when it exploded."

"Did you often row?"

He paused a moment, wondering what to say. "This isn't easy to admit, but I'd started to question her fidelity. I think this is why the rows had got so much worse. Last night's was worse than usual. Sarah told me she was going to her friend's in Avebury and told me to get lost."

"And was that the last time you spoke?"

"After she left, I asked her to come home."

"You spoke to her or left a voicemail?"

"A text message."

"What time was that?" Anna asked.

Matthew fumbled with his phone for a second, navigated to the texts and passed it to her. "See for yourself – just before eleven."

Jacob and Anna saw the message, sent just when he had said.

*Sarah, just come home OK? I'm sorry.*

Jacob frowned. "What is the name of her friend?"

"Sam Cowan."

"Did she often visit her?"

"She was an old uni friend," he mumbled. "She went over a few times a month depending on how much work she had on. Until you knocked on this door, I thought she was over there at The Crowne, safe and well in Avebury. Now I find out she was murdered there."

"The Crowne?"

"Yes, in Avebury. Sam and her husband are the landlords."

Jacob sensed Anna's eyes burning a hole in the side of his head, but he ignored her and took a slow, deliberate breath. "I'm sorry Mr Bennett, but I have to ask this question. It's a matter of protocol on all murder investigations. Where were you last night between ten and midnight?"

His jaw opened for a second, eyes widening as he leaned forward. "You can't honestly think I had anything to do with this?"

"As I say, it's basic protocol to ask, Mr Bennett. I have to do it. I can't presume anything based on personal feelings."

He rubbed his eyes, red and sore. "After the row I watched TV for a bit and finished my beer. Then I went up to bed around eleven o'clock after sending Sarah the text and watched a bit more TV before turning off the lights and going to sleep around midnight. The next thing I knew you're knocking on the door and telling me she's gone forever."

As he began breaking up, Jacob snapped his notebook shut and cleared his throat. "What car did your wife drive, sir?"

"A black Mercedes," he said, giving them the registration number.

"And her maiden name before she married you?"

"Taylor," he said. "Her name was Sarah Taylor."

"Thank you," Jacob said, lowering his voice. "I'm sorry to have to inform you that all the computer equipment and phones belonging to you and your wife will have to be seized and taken into our forensics department for analysis."

"Of course," he said weakly. "Anything."

Jacob gave him a sympathetic smile and slid his pad into his pocket as he rose from the chair. "Thank you, sir. You've been very helpful and I'll be in touch personally as soon as we have some information relating to the case."

\*

When they arrived back in Avebury, Jacob drove the Alvis straight past the murder site and started a short tour of the tiny village. Neat, well-kept homes and tidy, clipped gardens. Dry stone walls flecked with moss and rust-coloured lichen marked polite boundaries between properties. Thatched roofs, long straw and combed wheat reed, punctuated the quiet spaces between walnuts and wych elms as they patiently waited for the spring.

"Nice," Anna said.

Jacob said nothing.

"But I expect the most lively thing around here is the graveyard."

"Now, now."

"What exactly are we doing, boss?"

"We're looking for Sarah Bennett's car."

"Well, it's not going to take long with only a dozen streets to search, is it?"

"What did he say it was, again?"

She checked her notebook. "A black Merc."

Jacob drove past The Red Lion and then further along to The Crowne Inn. "No sign of it in either car park. Not surprising though. She drove over here after the argument with her husband, arriving late on a Saturday night, I'm betting all the car parks were full when she turned up."

As he cruised down the High Street, Anna said, "What about down there?"

She pointed to a small lane running a hundred yards to the west of The Crowne Inn, and when Jacob turned down into it they both saw what they had been searching for – a compact black Mercedes A Class parked up behind a red telephone box, pulled in tight against a high stone wall.

"That's it," Jacob said.

"So she definitely drove here last night."

"Which means she had to have been chloroformed in the village, too."

He pulled up and they climbed out of the car. Two doors slammed in the drizzle as they sought shelter beneath a plane tree hanging over the Mercedes. As Jacob peered inside the car, Anna took out her notebook and checked the number plate a second time. "It's hers all right, boss."

He tried the handle. "Locked."

"What now?" Her breath plumed in the air in front of her.

He stepped away from the driver's window and straightened himself up to his full height. Pulling the collar of his black peacoat up around his neck, he looked over to her with a glint in his eye and a crooked smile on his face. "Fancy a pint?"

# CHAPTER 6

The Crowne Inn was a traditional English pub with a fire blazing in the hearth and freshly varnished exposed beams criss-crossing the ceiling above their heads. Just before lunch on a Sunday morning and the place was already full of regulars enjoying a drink and waiting for their meals. When they approached the bar, the kitchen door swung open and a waitress stepped out holding a plate of hot, fresh garlic bread and salad.

They showed their warrant cards to another young woman at the till, and a man polishing a pint glass appeared from behind the bar.

"All right, Michelle," he said. "I'll handle this."

"Thanks, Jim."

Jacob slipped his warrant card in his pocket and gave a quick, professional smile.

"Mr Cowan?"

"That's me, and if that little bastard Kevin Hunter has put you on my doorstep he'll wish he'd never been born."

"Kevin Hunter?"

"I had to throw him out last night and he claims it was an assault. He's a shit-stirrer."

"We're not here to discuss any assault, and as far as I'm aware there's been no complaint made against you."

"Nothing outstanding on me, then?"

Jacob and Anna looked at one another before he replied. "No, Mr Cowan. I'm here as part of a murder investigation."

The stocky man gently set the glass down on the bar and his face changed into a study of shock and surprise. Glancing at the barmaid and lowering his voice to a confidential tone, he looked from Anna to Jacob. "So that's what's going on over in the circle is it?"

Jacob fixed him in the eye. "Is your wife here?"

"Sam!"

They heard Sam Cowan come down the stairs. When she turned the corner into the public bar, her hair was wet and she was holding a towel. "What is it?" she asked, staring at the two professionals in sombre suits in front of the bar. When she saw their warrant cards her face dropped.

"I'm Detective Chief Inspector Jacob and this is Detective Sergeant Mazurek. Can we speak somewhere privately?"

"Just through here," she said.

Jim Cowan caught the barmaid's eye. "Watch the place for a sec, Michelle."

"Will do."

They stepped into the private area behind the bar.

"What's this about?"

Jim placed his hand on his wife's shoulder and gave it a squeeze. "Murder."

Jacob nodded. "I'm sorry to have to tell you that earlier this morning a body of a woman was found not far from here up at the Avebury stone circle site. We're awaiting formal identification from the next of kin, but I can tell you informally that it's the body of Sarah Bennett."

Sam gasped, clutching her mouth with a free hand while the other gripped the damp towel. "You've made a mistake."

Jim shook his head and put an arm around her. "They don't make mistakes like that," he said, looking up at the tall detective in the black coat. "If you're round here telling us then it's not a mistake, am I right?"

"It's no mistake," Jacob said darkly. "We believe she was drowned in one of the waterlogged ditches surrounding the stones and then the killer moved her body across the field and placed it behind the sarsen called the Devil's Chair."

Jim swallowed and blew out a deep breath. "Bloody hell."

Sam was aghast. "But *why?* Why would anyone do such a thing?"

Jacob ignored the question. "We believe she was here last night?"

They looked at each other, confused.

"Not here, she wasn't," Jim said.

"I'm sorry?" Anna asked.

"Sarah wasn't here last night," Sam said. "What makes you think she was?"

"That's what we were told," said Jacob.

Sam said, "She'd texted me earlier in the evening to say she had something to tell me, but that was the last I heard of her."

"Are we able to see that message?"

"Sure," she said.

Jim frowned. "Don't you need a warrant to go through someone's private stuff?"

"Yes, unless you give us permission," Jacob said. "Anything that can help us establish the facts early on will help us catch the man who did this. Any objections?"

He shook his head. "Not when you put it like that. Just so long as everything's legal."

Sam ran upstairs and grabbed her phone. When she came back down, she held it out for Jacob to take while she was still on the bottom step. "Here, I just got the message thread up for you to see."

Jacob studied the phone's screen and saw the message just as she had described. When he handed it to Anna, Sam ran a hand through her hair and choked back more tears. "I don't understand why anyone would do this to Sarah."

"We're still in the preliminary phase of the investigation," Jacob said. "I'm sorry to say that motives behind murder can vary widely but at this stage my thinking is that the killer wanted to make sure the body was found fairly quickly so he left it in as public a place as he could find without putting himself at risk of being detected."

"Jesus," Jim said. "Sounds like a proper psycho."

Jacob ignored the comment. "And you're sure she was never here last night?"

"Totally, sure," Sam said. "You mentioned next of kin?" she asked. "You've told Matt, then?"

Jacob gave a simple nod. "Mr Bennett was informed earlier today by me personally."

"Bloody hell, he must be torn up," Jim said.

They all heard a glass break out in the bar, and Michelle cursing under her breath. A loud cheer went up from the patrons, but the faces of the four people in the stairwell behind the bar were grim and silent.

Anna got her pad out and clicked a pen into action. "I know it sounds bureaucratic at a time like this, but it would help us a great deal if you could tell us your movements last night."

Jim and Sam shared a quick, uncertain glance. "Well…"

"Anything," Sam said, talking over her husband. "Sarah was a good friend and I'll do whatever it takes to help you catch the bastard that did this to her."

"Mr Cowan?" Jacob asked. "Where were you last night between ten and midnight?"

The burly man sighed. "I'd rather not say."

"That's not good enough."

Sam stared at him as he shrugged.

"There it is. Take it or leave it," Jim said.

"It could be interpreted as highly suspicious."

"All right, I went out for a drive."

"A drive?"

"Yes."

"Think carefully, Mr Cowan," Jacob said. "If this investigation swings around in your direction you'll be required to give a proper alibi."

"Whatever."

"Mrs Cowan?"

She looked at her husband. He glared at her and she said, "I was here, working the bar just like most nights. If you ask around the village you'll find hundreds of people who can back that up."

Jacob nodded. "I'm sure I will, thank you. I don't suppose you'd care to tell me where your husband was?"

"He told me he went out for a drive."

Jacob changed tack and turned to Jim Cowan. "Is that CCTV out the front real or a dummy?"

"Dummy, sorry."

He and Anna exchanged a glance, and then Jacob turned to Sam. "Is there anything at all you can think of that would explain what might have happened? Did anyone bear a grudge against her? Had she received any threats?"

She shrugged, lost at sea with the gravity of what had happened her friend. "Not that I can think of, no. She was very focussed on her work as far as I know. You will let us know when you've caught him, won't you? The idea of him creeping around here makes me sick, and as for poor Sarah lying up there in that field all night…"

"Of course, you'll be informed as soon as we know what happened."

She nodded, her eyes red with tears.

"Thank you both," Jacob said. "We'll see ourselves out."

As they walked back to the car, Anna was the first to speak. "She seems pretty broken up."

"You're kidding?' Jacob said. "She's just been told her best friend was brutally murdered last night, not ten minutes' walk from her home."

Anna returned the sarcastic smile. "I *meant* that she seemed authentic, the real deal. You're so cynical."

"I find I have a better arrest rate that way." Jacob paused a beat. What did you make of Mr Cowan?"

"A bit nervous, maybe."

Jacob nodded. "That was my impression of him, too. Having said that, he did have two detectives in his home asking him to alibi himself in regard to the murder of a close friend." He opened his door, climbed in and pulled up the lock on the passenger door. "It can have an effect on people."

"Refusal to give an alibi?"

Jacob was sanguine. "Lots of reasons for that, but worth remembering."

As Anna slid down into the cream leather, she buckled up and said, "So what next?"

"I'll organise a full team briefing for this afternoon. It's getting a bit late in the day but there's still time and I'd rather get people up to speed today rather than tomorrow morning. Then they can start thinking about it tonight and sleep on it. In the meantime try and get hold of Dr

Bennett's employer in Oxford. And get Mia and the team out to go over the Merc with a fine toothcomb."

She pulled out her phone. "On it, boss."

"Let's get back to base." Jacob fired up the engine and pulled out into the lane leaving a cloud of dead leaves blasting up behind the car. "Something tells me this is going to get a lot worse before it gets better."

*

Nothing in this bin, either. The man in the torn, stained duffel coat cursed and smacked the iron rim of the rubbish bin with the heel of his gloved hand. Wiping his mouth, he lurched along the pavement until he reached the next waste bin and then began rummaging around in it all over again. Anything would do – a half-eaten burger, a discarded half-full can of coke, or even better, a plastic bottle with some cider sloshing around in the bottom of it.

One of the best bins was the one around the side of the pizza parlour, but when he approached it he realised it had just been emptied. Another curse as he tottered off down the street to find some shelter from the rain. This misery would soon be over, he thought. That old bastard lived like a king while he was out in all weathers eating scraps. But not for long, he mused. Something told him the old bastard would be much more generous this time around.

Then again, maybe he was in over his head. After all, the Saint had dropped off the face of the earth a few days ago. Maybe that had something to do with all this. Maybe he had killed him to shut him up?

He craned his neck up in the rain and stare at the towering vision of Salisbury Cathedral's iconic spire. Twisting up into the leaden March sky like a promise from God himself, it had been the highest in the country since 1549, at over four hundred feet. Now, the cloud was so low that the phosphor bronze cross atop the spire, the height of two tall men, was barely visible. It flashed in glimpses as the clouds raced over the wind-scratched town.

He nodded in agreement with some fleeting, mad thought and mumbled to himself as he staggered along the pavement and headed towards the cathedral. Somewhere under that cross was the bastard, and only the bastard could help him escape this living hell.

# CHAPTER 7

J acob watched a police helicopter swoop down out of the sky and land on the helipad to the west of the police headquarters. The flight crew had been engaged in a search for a car thief on the Somerset border but were now back in HQ. Behind the chopper, the sun was sinking towards a ribbon of crimson clouds on the horizon, lighting the rolling fields of western Wiltshire a gentle tangerine colour. Somewhere high above, the first stars were appearing as night grew from the east.

Turning back to the expansive open-plan CID office, he scanned the faces of his team as they prepared for the briefing on the Bennett murder. His old friend Detective Sergeant Bill Morgan and DC Innes were sitting at the front, pads out on desks in front of them, Anna Mazurek was frowning as she checked a message on her phone. Holloway entered the room at a clip, muttering his apologies as he found a desk at the rear among several young men and women in uniform.

Jacob raised his voice. "All right, let's quieten down, please."

When he had everyone's attention he turned and wrote OPERATION AVEBURY on the whiteboard at the end of the briefing room. Turning and looking at his team, he registered a blend of anxiety and excitement on their faces. The Witch-Hunt murders had rapidly escalated into a major international news story and brought a lot of unwanted attention and scrutiny onto them all. Now, everyone felt like the eyes of the world were upon them no matter what they did. A murder at a world-famous pre-historic site wouldn't go unnoticed for long and they all had to be ready for when those eyes turned in their direction once again.

Using a black marker pen from the desk in front of him, he pointed at a blown-up copy of a passport photo stuck to the murder board. "Dr Sarah Bennett, forty-three years old," he began. "She had a successful career at Oxford University and was respected around the world for her academic knowledge in the field of classics. She had a brilliant mind and got a first class undergraduate degree before going on to write a seminal PhD."

"A professor?" Holloway said.

"No, she was a reader."

The young man looked confused. "Not heard of that one, sir."

"It's a rank in between senior lecturer and professor."

Holloway made a note on his pad. "OK, got it."

"Dr Bennett was last seen by her husband at her home yesterday evening at around ten o'clock. Following a heated row with him, she left the property, climbed into her car and drove over to The Crowne Inn in Avebury. As far as we currently know, she never made it inside."

"Must have been a ripper of an argument," called out a man in uniform at the rear.

"All right, settle down," Jacob said. "The pub is owned by one of the deceased's close friends and her husband. That's why she went there, not because she wanted to drown her sorrows. Sorry, poor choice of words."

"You can say that again."

"You said her husband was the last to see her?" Innes asked. "Is he a suspect, sir?"

Jacob paused, thinking back to the image of the hollow-eyed Matthew Bennett sitting with a cigarette in his hand. His grief seemed real enough, but he knew guilty people were capable of doing or saying anything to save themselves. If he was to have any chance of solving the case he had to distance himself from everyone involved, and that included the grieving widower.

"The husband has a motive, of sorts, which is that he suspected his wife was having an affair. He didn't have to tell us of his suspicions, but he did. Having said that, he might have known we would find out about it in the course of our investigation and decided to come clean early on. Also, he has no alibi because he was at home alone when she was killed."

"So that's a yes, then," Morgan said. "I like yeses. Thinking back, maybe that's why I never got on with my ex."

This produced the laugh the Welshman had been hoping it would, but Jacob soon brought it crashing to a halt.

"So not only is Matthew Bennett a suspect, he is at this time the prime suspect. Another man I suspect may have something to do with the murder is James Cowan, the landlord of The Crowne Inn. He claims he was out driving until after midnight which is just not good enough as far as alibis go. We will be looking further into that."

The team made notes as Jacob continued with the briefing.

"Back to Matthew Bennett. He claims that his wife was a popular woman whom everyone loved and got along with, and a quick trawl of her Facebook page suggests no reason to doubt this. She was a successful academic with a strong publication record in the classics, specifically Latin, and she had a wide social circle of friends. No one we have spoken to so far has had a bad word to say about her."

"What about work colleagues?" Innes said. "A cousin of mine works at a university and he says they're always fighting like rats in a sack among themselves. Insecure, he reckons."

"We're going to pay a visit to her workplace as soon as we can arrange a meeting with them before the break for Hilary Term in a few days' time, right Anna?"

She nodded. "I called them earlier today. Her line manager has agreed to meet with us on Tuesday. A Professor Seward."

Jacob continued. "And we'll take the opportunity to look around the college in more detail then as well. If anything comes up concerning any of her students, then it means acting fast. Waiting for them to return to Oxford once they break up isn't an option because Trinity Term doesn't start for another seven weeks."

"Have we got the PM results yet?" Holloway asked.

"Not in a formal paper report, but the PM has been completed."

"Blimey," a uniform said. "That was quick."

Jacob smiled. "Knowing he had nothing better to do, we called the new Home Office Pathologist into work nice and early on this glorious Sunday morning."

With rain lashing down the windows, the small gathering laughed for a moment until Jacob called them back to order. "Dr Richard Lyon is one of the very best and he stepped up to the plate without any complaints. He's already told me his findings, although as I say, he hasn't had time to produce a formal post-mortem report yet."

"Doesn't have an interest in druids, does he?" Holloway said.

"No, he doesn't," Jacob said. "And thanks for that, Matt. The bottom line is that after being drugged with chloroform, Sarah Bennett was drowned in one of the waterlogged ditches surrounding the stone circles and then her body was dragged up onto the site and dumped beside a sarsen called the Devil's Chair. For those unfamiliar with prehistoric Wiltshire…" a short titter of laughter in response to this, "this is an ancient stone circle to the west of Marlborough that dates back five thousand years."

Holloway shifted in his seat. "Why drag her up onto the site?"

"Yeah," Morgan said. "Me and Leanne went to the Devil's Chair once. It runs close to the road. If he took her from the ditch to the sarsen stone, he was taking an unnecessary risk. He must have had a reason to do it."

"Ritual significance?" Innes asked.

Jacob pursed his lips as he considered it. "Maybe, but another theory we're working on is that the killer simply wanted to make sure the body was found, or even as a warning to others who might see some greater significance in her death. We have two reasons for thinking this, the first is that the Avebury stone circles are a fairly well-known landmark attracting a reasonable number of visitors most days and second is that this was found in the dead woman's hand."

He turned and pointed to a picture of a crude wooden crucifix up on the board behind him.

"We believe the killer made this cross before leaving it on the body." A murmur went around the briefing room. "Settle down, please. There's more." He changed to the next picture of the cross which showed the letters carved into the horizontal beam.

"What's that say?" Holloway asked.

"It's Latin," Jacob said. "And it means the Angel of Death is coming."

A deep, tense silence filled the room.

"In that case," said Holloway. "Let's hope the press don't get hold of it."

"No," Jacob said with a withering glance at the young detective. "But I want to know the significance of this cross and its message. There's no way the killer leaves something like that behind without a serious reason and I'm having a hard time believing it belonged to the victim."

"No disagreement there," Morgan said.

Jacob said, "There has to be a reason he left it behind, and we'd better hope it was a personal matter between him and the victim and not because he's playing games with us and plans more murders. This could be a signature, or a calling card and we all know what that means – a serial killer. Maybe this is a message for us, for *me*, or maybe it's a message for someone else – another potential victim. Either way, the last thing we need after Grovely is any more hysteria, so I want a lid kept on this at all costs as far as the press is concerned."

"Yes, sir."

He looked at Innes. "I want a house to house done first thing tomorrow morning in a three mile radius from the murder site. It's a relatively isolated area with small villages and farmhouses so the same approach you took during Grovely should be fine. I also want a team asking questions all over her part of town over in Marlborough and also run her name through the records – both married, Sarah Bennett and maiden, Sarah Taylor. That's your job."

"Sir."

Looking at his old friend, he said, "Bill, you and Holloway here can get all over her online life. Her computers were all seized from her home this morning, as were her husband's as well, and both their phones, although hers is damaged and still with Mia at CSI for the moment. Go through them like a dose of salts and see if anything turns up. Matthew Bennett told me he had suspicions she was having an affair. That's as good a place to start as any."

"Leave it with us, boss." Morgan gave Holloway a broad smile. "If there's anything there, we'll find it."

Jacob clapped his hands together. "All right, let's get on with it, and remember – no talking to the press. Not every suspicious death has to be splashed all over the TV and internet. This woman was brutally murdered in cold blood and it's our job to catch her killer, not turn her life and death into a public spectacle."

After a murmur of excitement, everyone got up and filed towards the door.

Jacob watched them go and breathed a sigh of relief. When they had all left the briefing room, he gathered up his notes and walked over to the long, tinted window. The day was almost gone now and somewhere over there in the setting sun was the Old Watermill, not half an hour's drive away. For the first time since moving into the place, he wished he was there right now. He'd started to visualise himself doing it up and turning it into a proper home. He'd even imagined Sophie living there, too.

Switching off the lights, he closed the door and got his car keys out of his pocket. It was time to go home and get a good night's sleep.

\*

"What are you doing here?"

The old man looked at the visitor like he was some kind of rare insect as he padded up the path toward his freshly painted front door.

Looking up at the man in all his finery, the visitor curled his lip in disgust. "You remember what we talked about a few days ago?"

"Yes, I remember," the man replied. "I'm hardly likely to forget, am I?"

"I suppose not." He grinned and pushed his way into the large house. Moving over to the fire, he sat in the other man's chair beside the hearth and warmed his hands. The fire crackled and popped and a sharp squealing noise emanated from one of the beech logs buried deep in the flames.

"Sounds like some old wild thing screaming in pain," said the unwelcome visitor.

"Don't be ridiculous. It's no more than the intense heat of the fire decomposing the cellulose inside the wood, heating the sap."

"Whatever you say, chief," he said with a cackle. "I trust you've got a bit more for me this time?"

"Yes, and when you get it I never want to see you again, got it?"

The visitor produced a cheap half bottle of whisky from the pocket of his filthy trench coat. He hastily swigged from the bottle before passing it to the other man with a trembling hand. "That depends on what you have and how much it's worth to keep your vile little secret from the world, your holiness."

The man sat down opposite him and declined the whisky with a grimace, his face turning a sickly pale shade. His voice softened to a terrified whisper. "You'll get what you asked for."

The visitor finished the drink with a loud smack of his lips and set the empty bottle down between his two muddy boots. He didn't like the way this old bastard was looking at him now; any fear seemed to have been replaced by contempt. Still, no sense making this go on any longer than it had to. "When I have it in my hands, you'll never see me again and all this will be over."

"It had better."

"No threats, your worship, please. I'd hate to have to let the world know what you've been up to in your spare time. God's house has a big roof, don't it? You wouldn't want it crashing down on your head, I'm sure."

"No, please. I'm sorry. You'll get what you want."

"I thought I would," he said, his lips twisting into a wicked grin. "I thought I would."

*

Jacob changed into third and the Alvis's three litre engine responded with a satisfying growl. He'd been too busy with work over the last few weeks since the Witch-Hunt murders to do much restoration work, but the driver's door had been cleared of rust and resprayed to match the bonnet's sparkling powder blue. He'd also found the time to restore and condition the seat in the back, bringing the cream leather seats to a rich, deep shine. The rest still needed work.

Or still looked like a skip, according to his sergeant.

Relieved after such a long and stressful day to see his home silhouetted beneath a sea of sparkling stars, he slowed down and pulled onto his gravelled drive. Killing the engine, the interior of the vintage car was still lit a soft amber by the instrument lights and the smell of worn leather hung in the warm air. For a moment, he couldn't think of a greater sanctuary than to be sat right here, in his father's old car, but then visions of Sarah Bennett's face appeared in his mind like a monster rising from a bog.

Drowned and dragged from the ditch that killed her, her body had been dumped in a public place for all to see. Head to the west in the old Christian burial ritual and the strangest thing of all was the wooden crucifix he had left in her hand. What did it mean? Was the killer leaving a message for him or for someone else? Was it a warning? He peered over the steering wheel and watched the water tumbling along the river until it vanished into the darkness beyond his kitchen.

Again, he felt the weight of others' hopes on his shoulders. Loved ones, friends and relatives all expecting him to catch the killer and bring him to justice. Thanks to the Witch-Hunt murders, Tom Jacob had become a national household name, with his details broadcast all over not just this country but all over the world. That only increased the pressure he felt to get it right and not make any mistakes. He'd had big successes in the past – most notably Cameron Sackville, the famous fraudster, and Kyle Marsden, the man who had burnt his house down and murdered his fiancée. Putting those two behind bars had brought him a lot of satisfaction, even though Marsden's brother Kurt was still at large.

But he'd had his failures too – three of them. Three killers he had been unable to hunt down – one from his days in the Met, the Camden Town killer, and two from his time at Thames Valley, the Oxford College killer and the White Horse killer.

Those cases kept him up at night almost as much as the memories of the fire that took Jess's life. He couldn't let the Angel of Death become number four, to torture him like these other failures.

But the other cases were in the past, he thought, and climbed out of the car into the cold. Now, it's time to look to the future. Lay those ghosts to rest, he thought. Get some sleep. Find the Angel of Death before he strikes again.

# CHAPTER 8

*Monday, 11ᵗʰ March*

Detective Inspector Bill Morgan heard the phone ringing in the front room but played his usual trick and ignored it. He'd got up with the lark, as his grandfather used to say, and gone for a long, hard run around the wet, dawn streets before coming back in and grabbing a shower.

This time of the year his body needed the extra exercise and at his age this demanded more effort than ever before. Long gone was his life in the Royal Marines Commandos. These days the fat built up a lot easier than it burnt off, and his recovery time from training injuries was worse than ever. He sighed at the thought of it all and pulled a box of cereal from one of the cupboards.

As he stepped through into the cramped front room of his rented flat with the cool china bowl in his hands, he listened to the answering machine take the call. With a heavy heart he had presumed another brutal message from his wife's divorce lawyer but instead he heard the familiar oily tones of Marcus Kent, and he didn't sound very happy. The discovery of Sarah Bennett's body the day before had rattled everyone and he guessed Kent was on the warpath for a speedy resolution to the case.

"If you're there, Morgan, do me the courtesy of picking up the phone. It's important police business."

He relented, set the bowl down and lifted the phone from its cradle, grateful not to be discussing costly pension splits and other assorted nasties with Leanne's legal army.

"Good morning, sir," he said.

He turned his head and peered through the kitchen window. A blackbird hopped around on his patio for a few seconds and then flew away in disgust. Since the separation from his wife he'd been renting a small semi-detached house in Swindon's Old Town. It was nice enough, but the garden was what Kent might call *bijou*.

Morgan called it crappy, but the view over the fence was nice enough. Seeing the rain had relented for a few minutes, he stepped out of the French windows onto the patio and took in the view of Town Gardens, a large parkland of trees and lawns nestled behind a black wrought iron fence. "And what a wonderful morning it is, too, sir."

"Not anymore, pal. We've got another dead body on our hands."

He closed his eyes and stifled a sigh. He knew Kent's tone of voice well enough by now to know how his day was about to change, and not for the better. The Chief Super was not renowned at the station for his sense of humour, so Morgan quietly dismissed any silly notions that this might be a wind-up and threw himself into the conversation.

"Another body, sir?" he asked.

"I want you down at Salisbury in a hurry." His words were delivered in their usual clipped, businesslike manner. "We've had a call about a dead body floating about in the river there and since Jacob's engaged on the Avebury murder, I thought I'd send it your way."

"You're very kind, sir."

"You know me, Morgan. I aim to please."

"You think these two deaths are connected, sir?

Kent sighed. "Why do you think I'm sending you down there, man? I could easily hand it over to someone from the local nick in Salisbury."

"Sir."

When Kent disconnected the call, Morgan reluctantly said goodbye to his breakfast and slipped his suit jacket on over his freshly laundered, crisp white shirt. Picking up his mobile, wallet and car keys, he paused at the little table in the hall when he saw the photo of his daughter smiling back at him. She was standing in the sunshine at her graduation in Cambridge. He remembered the joke they had shared just as he snapped the picture. He finished his tea, locked the front door behind him and walked to the communal garage.

*

Churchill Gardens was a large park on the north bank of the River Avon just south of Salisbury. Locals used the area for walking, jogging or cycling and not long ago the council had installed a brand new skatepark there. Today, in the drizzle, there were no skaters. Instead, a quiet gathering of police officers and CSI specialists were unpacking a forensic tent in the field to the east of the park, just beside the river.

Morgan and Innes stepped out of their car and took in the scene. As they wandered over to the riverbank, two uniformed constables were standing grim-faced either side of a dead body snagged in a bend of the river. Another young constable was busily stretching barrier tape across all the park entrances beyond the field.

As they approached the men standing by the river, both of them stood up in a vague facsimile of attention. "Nothing's been touched, sir," one of them said.

Morgan gave a nod of appreciation as he peered down at the fully-clothed corpse. "Thanks," he muttered. "Who called it in?"

"Chap on a narrowboat, sir. Just over there."

Morgan followed the constable's pointing finger to a smart red and black narrowboat moored up on the north bank a hundred yards to the east. "Good work. I think it's time to get this poor sod out of the drink, don't you?"

"Yes, sir."

As they dragged the dead man out of the water and hauled him up onto the muddy grass, Morgan saw Mia Francis's Volvo pull up and come to a stop near the skatepark. She climbed out of the car and grabbed her medical bag which she placed on the bonnet while she changed into a white forensic suit.

As she slipped on some disposable shoe covers, a brief ray of rogue sunshine broke through the clouds and lit up her hair, forming a sort of halo. Then the clouds swallowed the sun and it was gone again. Thinking of Leanne and the trail of destruction bobbing about in the wake of his personal life, Morgan realised that Mia Francis really was a very good-looking woman, and sighed.

"Sir?"

He turned to Innes. "I'm sorry?"

"They want to know where to bring the body."

He looked at the two young constables. They were staring back at him, each one holding an arm of the dead man. "Right over there," he said.

They dragged him further up the bank, still face down.

"All right," Morgan said. "Turn him over."

The uniformed men complied and pulled the man over onto his back. Seeing the decomposed face they took a step back in disgust and covered their mouths. "Bloody hell!"

Morgan stepped closer. It was hard to see because of the water damage, but it looked like his clothes were old, filthy and stained before he went into the river. He wasn't a big man and from what was left of the face he saw that he hadn't shaved for weeks, but it stopped short of a full beard. His dead, sightless eyes sat above two soft purple bags and his forehead was criss-crossed with deep, craggy frown lines. Most of the nose was missing.

"Not going to be easy getting an ID from that," Innes said quietly.

The Welshman shook his head and lowered his voice. "Looks homeless to me."

Innes looked up at him. "Sir?"

"Look at his coat and his boots. Look at his hair."

"Yes, sir."

The former commando sniffed and fixed his hazel eyes on the young uniformed constables. "Either of you two recognise this man from about town?"

They each peered down into the dead man's face before returning their verdict. "Can't really see much of the face, sir, but no, not me."

"Nor me," said the other. "But I would agree he's homeless, sir."

Morgan nodded.

"Accidental drowning?" Innes asked. "Maybe he got drunk and fell in."

"Not with bruises like that on his neck and throat," Morgan said darkly. "I don't want to play a guessing game here, but it looks like exactly the same cause of death as the boss's case up in Avebury."

"Shouldn't we wait for Dr Lyon's report before making a leap like that?"

Morgan looked at the young detective and gave her a warm smile. He knew he was right, but he knew she was right too. "We should, Laura, we should."

Mia reached them, looked at the body on the ground and sighed. Two of her CSI team were making good progress setting up the forensics tent beside it. "Not there," she snapped. "For goodness sake... *men*."

Morgan smiled. "What's wrong with over there?"

She ignored him and spoke to the two young policemen. "Put it over there to the lee side of those trees."

They looked at her, confused.

"Out of the bloody wind, over there!"

The men moved the corpse, and Morgan and Innes exchanged a subtle glance as Mia padded over to the body. "Bloody hell, he's been in there a long time."

"That's what I thought," Morgan said.

"Looks like he just couldn't *face* life anymore."

Morgan looked at her. "Really? Here and now?"

"Sorry," Mia said with a slight shrug. "It's the gallows humour that keeps me going." She looked up at the sky. For now, the rain had stopped and made the job a little easier, but the leaden grey clouds whipping over the city promised more to come. "Anyway, let's get this over with."

Morgan drew in a deep breath and shoved his hands into his pockets. Mia Francis crouched down on her knees on the wet grass and lifted the dead man's head to see the back of the skull. She worked methodically and very much at her own pace. They all knew better than to interrupt her.

Mia had been working as the senior CSI officer for so long she was counted as part of the furniture on the office inventory. She could always be relied upon to deliver whatever compliment or insult was required at any given moment and such was her encyclopaedic knowledge, rarely was it a good idea to cross swords with her. Outside of her forensic career, her specialist subjects were in a terrifyingly wide arc, ranging from real ale to rugby to the classical world. Her gastronomic knowledge was unrivalled. Those who dared to challenge her always came off worse.

"I'll get to work then," she said sharply.

Morgan nodded. "Righto."

She sighed and her shoulders slumped down. "You're not going to watch me working? If there's one thing I can't stand it's…"

"I know, I know," he said. "If there's one thing you can't stand it's someone watching you work over your shoulder. Don't worry, I need to have a little chat with a distressed narrowboat owner."

"What about me, sir?" Innes asked,

"You can stay here and watch Mia work over her shoulder."

# CHAPTER 9

He walked over to the narrowboat where a glum-looking man was idling his time away by pacing up and down the riverbank, just in sight of a female police constable. Morgan gave the PC a friendly nod and gestured towards the boat owner. "How's he doing?"

"Not well," she said.

"Name?"

"Michael Slade."

"Thanks."

Morgan casually approached the man as if he were going to ask him directions. "Mr Slade?"

"That's me." He offered a pale hand, which the Welshman accepted and the two men shook hands for a few seconds.

"I'm Detective Inspector Morgan. Could you spare me a few minutes?"

"Of course… dreadful business."

"All part and parcel of a normal day's work for me, I'm sorry to say."

The man widened his eyes in a show of respect and shook his head. "I don't know how you do it."

"I get by. Tell me, sir, are you on some sort of boating holiday?"

"Me? No, I live on the boat."

"You live on the boat? That sounds idyllic."

"Under normal circumstances I would agree with you, but now this has happened I'm not so sure."

"Do you live alone on the boat?"

"Yes. I'm divorced."

Morgan considered using his own broken marriage to build a bridge to the man but thought better of it. "I'm sorry to hear it."

"Don't be."

Morgan gave a nod and sucked in some cold air, turning for a moment to study the surface of the water as it rippled downstream. With nearly half the county designated as an official Area of Outstanding Natural Beauty by the British Government, it was typically beautiful. Just a few yards away, two mute swans sailed past the starboard side of the boat and turned a bend in the river.

Beyond the boat's bow, he heard the high-pitched *weet weet* call of a sandpiper hiding somewhere in the reeds. For a moment, more sun broke through the cloudbank and sparkled on the dappled surface of the Avon. He almost forgot why he was here and studied a skylark turning above his head, tearing open the wind's cold silk with its beak. Sniffing again, he turned back to Michael Slade. "So, what happened exactly?"

The man puffed out his cheeks and shrugged. "It's simple really. I was making my way downstream en route to the south, a journey I have made many times, when I turned this bend and saw something bobbing about in the water over by the north bank. It was sort of tucked into the reeds and at first I thought it was just a pile of old clothes someone had dumped in here. You'd be surprised what some people use our waterways for."

Morgan gave a weary smile. "I don't think I would be, sir."

"No, probably not, considering your line of work."

"And what's *your* line of work?" Morgan asked suddenly.

"I'm an artist."

"Very nice. I can see why living on the river appeals to you."

"Yes."

"Anyway, what happened next?"

"I steered the boat over to the clothes and then I moored it up just beyond so I could have a closer look. That's why the boat's just east of where the body was."

"Go on."

"I got the boathook and gave it a bit of a poke and that's when I realised it was a body. Gave me quite a shock, I can tell you. I've been on the river for over ten years and I've never come across anything like this."

Morgan put his pocketbook away and his fingers brushed against his cigar packet. Wishing he could light one up right now, he almost considered asking Michael Slade if he smoked.

"All right, we have your details I believe."

The police constable nodded. "Yes, sir."

"In that case you're free to go, Mr Slade."

\*

Morgan wandered over to Innes and briefed her about Slade while he watched Mia and her CSI team efficiently buzzing in and out of the forensic tent. She'd already ordered a fingertip search of the riverbanks and called into HQ to organise a police diver team to come out and search the riverbed. All very efficient. All typically Mia.

Approaching the senior CSI officer, he said, "Any preliminary findings?"

"Age is too hard to call right now, but judging by his left arm he was a regular user of intravenous drugs."

"Heroin?"

"How should I know?"

Morgan and Innes exchanged a glance and then the Welshman turned back to Mia. "Your best guess."

"It would be wild speculation."

"It's a lovely spring day, Mia," he said. "Feel free to speculate wildly."

"It was *never* a lovely spring day, Bill, and now it's even worse, now it's – well this." In the drizzle, she jutted her chin towards the dead man on the plastic sheet in front of them. "I was about to start packing for my little sojourn to Ireland, and then your people call me out for this."

"Mia?"

"What?"

"You were about to speculate wildly."

She sighed. "He could have been using heroin, yes. It may also have been morphine, amphetamine, methamphetamine, cocaine or any number of prescription drugs. Hell, Bill – you can inject liquid suppositories into your arms if you're mad enough. Impossible to tell until you get him back on the slab and Dr Richard has passed his expert eye over him, so you'll just have to wait until then."

"Fair enough. What *can* you tell us?"

"For one thing, it's not going to be easy to get an ID. He's been in the water so long that the decomposition is fairly extensive. There's no easy way to say this, but the face and hands have been mostly consumed by various nasties, as has every other piece of exposed flesh. Might be a dental records job."

Morgan winced. "Fell or pushed?"

"No way to tell," she said. "I *can* say that a quick look at the riverbank in this area doesn't show any signs of a struggle, but that's not saying much. First, he's been in there a long time so the weather could easily have removed any signs of a fight, and second he could have gone into the river at any one of a hundred locations anywhere upstream of here."

Innes frowned. "That's what I was thinking. He could have gone in anywhere in the city or even further out to the west."

"I'm not so sure," Morgan said. "Even at this time of year this is a busy city and lots of people walk and run along the river. I'm pretty sure someone would have given us a call if they'd seen a corpse floating about in the water over the last few days. I doubt he could have drifted too far without being seen." He paused a beat. "You know what I think?"

"I do *not*," Mia said. "My career as a circus telepath was a total failure."

He returned her smug smile. "I think he went in not far from here, got to this part of the river quite fast and was snagged in here for most of the time he was in the water. This is just far enough from the park to be out of things a bit and you can't see it from Churchill Gardens or the skatepark."

"Go on," Mia said.

He nodded at an unspoken thought as his eyes worked their way along the riverbank. "He went in at night, drifted for a few hours before getting snagged up here. How fast does a corpse travel down a river, Mia?"

"Finally, a question on my favourite hobby!"

He raised an eyebrow. "Mia, *please.*"

She crossed her arms over her chest and sighed. "Human bodies are heavier than freshwater, so when you lose consciousness in it you go down to the bottom. This is basic physics."

"Basic physics," Morgan repeated.

"Seawater is an entirely different dynamic, but we're talking about freshwater."

Morgan nodded. "Freshwater, right."

"However, a dead body that has sunk in freshwater will eventually return to the surface because of the gasses which form inside a decaying corpse."

"Delightful," Innes managed.

"As the gasses grow and inflate the tissues, the body becomes steadily more buoyant until it reaches the point where it's able to float in the freshwater again, hence arriving back on the surface. There are other factors such as the temperature of the water and the percentage of body fat and so on, but looking at this chap it's pretty clear he was as thin as a rake when he went in. It's impossible to be sure, but I'd say he's already done the sinking to the bottom bit and now he's come back up to the surface, so he's been in a long time."

"One for Richard, I think," Morgan said, scratching the back of his head.

Mia nodded. "Yes, one for Dr Richard. There are too many variables here, and don't forget that surface current can vary quite a lot from the current at the bottom of the river. Plus there's going to be other obstacles down there like reeds, rocks and junk thrown in by people, all of which is going to have an impact on the speed he can travel down the river."

"Which in turn has an impact on where he went into the river to get here by today," Innes said.

Morgan sighed and looked out across the water once again. To the west, he watched Michael Slade's narrowboat as it made its way gently downstream, its bright red paintwork in stark contrast to the muted early spring landscape of bare trees and muddy grass.

Turning back to the corpse, he blew out a breath and felt a wave of sadness. Was he lured out here, killed and dumped in the water? Was he killed elsewhere and driven out here? Was this linked to the dead woman up in Avebury? If he was here by his own choosing, what was a homeless man doing out here near the river, in a place like this on his own at this time of year? Was he high? Got drunk, fell in and banged his head? No, don't forget those bruises. The questions raced in his mind.

"Maybe he just slipped," Innes said. "Up here in the dark, drunk maybe and in you go over the edge."

"However he went in," Morgan said quietly. "He had to get here first, and that means we need to find out his movements leading up to his arrival."

"Yes, sir."

Mia Francis was making her way around the body.

"At least can you tell us if he drowned, Mia?"

"Too early to say. Diagnosing death by drowning is notoriously difficult, especially in the field."

"But Richard will be able to tell us after the post-mortem?"

"Maybe."

"Maybe?"

"Is there an echo around here?"

Morgan frowned. "I'm just asking a question."

"And I'm giving you an answer, Bill. Even PMs sometimes fail to render a reliable diagnosis of death by drowning. Very often they have to do a full laboratory investigation and even then, they might not be certain. The technical definition of death by drowning is submersion not just in water but in any form of liquid. I simply cannot say what caused this man to die at this stage of the investigation. For one thing, just look at his head. Cause of death could easily be head trauma. You'll have to wait for the fun stuff."

"All right, all right... I give up. Did you find anything ID-wise on the body?"

"Not much." She handed him a transparent evidence bag and he slipped on a pair of nitrile gloves from his pocket and started to rummage around in the bag. "And there was definitely no wallet or any kind of ID?"

"Just what's in the bag."

He sighed and looked at Innes. "No wallet and no ID."

"Helpful," Innes said.

"But apparently, he had a very expensive water resistant watch." He pulled it from the bag and held it up in the light so she could see it.

Innes whistled. "Blimey, what's that?"

"This, my young *padowan* is a Rolex Submariner."

"Is that important?" she asked.

"This little baby has eighteen carat yellow gold, a beautiful blue dial and a blue scratch-resistant bezel. At least twenty grand."

Innes was shocked. "Twenty thousand pounds?"

He nodded. "It's a thing of beauty." Peering at the shiny navy blue dial, he couldn't resist grinning at it. "And water resistant to one thousand feet. They're famous for their water resistance, see."

"I should bloody think so for that price," Innes said. "That costs three times more than my car."

Morgan sniffed as he dropped it back in the bag. "I have a question. What is a twenty thousand pound watch doing on the wrist of a homeless man?"

"Stolen?"

"Possibly."

"Maybe you're wrong about the homeless thing," Mia said. "Maybe someone changed his clothes to make him look homeless?"

Morgan looked at the body one more time, specifically what was left of the face and his hands. "No, we're not wrong. You can switch clothes on a dead man, although it's a lot harder than the films make it look, but you can't switch faces, and from what's left of that face I'd say he's been sleeping rough for years. Trust me, I know."

"Sir?"

"Never mind... forget about it. Let me just see what else is in Mia's little bag of tricks."

"You're not going to like it," Mia said.

He paused. "Why not?"

"See for yourself."

He took another look through the bag and pulled out a homemade wooden crucifix. Innes stared at the tiny object with wide eyes as he slowly turned it in his hand to reveal the same Latin inscription carved into the horizontal beam.

"Bloody hell," he said. "The boss is not going to like this."

"It's got be the same killer," Innes said.

"Unless it's a group of them," said Mia. "Found it stuffed in his inside pocket, by the way."

No one spoke, then an ambulance turned in the car park and squashed its way over the muddy grass of the field before parking up just beside the river.

"Looks like his taxi's here," Innes said.

Morgan watched them zip the body inside a bag and load it up into the back of the ambulance. He followed suit and zipped up the evidence bag containing the crucifix, the watch and other items. He passed it back to Mia. "Go through all of this with your usual proficiency, please."

"Naturally."

"All right, then." Morgan smacked his hands together and rubbed them. Then he reached into his pocket and grabbed his cigars. "We'll start by checking the homeless shelters, and while we walk I can have a smoke. If this isn't connected with the murder in the Avebury, I'll eat my hat."

# CHAPTER 10

The senior officer of Wiltshire Police's CID department drew in a weary breath and glanced at the wall clock above his filing cabinet. After a Saturday spent largely avoiding his wife by hiding at the local golf club, he had spent most of yesterday dealing with the after-effects of the discovery of the dead woman found near the small village of Avebury. Now it was Monday morning and he had summoned the SIO of the case into his office for an update.

The glance at the clock had told him he had a few minutes before DCI Jacob arrived so he took the time to make himself a cup of coffee and check his appearance. He walked the freshly-made coffee back over to his desk and set it down before admiring himself in the mirror on the back of his office door. He liked what he saw. Steadily approaching the big Five-Five but he was still leaner and fitter than most men half his age. He smugly patted his tight stomach and blew out a loud breath of satisfaction before returning to his desk.

When he heard the knock on the door, he sank into his leather captain's chair and called out for Jacob to enter the room. "Come!"

The younger man was also trim and in good shape. His height probably helped with that, he thought with a sneer. "Please," he said, gesturing at a seat in front of his desk.

"You wanted to see me, sir?" Jacob sat down and linked his hands in his lap before looking up and offering a peaceful smile at his boss.

"After the discovery of the dead man down in Salisbury, I wanted an update on Operation Avebury. Two violent murders in as many days in a quiet rural county makes alarm bells go off in my head. Do you have any leads?"

Jacob paused. "Well, not at this time…"

Kent darted out of his seat and padded over to his favourite window. "In my dreams, Jacob, I run a department where you're able to solve a murder in good time and without any problems from the press."

"I'm in your dreams, sir?"

He spun around, red-faced. "Don't get funny with me, laddo."

"No, sir."

Kent shook his head in response to some unspoken despair. "There's no way we can keep this out of the press for much longer."

"We may need them, sir," Jacob said. "For a public appeal, I mean."

"If you can't catch the killer, then we certainly *will* need them. We've had a woman drowned up at Avebury stone circle on Saturday night, and now a man who has been killed the same way has been found in the river at Salisbury. Tell me, who's doing what on your team?"

"I've reallocated responsibilities following the discovery of the second murder victim, sir. Bill Morgan and DC Innes are looking into the Salisbury murder, and DS Mazurek and I are investigating the death at Avebury. We have DC Holloway looking into computer records. He's liaising closely with Mia Francis in CSI."

Kent seemed pleased. "I was very impressed with how fast the pathologist got the first one turned around. Let's hope he's as efficient with number two."

*The first one*, Jacob thought without passing comment. "Yes, sir."

"I read your summary. I see he confirms your suspicions that she was drowned in the ditch surrounding the monument."

"That's right."

"So what the hell was she doing several dozen yards away under a sarsen in the middle of a sodding ancient monument? Why not just leave her in the ditch?"

Jacob crossed his legs and resisted the urge to sigh loudly. "This is something we're actively investigating, sir."

"Which is exactly what you told me yesterday when we discussed this matter last. I want progress, Jacob." He leaned forward and raised his voice. "Progress."

"Of course, sir."

"Tell me about the second one, the dead man in the river."

"Not much to report at this time, sir. Morgan tells me that he believes him to be homeless, but the body had spent a considerable time in the Avon before being discovered. As a result of this, there was significant decomposition so facial recognition is impossible. Richard Lyon is going to run the usual DNA tests and also order a dental record check, and in the meantime Morgan's trying to ID the body using his clothes."

"His clothes?"

"The body was dressed in a unique woollen trench coat with some badges pinned to the lapel, and also there was a fairly individual sort of bobble hat as well."

"Could have been a clothes switch."

"Maybe, but he's aware of that. And there's something else."

"What?"

"They found another crucifix on the body."

Kent's face dropped. "The same sort as you found on the Avebury woman?"

"Yes, sir. It looks that way. The same Latin inscription."

"Christ, this could get nasty. Wait, didn't you say he'd been in the river some time?"

"Yes, sir. It's just speculation based on visual observation, but we're expecting Dr Lyon to confirm it after the PM."

"Then if it's the same killer, the man in Salisbury was his first victim, not the woman at the stone circle."

"Exactly, sir. We'll know more when we get the medical tests sorted."

"And talking of which," Kent said sharply, "I want the PM expedited as a top priority. Get on the blower to the pathologist and make it happen as fast as yesterday. Two murders in two days in this county is too rare for them not to be connected. That crucifix worries me."

"Sir."

A long silence followed, filled only when a car alarm went off down in the HQ car park. Kent frowned and walked to his window again to see a young uniformed constable running across to his vehicle in the low light and deactivating the alarm. "Bloody thing. I do wish he'd sort that out."

"Sir?"

Kent ignored him and returned to the subject. "What links an educated and wealthy woman with a successful career to a homeless man with not a penny to his name?"

"That's what we're working on, sir," Jacob said. "We're looking into their backgrounds but without a positive ID on the homeless man there's not much more we can do in terms of seeing if they had anything in common."

"Well they had something in common, Jacob," he snapped. "And you're going to bloody well find out what it was and report it back to me before the press get wind of it, got it?"

"Got it."

He turned sharply on his heel and fixed two laser-eyes on him. "Your next move?"

"DI Morgan and DC Innes have a meeting scheduled with Richard Lyon over at the Great Western to discuss the homeless man's post-mortem and in the meantime they're going to pay a visit to the homeless shelters down in Salisbury. DS Mazurek and I are looking into Sarah Bennett's background a bit more thoroughly, including finding out what DC Holloway's got out of the computers."

Kent thought about this for a few moments. "All right, sounds like you're doing all you can for now. As I have said, I want this tidied up nice and neat with a little bow tied on it within two or three days, long before the press get hold of it. This is people's lives we're dealing with here. We're not here to provide an exciting bounce for the next news cycle."

"Of course not, sir."

"Dismissed."

He watched Jacob rise from the chair and unfold to his full height before leaving the room and closing the door behind him. Then he sighed, collapsed down into his chair and swivelled around until he was able to look out across the car park to the west and the fields beyond.

Sometimes, he thought he should do as his wife suggested and take early retirement. In these days of austerity they were always trying to bundle the senior officers out of the door. It cost a lot of money to run a Detective Chief Superintendent, after all, and then there were the pension contributions. But if he left, Jacob would probably get his job. Did he care? Should he just walk away?

No, he hadn't come this far to roll over now. He was still young enough to harbour a realistic ambition of getting Chief Constable when Bernard Portman finally called it a day. He had worked hard and come a long way, but one screw up and his chances would be dust.

He thought of Jacob and his fast and loose way of playing the game, and for a moment a wave of apprehension washed over him. Jacob was a brilliant detective when the mood took him, but he was unpredictable and disrespectful of the rules to a dangerous degree. If he could get rid of him, his life would certainly get back to a more even keel, but it was easier said than done.

Still, he thought with a smile, give it time – looked like Laura Innes was safely in his pocket, and Rome wasn't built in a day, after all.

There was still plenty of time for Jacob to screw up, and when he did, he would strike.

*

Twenty miles south in Salisbury city centre, Morgan and Innes pushed Sherard House's door buzzer and waited patiently under their umbrellas for a response. To their right a commuter train rattled over the railway bridge on its way out of the station. Beneath it, a long line of cars was backed up at traffic lights, full of drivers with sad faces intermittently visible when their wipers cleared the rain from the windscreens.

The intercom crackled. "Hello?"

"I'm Detective Inspector Morgan and I'm here with Detective Constable Innes with regards to the death of a homeless man here in the city."

After a short pause, the door buzzed and opened and they walked inside out of the wet. Shaking the rain off their umbrellas, they made their way along to the front desk and both showed their warrant cards to a young woman.

"Is there someone senior we could talk with?" Morgan asked.

"Mr Burroughs is in."

"Mr Burroughs?"

"The shelter manager."

Morgan gave the nervous young woman a warm smile. "Then lead the way."

They followed her to a busy canteen where dozens of homeless people were sitting around long trestle tables eating bowls of stew. Gathered at the head of a line of people queuing up for food was a small staff of people standing behind a counter. The woman approached a man in his fifties with a pointy goatee beard and a serving spoon in his hand and caught his attention.

"Janet?"

"It's the police, Robin."

He looked up from the counter, pale and startled. "The police?"

"Yes."

A pause. "Well, send them over!"

Morgan went first, then Innes joined him in the cramped kitchen space. He went through the procedure of extracting his warrant card wallet all over again.

"That will be all, Janet, thank you."

The woman left and padded back through the crowd to her office.

"I'm DI Morgan and this is DC Innes, Wiltshire CID. I was wondering if you could spare five minutes to talk to us about a homeless man who was found dead this morning."

The man's jaw opened slightly as he scanned the faces of the two police officers.

"Yes, of course," he mumbled. "Dead, you say?"

"I'm afraid so, sir." Morgan glanced around at two people who had just entered the hall, both wrapped up in old coats and with thick-woollen scarves obscuring much of their faces. "Is there somewhere we could discuss this in private?"

He scratched his head and swallowed. "Yes, my office is just through here – please, walk this way."

They walked along a short corridor, all creaking floorboards and poorly fitting carpets until reaching a white-painted door. Robin Burroughs fumbled with some keys before opening the door and ushering them both inside his office.

"Would either of you like some coffee or tea?"

"Not for me, sir," Morgan said. "But thanks for the offer."

Innes followed the inspector's lead and raised a polite hand. "Nor me, but thank you."

"So it's straight to business," he said with a nervous laugh.

Morgan ignored the comment. "Now sir, first I'm hoping you may be able to identify the man, but unfortunately the only post-mortem images we have are unsuitable for identification purposes. Instead, I was hoping you could identify the body from some pictures of his clothes and personal effects?"

"Oh, I see – of course."

Morgan pulled out his mobile phone and lifted it up so Burroughs could see the screen. "Do you recognise these personal effects, sir?"

Burroughs took a long look at the image, squinting slightly to reduce the glare of the overhead lights as he peered into the phone. "Oh dear, yes, I think these are the Saint's."

"The Saint?" Innes asked.

"That's the only name I have for him," he said. "He got the name because he was always talking about how God would punish sinners and so on and he spent a fair bit of time up at the cathedral. He came in and out of here quite regularly."

"If you have any other information about him, sir," Morgan said, slipping the phone away, "that would be of great use to us. I'm afraid with the Saint being homeless and all, it's not always straight-forward to gather the information you need to build a picture, if you know what I mean."

Burroughs sighed. "Many of the people who come in and out of here lead very transient lives, Inspector. The Saint was one of them, I'm afraid. I can tell you that he was around forty-five," he paused, noting their reaction. "I know, but living on the streets and sleeping rough ages a person terribly, as you realise."

"I do realise, sir," Morgan said softly. "Only too well."

Innes shot him a glance, noting the change in her boss's voice, but said nothing.

Morgan felt her eyes on him, but moved things along with another question. "Did you know he owned a very expensive wristwatch?"

Robin shook his head. "I didn't know him that well, sorry. He came originally from a small village I believe, and there were rumours he was a very successful businessman in his youth, or so he used to boast around here, anyway. That's about all I have, sorry."

"Tell me, how often did he sleep here at Sherard House?"

Burroughs pursed his lips. "Well, we don't have limitless space, I'm afraid, and we operate on a first-come, first-serve basis. Getting in for the night can be tough."

"Do you keep a record of who sleeps here, sir?" Innes asked.

The thin man with the goatee beard gave her a look of sympathy. "That's just not feasible, I'm afraid to say. They come and they go. Here, they can get a warm bed and something decent to eat but then they must go back out into the world. It's not a hotel. I only wish I could do more."

Morgan kept his calm, hazel eyes fixed on Burroughs. "I'm sure you do, sir. Now, when was the Saint last here?"

"Hang on a sec."

Burroughs picked up his phone and called the woman at the front desk. She appeared moments later, sheepishly poking her head around the door. "Robin?"

"Come in, Janet, come in."

She shuffled into the tiny space and took up a position to the side of Burroughs, her arms dangling down awkwardly at her side. "How can I help?"

"I've got some bad news. The Saint was found dead this morning."

She gasped and looked down at Robin Burroughs. "That's terrible."

"I know."

She opened her mouth to speak again, but Burroughs interrupted her. "The police here are trying to find out when he was last here at the shelter. I can't recall, but do you have any idea?"

She thought for a moment, her eyes wandering up to the ceiling as she counted some dates off in a breathy mumble. "Yes, I think so. It's Monday today so he was here a just over a week ago – last Saturday."

"Are you sure?" Morgan asked.

"I am, yes. It was my birthday and he wished me a happy birthday."

Morgan asked, "And what else did he say?"

She gave a quick, shallow shrug. "Not much, they never do. Wait – he did say he would buy me a present but for my next birthday. He said he was going to be a very rich man soon."

Morgan heard Innes writing everything down in her pocketbook beside him.

"Any idea what made him say that?"

"Not really. I think he was just messing about."

There was a steady, quiet pause. "Why don't you try Heron House?" Robin said. "That's another popular shelter. It's run by the Samaritans. It's just on Trinity Street."

"I know where it is, sir," Morgan said. "And thank you for your time today."

"You're most welcome."

*

Dr Sophie Anderson clicked the door of her modest home behind her and locked the deadbolt. Taking hold of her suitcase's pull handle she trundled it along the path on its tiny plastic wheels until she reached her car. Lifting the boot of the Audi, she set the case inside and shut it back down again. Car keys in hand, she opened the door and climbed into the soft leather seat.

Fired up the engine.

Wipers on and checked the mirror.

She didn't notice the small white van parked up at the end of her street.

Then as she reversed out of her drive and pulled out onto the quiet cul-de-sac, she ran through a mental list to make sure she had everything she needed for the conference. She pressed the throttle and the powerful coupé moved away from her flat. She turned on the radio and tuned into the news as she signalled and slowed to pull onto the main road.

She found herself quietly hoping the body Jacob had told her about at Avebury was a suicide. It was a grim, dark thought, she knew, but it was better than the prospect of another killer on the loose. The Witch-Hunt murders had left him tired and shocked and he was damaged enough by the terrible fire that had taken Jess from him the year before. Finding out that his colleague Ethan Spargo had been the mastermind behind the killings up at Grovely Wood was another hefty blow and she worried about what it was doing to him.

She changed up into third and gained some speed. She looked to her left as her car cruised along the A36 past the very same woodland where it had all happened just after last Christmas. Since then, they had grown closer and spent a lot of time together. He was still reluctant to talk about the fire, but he had described to her the feeling of failure he got whenever he thought about how many had died during Operation Grovely because he had not worked fast enough.

Checking her mirror, she saw some light traffic behind her, but paid no attention to the white van lagging two or or three cars back. Driving safely, obeying the speed limit. Drawing no attention to itself.

As a psychologist she knew these were misplaced feelings, probably connected to the heavy sense of guilt Jacob felt over Jess's death and his inability to fight through the smoke and flames and save her life during the blaze. She also knew it would take more than a few sessions with police therapist Dr Amelia Lovelace to get him to a more peaceful place in his mind.

Onto the A303 and into fifth. At the limit now, she dumped the radio and played one of her favourite CDs. Jacob was a grown man and could look after himself, and she had a week-long conference to attend down in Exeter. Smiling as she pushed back into the comfortable seat, she relaxed for the long journey down to Devon.

Behind her, the driver of the white van was keeping a safe distance from his victim.

# CHAPTER 11

When Anna Mazurek saw the caller ID, she breathed a sigh of relief. Even here in her office at the heart of the CID's headquarter building she had started to feel unsafe and vulnerable. Her ex-husband's recent release from prison was something she had dreaded for a long time but when he'd started sending her intimidating messages on her phone her paranoia had really kicked into overdrive. When she saw the name of the senior CSI officer on her phone screen she felt her nerves settle down once again.

"Hi, Mia. Any news?"

"As much as I like you, Anna, I'm not calling to arrange a night out. Of course there's news."

"But we should do that."

"What the night out thing?"

"Why not?" Anna said.

"And drag Bill and Jacob out, too?"

"Sounds good to me. If you haven't seen Bill Morgan on the dancefloor, you haven't lived."

"Sold, but back to business."

Anna took out her pad and a pen. Mia wasn't exactly the type for small talk so she wasn't offended by the cool response to her suggestion of a night out. "Go ahead."

"My team in the computer forensics section have got Sarah Bennett's phone up and running despite the water damage and I can confirm that she received a text on Facebook Messenger from her husband in which he told her he wanted to apologise and that he wanted her to come home. She never replied."

"Sure?"

Mia sighed. "No, I'm just having a laugh. Of course I'm sure."

Anna rolled her eyes. "I'm just checking, thanks. Anything else?"

"The watch on the wrist of the dead man in the Avon is brand new. Each Rolex has a specific six-digit serial number. In the good old days, it used to be engraved between the lugs on the side of the case just below the six o'clock mark. These days it's engraved on the rehaut."

"The what?"

"The inside flange."

"Right."

"So you can use this serial number to find out a lot about a watch, including where and when it was made, and in this case it's brand new – manufactured this month. Unless the dead man had a car tucked away somewhere, it's probable he bought it in a shop in the city, very recently."

"Great stuff, Mia, thanks. I'll check on it right away."

"You sound glum," Mia said. "I thought that would cheer you up."

Anna sighed. "If it's brand new then it's less likely that it's stolen. It's possible, but robbing someone and getting a brand new watch is just too lucky. I think he bought it and that makes things more complicated, more likely that he had come into some money. But that problem belongs to Bill and Laura so I'll pass it along."

"Sounds like a plan."

"Any word on Sarah Bennett's computer equipment?"

"Nothing dubious on any of their stuff," Mia said with a note of disappointment. "So they're ready for you to spend your day trawling through all of their boring emails."

"Oh, joy."

"What about the PM on the homeless chap I saw this morning?" Mia asked. "Any word on that?"

"Later today, apparently."

"Dr Richard surely is working fast these days."

"I think the top brass are worried we might have a serial killer on our hands so the PM was ordered as a top priority, especially after yesterday. He drove down to Salisbury and arrived at the hospital an hour ago. Attending the PM of Sarah Bennett yesterday was more than enough for me this week."

"Cheer up," she said. "It's a lot worse for the one on the gurney."

Anna huffed out a sad laugh. "I worry about your sense of humour, Mia."

*

Heron House was half a mile closer to the river and with most of the cathedral well in sight from its front path. A two storey red-brick building built just after World War I, its sash windows were all firmly shut against the wind and rain as Morgan and Innes walked inside and reached for their warrant cards.

"Is the manager available?" he asked.

"He's just through here," said the man. "But I'm afraid we've had some trouble."

Morgan fixed his eyes on him. "What sort of trouble?"

Before he answered, another man's voice boomed down the corridor. "Is that the paramedics, Tim?"

Tim looked at them. "You'd better follow me. That was the manager."

He led the way down a narrow corridor lined with several bedrooms. When they reached the room at the far end, they found the manager on his knees, putting a young woman in the recovery position. He turned and frowned.

Morgan crouched down beside him. "What's happened?"

"Looks like a deliberate overdose," he said. "Where the hell is the ambulance?"

As he spoke, they heard a commotion behind them and Morgan turned to see two paramedics rushing through the lobby. Dressed in the familiar green paramedics' uniform, they rushed past him and Innes and while one immediately set about unpacking equipment, the other began to check the woman's vital life signs.

"Can we have some space, please?" the woman said.

The manager pushed up off his knees and got out of their way. He turned to the two detectives and asked them to move outside.

"Sorry about this," he said. "It's not common but sadly it's not unusual, either."

"You're the manager, I believe?" Morgan asked.

He nodded gravely as he watched the paramedics stretcher the woman out of the door. "Yes. I'm Simon Marshall."

He extended his hand and shook Morgan's and then Innes's hands. As the paramedics passed him, he asked, "Will she be all right?"

"I think so," one of them said. "We've cleared her airway and she'll be in hospital in a few minutes."

"Thank goodness."

He watched them take her along the corridor towards the car park where their ambulance was parked. "I'm supposed to look after things around here, but I didn't do a great job today, did I?"

Morgan puffed out a deep breath. "It's a tough job, what you do, sir."

"Someone has to care for these people, Inspector. Now, is there something I can help you with?"

Morgan explained the situation.

"I see. Let me clean my hands and I'll be right with you," he said. "You can wait in my office. It's just down there off reception."

They waited in the office as instructed, and a moment later Simon appeared, smelling of hand soap. "Thanks for waiting."

"What's her name?" Innes asked.

"Lucy," he said. "She's still a teenager. From what I can gather she ran away from home a few weeks ago, but no one knows why. She won't talk about it. We've all tried to help her but recently she's got very depressed. Someone's giving her trouble I think."

"Trouble?"

Simon shrugged. "That's all I have, sorry. We do our best with limited resources. The homeless aren't one homogenous group. Each has his or her own story, but the one thing they all have in common is that they live on the periphery of society. Right here among us in our towns and cities, and yet no one sees them. It's like they're invisible."

"I understand," Morgan said.

He sighed. "We do what we can, as I like to say."

"The rooms are impressive," Innes said. "I pictured a dormitory with about twenty beds in it."

Morgan looked at her and nodded with understanding. "That's what most people think, but it's not like that these days, at least not in many night shelters."

"But there are still far too many that need a lot of updating," Simon said. "But we were lucky. After the Novichok scare they had to evacuate John Baker House and everything inside was seized and destroyed for fear of contamination. A lot of people think of Salisbury as this

116

beautiful tourist town, which it is, but what many don't realise is that we have the county's highest number of rough sleepers here, plus a lot of problems with heroin as well."

"You don't have to tell us that, sir," Innes said.

"No, of course not," said Simon.

Morgan took out his pocketbook and paused for a moment. When he spoke, his voice was low and level. "I'm sorry to have to tell you that this morning we attended the scene of a dead man across town in the river. We believe him to be a homeless man, and the manager at Sherard House has made a preliminary identification of the body based on the deceased man's clothes."

"And you want me to do the same?" he said sadly.

"I'm sorry, but yes."

Morgan showed Simon the pictures and his response was instant.

"Yes, those are the Saint's clothes."

"That's what Mr Burroughs said, too."

"What a bloody shame, and after what we had here this morning as well."

"You knew him well?" Innes asked.

Simon shook his head. "Not at all. He kept himself to himself. Some of them do, others are more sociable. He was one of the quieter ones. I always got the feeling he was very resentful about what had happened to him. There was never any sort of acceptance. On the rare occasion that he spoke, he always sounded very angry and talked a lot about divine punishment for sinners. Hence the nickname."

Morgan made a note. "Can you tell us anything else about him?"

"Not really, but perhaps I know a man who can."

"Oh, yes?"

He nodded as he got up from his desk and glanced at his watch. "It's still early enough for him to be here, but we'll have to be quick."

# CHAPTER 12

Jacob watched the rain streaking down the window and sipped his steaming tea. Turning, he set the cup down beside Anna's and joined her at her desk where she had been meticulously working her way through the various, files, folders and emails on Sarah Bennett's laptop. When she let out a long sigh, he gave her a sympathetic smile.

"You sound depressed," he said.

She looked up at him. "It's nothing, boss. I'm supposed to be going to some bloody stand up show tonight with Gaz and I could do without it."

"I can sympathise with that. The last stand up I saw was about as funny as income tax."

"You can say that again, but he thinks he's hilarious. Let's put it this way, I'd rather be at work."

"I won't take that personally."

"Thanks."

"Found anything interesting on the laptop?"

"Not really," she said, taking a sip of her coffee and lifting her tired eyes from the screen. "Just the usual stuff. Lots of quick and simple messages to friends and family, but nothing indicating any kind of meeting at the time of her murder. On that score the only thing we have is the text her husband sent her asking her to go home."

"What about the work stuff?"

"Most of it is just admin, but some of the academic stuff is just going over my head – look."

She opened an email thread entitled *Lecture on Homeric Intertextuality* and a heavy silence fell as the two of them made their way down through the messages.

"Get any of that?" she asked.

They shared a glance and laughed. Jacob said, "No, you?"

"Not a frigging word." She continued to scroll back through the emails. "They might as well be speaking in Ancient Greek."

"Very good, Anna. Wait, what's that there?"

"Where?"

He pointed to an email down at the bottom of the page. "There, back in January. The one with *Iachimo* in the subject heading."

She squinted at the screen. "Eh?"

"Iachimo," Jacob said. "It's a character from Shakespeare's *Cymbeline*."

"Never heard of it."

"You didn't study Shakespeare in school?"

She turned and gave him a sarcastic look. "I think we might have gone to very different schools, guv. Mine had cardboard boxes taped over broken windows and if you made it to the going-home bell without a black eye that was a successful day of learning."

"My condolences," he said. "How long is this email thread?"

She clicked on it. "Looks like this is a *massive* email thread." They started to read the first message: *My dear Imogen, let me service tender on your lips?? I xx*

"Woah, looks like we got to the good stuff," she said. "But who the hell is Imogen?"

"She's another character in Cymbeline – the king's daughter. She marries Posthumus in secret so the king exiles him to Italy. While he's there he meets Iachimo, a villainous lothario who claims he can bed any woman in the world."

"Tell me more," she said with a vampish wink.

He laughed. "He makes a bet with Posthumus that he can seduce Imogen and then he goes to England. When he's there, he tells Imogen that Posthumus is using the gold to pay for prostitutes and gambling while living in exile in Italy. He tries to convince her to get revenge on her husband by sleeping with him instead, only in Cymbeline, Imogen is faithful."

"I think we're straying way out of my comfort zone."

"The point is that Matthew Bennett told us he had suspicions his wife was having an affair, and now we have an email thread between her and old Iachimo here."

"You think she really was having an affair, then?"

"I think we have two clever people carrying on with each other and trying to hide it behind a Shakespeare play. The big question is, who the hell is Iachimo?"

"Someone at her work, has to be." Anna said. "Oxford Uni has to be chocked full of people who could use references like this."

He nodded. "A safe start. We'll ask around when we're there, and in the meantime give Mia a call and see if she can isolate the ISP on Iachimo's email account. If there is another man involved, he's a prime suspect in her murder."

"Could be the break we're looking for."

"Let's hope so. I'm going to print off Iachimo's email thread and read the whole thing. You go through the other emails and let me know as soon as you hear from Mia."

\*

Thirty miles south in Salisbury, Morgan and Innes followed Simon Marshall into the shelter's soup kitchen and watched him scan the room for someone.

"I see him," he said. "Over there."

They made their way through the steamy, noisy hubbub until they reached a young man in a stained trench coat and a thick woollen jumper with a large hole torn in the front. A scraggly salt-and-pepper beard obscured much of his facial features and a navy blue beanie was pulled down over his forehead. He wore gloves with the fingers cut off, exposing filthy, chewed fingernails.

"This is Denny," Simon said. "Denny Marks. He came up from Devon and he's been sleeping rough in the city for a few months now. He stays with us when he can get a bed."

The man looked up from his soup. "All right?" He stared up at Morgan with two keen eyes buried in a filthy face, the detective made eye contact with him and gave him a smile heavy with sympathy. "Hello, Denny."

Simon pulled up a chair, the metal legs scraping on the tiled floor. "These are police officers, Denny."

"Coppers?"

Simon nodded and dipped his head closer to him, lowering his voice. "I'm sorry to tell you this, but the Saint was found dead this morning."

Denny dropped his spoon in the soup and widened his eyes. "Dead?"

Morgan said, "I'm very sorry, but it's true. I know he was a friend and I'm sorry."

Denny grunted something none of them caught and started to eat more of the steaming vegetable soup.

Morgan said, "I was wondering if…"

"I don't know nothing about what happened to him," Denny said, interrupting him. He pushed the bowl of soup away and got up to leave. As he moved, the bitter smell of urine drifted up, causing Innes to take a subtle step back.

Morgan saw her move but said nothing. He grabbed Denny's arm to stop him moving away and the man sank back down into his seat. He crouched down closer to him; he had recognised the west country accent at once, and now gave a reassuring smile. "Just relax, we're not here to accuse you of anything."

"No?"

"No."

A long pause. "Is it really true?" Denny's eyes were now hollow with fear. Living on the wastelands of society since his teenage years, he'd lost all trust in others, and all faith in humanity. Morgan read it in his face.

"Yes, I'm sorry. The Saint was found dead this morning not far from here, over in the river near Churchill Gardens."

Denny shivered. The spring might be almost on the horizon, but the winter was still deep in his bones. "It's not fair."

"No, it's not. Tell me, is that area somewhere the Saint spent a lot of time during the day when he wasn't in here or the other shelters?"

The man shook his head and pulled his woolly hat down lower, almost obscuring his eyes. "Not that I know of, no. He wandered all over the place in the daytime. He was out of his face half the time. This life can do that."

Morgan and Innes shared a sad look. The Welshman placed a heavy hand on the young man's shoulder and gave him a reassuring squeeze. "I know, Denny. I know. You smoke?"

A quick, furtive nod, and a glance over at Simon.

"But not in here," the manager said.

Morgan gave him a disapproving look, then pulled a thick Robusto cigar out of a packet in his pocket. "This'll help warm you up, lad."

Denny took the cigar. A mumbled, embarrassed *thanks* was hidden by the rustling of his filthy woollen trench coat, and then the Robusto was gone, snatched down into the folds of the coat to be enjoyed later. Maybe traded for a drink, Morgan considered with a sad sigh.

"Tell me, Denny – I've heard the Saint had a bit of cash lately. Any truth to that?"

Denny shot a quick glance up at the manager.

"It's OK, Denny," the manager said quietly. "You can tell them."

"He might have had some." A low whisper.

Morgan frowned. "Speak up, Denny. I didn't catch that."

The young man cleared his throat and shifted nervously in the seat. "I said he might have had some, but I don't know where he got it from."

"I never said you did, did I?" A broad smile crossed the Welshman's lean, freshly shaven face.

"No, sorry."

"But you *do* know, don't you, lad?"

He looked up at Simon with desperate eyes. "Do I have to talk to him?"

"No, I don't think so. Not without a solicitor. Isn't that right, Inspector?"

Morgan sighed. "There's no need for any of that. You're not a suspect, Denny, and no one needs a lawyer." He lowered his voice to a smooth, fatherly tone. "You want me to catch who killed the Saint, don't you, lad?"

A shrug.

"You don't mean that. You could be in danger, for one thing. What if the killer has a problem with homeless people? What if he has his eye on another target?"

Denny's face turned ashen, but Simon answered. "Look, just between us, I think the Saint *had* come into some money, to be honest with you."

"What makes you say that?"

"Most people who live on the streets and sleep rough never really have any money. What they get, they spend, fast. Sometimes on food, sometimes on drink or drugs – but it's usually gone within minutes of getting hold of it. The thing is, the Saint had started to buy food and drink for some of his friends, and it's not often any of the poor souls we get in here have enough to share it around."

"But not unheard of?"

"No, not unheard of, but he was buying quite a bit of stuff for other people. He had started to drink and smoke much more heavily as well, but where he got the money from to fund it all beats me. Vice is not cheap, Inspector Morgan."

"No, I don't suppose it is. Tell me, when did this increased interest in vice start?"

"Just in the last few weeks, I'd say."

"He drank on the streets or in pubs?" Morgan asked.

"Most pubs around here won't let any of the homeless people in, but some do," Simon said.

Innes said, "Any idea which ones?"

He shrugged. "Sorry, I have no idea."

"I'd try The Mitre," Denny mumbled. "He was in and out of there a bit lately."

Morgan let out a heavy sigh. "Thank you both for your help. I know where to get hold of you if anything else comes up."

"Anytime," Simon said.

Denny got up from the table and turned his back on them, wandering away into the noisy chaos of the soup kitchen. He found a group of friends and they started to talk together in hushed, suspicious tones.

*

Morgan and Innes stepped back out in the cold, and noticed with something approaching relief that it had finally stopped raining. Thinking of what she had just seen, Innes felt another sort of relief as well, when she thought about her cosy flat with her sofa and TV set and central heating system.

Morgan checked his pockets for his phone and keys and then gave a low, weary sigh. He'd investigated more crimes than he could remember but something told him this one was going to be very hard to get a handle on. "Sounds like the Saint was a bit of an iceberg."

"Sir?"

"A hell of a lot going on under the surface."

"Gotcha."

Morgan relit his cigar and turned it in his fingers to get a nice, even burn. "After years of nothing he suddenly starts to get his hands on some cash, and then he gets knocked off one night. A lot to think about there, wouldn't you say?"

"And I'd say the best place to start is *The Mitre*, sir."

Morgan looked at his watch and then back to her. "What a bloody good idea, Innes – and we're just in time to squeeze in a late lunch, too!"

"So we are," she said with a smile, and the two of them started off down the street, thoughts of murder suddenly eclipsed by what they were going to find on one of the best menus in town.

\*

Sophie Anderson pulled off the A303 and parked up on the forecourt of the BP petrol station. She was well into Somerset now and nearly halfway to her destination in Devon. After filling the car up she walked inside the Londis and pulled a chocolate bar and a bottle of still mineral water off one of the shelves. Standing in line to pay, she watched the rain trickling down the window and found herself praying for it to stop.

She also found herself thinking about Tom Jacob again. A few short weeks ago she had never heard of the man, and yet now she was in a relationship with him and it looked like it might get serious. On the surface he was everything any woman could wish for – tall and handsome with striking black hair and cobalt blue eyes, but also kind, brave and funny.

But he was a serious, quiet man, and as a psychologist she knew better than most that still waters ran deep. She also knew he was scarred by personal tragedy and that he largely blamed himself for what had happened. She knew she could help him, but only if he let her.

The rain tumbled down and the queue of customers shuffled forwards, one step closer to the till to make payment for their fuel and snacks. They were a group of perfect strangers who had joined together from all over the country for a few short moments while they paid for their fuel, and then they would break up and go in their own directions, never to see each other again.

All except one man, who was standing at the back of the queue with a newspaper held up to obscure his face. As he pretended to read it, he snatched some chewing gum from a shelf and pulled a black leather wallet from his pocket, all the time never taking his eyes off the back of Sophie's head. The headlines on the paper in his hands reported a sharp rise in violent crime in the area, including murder.

*You ain't seen nothing yet*, he said to himself.

Nothing.

# CHAPTER 13

*T*he *Mitre* on Crane Street was Salisbury's oldest pub, starting its long life as a brothel in 1319, during the reign of King Edward II. Centuries of use and abuse had taken their toll, but the building had recently undergone extensive reconstruction inside and out, and now Morgan and Innes stepped down over the smooth stone doorstep and walked into a cosy, firelit saloon bar.

The cold of the outside world was banished and suddenly they were surrounded by oak beams and landscapes in oils and cheery laughs.

And with luck, the Welshman thought, some answers.

"Nice place," Innes said. "Never been in here before. The price list looks a little steep for your average rough sleeper."

"That it does," he said quietly, scanning the faces of the drinkers. "That it does."

A waitress smiled as she walked past them with a plate of steaming food, the delicious smell of chicken and leek pie drifting in the air behind her.

Innes looked at the food with greedy eyes. "How long have we got, sir?"

Morgan was staring longingly at the menu of bangers and mash, a full ploughman's lunch and roast beef and

Yorkshire pudding. "Not *that* long, unfortunately, but a quick sandwich might just be on the cards."

As they approached the bar, a chunky man with a broad, well-worn face looked at them from behind the till. He had soft bags under his eyes the colour of aubergine skin, his nose broken in two places and when he smiled he revealed a gold tooth on his upper jaw.

"Can I help?" he asked.

They showed their warrant cards, keeping them low on the bar to make things private. "I'm DI Morgan and this is DC Innes."

"I'm Eddie Harrington," he said. "Don't tell me. You're here to break the rule about never drinking on duty?"

Morgan's expression quickly wiped the smile from the other man's face. "No, sir. We're from Wiltshire CID investigating the death of a homeless man discovered earlier this morning in the River Avon. We are treating it as a suspicious death."

"Christ," he said loudly. "What brings you in here?"

"We think the man went by the name the Saint," Morgan said, totally ignoring his question. "He wore a long, brown woollen trench coat with a lot of badges on the lapels, and a…"

"A dark blue beanie?"

Morgan and Innes caught each other's eye.

"That's the one, sir," Morgan said. "So you know him?"

"I don't *know* him," he said defensively. "I didn't even know his name was the Saint, but yes, I've seen him in here."

"You allow homeless people in here then?" Innes asked.

"They're not lepers," he said. "So long as they can pay for their drinks and they don't cause any trouble then they're welcome to come in and get a drink, just like anyone else."

Morgan lowered his voice. "Not all landlords share your attitude."

"We don't have a hive mind, Inspector."

Morgan fixed his hazel eyes on him. He respected his views on serving the homeless, but he thought he detected some attitude. "You get any trouble in here?"

"Sometimes. We get all sorts in here," he explained. "In the daytime it's all fairly cosy with shepherd's pie and half pints, but things can get a bit tasty on Friday nights from time to time. Depends on the clientele. Mostly locals but sometimes we get outsiders here, too. It's a buzzing little city."

Warrant card wallet slipped back inside his suit pocket, Morgan once again looked at the big man behind the bar. "You've been here long?"

Eddie gave a subtle nod. "Nearly ten years. I've worked every angle of the pub trade since I was a kid at my father's knee. He was a publican too. His first pub was the Royal Oak in Thame, then came the Fox and Hounds in Abingdon. My first as landlord was The White Hart in

Blunsdon, then The Bell in Chippenham and then I finally settled down here. As soon as me and the wife arrived we knew we wanted to stay forever."

"It's a nice place to be," Innes said.

Eddie's face turned to a frown and he lowered his voice. "We lost our son in a hit and run, you see. It broke both of us, and there was something about the beautiful nature of this place that offered us some peace. Mind you, life in the old cathedral city isn't all champagne and strawberries. Like any English city, the winters can be long and that Russian nightmare drove many of the drinkers away, especially tourists."

"It hit the city hard, I know," Innes said.

"Takings go down and the worries claw their way up to the surface. Some of the youngsters have a real attitude problem and sometimes fights break out. I've been handling brawling drunks most of my life, but I'm getting older. Luckily, pub fights are rare in this part of the world."

Morgan glanced around the bar and then brought the conversation back to the investigation. "When was the Saint in here last?"

"Last week," he said quietly. "He was in here last week – maybe last Saturday, I think."

"What time did he leave?"

"Throwing out time. He was fairly well-oiled, too."

"Drinking what?"

"You name it. Mostly beers but also some single malts."

"Who paid?"

"As far as I can tell, he did."

"Was he drinking alone?"

"No, he was with another younger lad. He looked like a rough sleeper too, if I'm being honest. Scratchy little beard."

Morgan thought of Denny back at the shelter. "Where did they sit?"

Harrington pointed to a table between the fire and one of the bay windows in the front. "Right there."

The Welshman turned and pictured it. He was good at this, and he took his time as he reconstructed the scene. No one ever rushed Bill Morgan, and now he saw them, the Saint and Denny sitting in the warmth of the fire with pints in their hands. Drinking, talking and laughing. Shooting the breeze before drifting back out into the night, back out to the cold, far edges of civilised society. He felt a wave of anger rise in him, a rush of hatred for the man who had killed him.

He turned back to Harrington. "Did they leave at the same time?"

"Yes, they did. They went right at the very end, and they got a taxi too. The one you called the Saint asked me to call it for him."

"Which company was that?"

He eyes crawled over the horse brasses nailed to the exposed ceiling beams as he tried to recall the name of the taxi firm. "I think it was Rossiter's."

Innes made a note on her pad. "Are they a local firm, sir?"

"I think so, yes. It's a one man job based in Laverstock, I think."

"OK, thanks."

"I see you've got a CCTV camera fitted on the front of the building," Morgan said.

"That's right and before you ask – yes, it is real, and yes, you can have the footage from last week if I still have it."

"Thank you sir. I'll send a uniformed constable around to collect it in due course."

\*

The drive out to Laverstock was less than three miles and during the short journey Morgan's mind had turned into a maze of problems and unanswered questions. Until the CCTV footage from the pub was recovered, the last sighting of the Saint and Denny was when they were sitting in the saloon bar of *The Mitre* sharing a few drinks and laughs.

Denny had neglected to tell him that, but he could understand why. Still, it was another cause for suspicion. The questions piled up. Where had the money come from to buy brand new Rolex watches and single malt whiskies in the pub? Where had they asked the taxi to take them? Not the shelter – that was only a few minutes' walk from the pub.

"This looks like the place, sir."

He looked over at Innes who was now steering the car into a small car yard on the northern edge of the small parish. A silver Ford Tourneo was parked on the tarmac outside a portacabin and as they pulled up and killed the engine, a man swung open the door and peered out at them.

As a man who kept himself fit, Morgan instantly knew that Preston Rossiter had once been fit but was slowly running to fat. He was in his late forties with a shock of bright blond hair, a small, chiselled nose and slightly manic, beady eyes. The early stages of a double chin were just visible beneath his jawline, as was the small roll of fat starting to tumble over his belt.

"Hello Mr Rossiter," the Welshman said, flashing his warrant card. "I'm DI Morgan and this is DC Innes."

"What do you want?"

"I want to ask you about one of your fares."

"Oh, yes?"

"Yes."

A long pause.

"Which one?"

"Two homeless men, one of whom went by the name the Saint. We believe he hired you to pick them up from *The Mitre* last Saturday evening. Can you recall that?"

"I drive hundreds of people a week, Inspector."

"But how many homeless people in trench coats do you pick up from *The Mitre*?"

The man's eyes danced over the tarmac for a moment. "Ah, yes! Now that you mention it I *do* remember that particular passenger."

"Just one passenger?"

"That's right, two of them came out of the pub together but they said goodbye to each other and only one got in the cab. Didn't smell too good as I recall."

Morgan bristled, but kept his cool. "You picked him up from the pub at what time?"

"Throwing out time. I remember because there were pissheads everywhere chucking up in the gutter and I was worried they were going to do it on my cab."

"And where did you drop him off?"

"That's the funny thing," he said quietly. "He wanted me to drop him off in the middle of nowhere."

"Where?"

"I took him out past the Alderbury Trout Farm down near Harnham on the River Nadder."

"And?"

"And he told me to wait while he disappeared for a few minutes, then he came back about ten minutes later and told me to drive him back into town."

"Where to, exactly?" Morgan asked. "The Samaritans shelter?"

"No, he had me drop him off on Exeter Street, next to the cathedral. He told me he had some business to attend to. That was the last I saw of him, I swear."

"Did he mention what this business was, sir?"

The man paused, then raised his chin. "As far as I recall, I'm not being interviewed under caution."

Morgan and Innes caught each other's eye. "No, you're not," Morgan said.

"Then you have no right to ask me that question, Inspector. Establishing my identity and what I was doing is one thing but trying to obtain information that will give you further lines of enquiry would require a caution. At least, that's the idea, no?"

"Don't take this personally, sir," Morgan said. "But you seem to know a lot about the law for a taxi driver."

He glowered at them for a moment before leaning up against the Portacabin wall and folding his arms over his chest. "I was a lawyer," he said sullenly. "A barrister, in fact."

Morgan and Innes exchanged a glance. Morgan said, "Not every day you find a barrister driving a minicab, sir. As someone in the middle of a lengthy divorce with lots of legal bills, I'm quite sure you'd earn more in your previous occupation."

"That's rather hard to do if you've been disbarred, isn't it?"

"Disbarred, sir? What on earth for?"

He climbed down the portacabin steps and squared up to Morgan. "That has absolutely nothing to do with you."

"All right, Mr Rossiter," Innes said calmly. "Take it easy."

"I know my rights, and don't you forget it."

Morgan smiled at him humourlessly. "Alderbury Trout Farm, you say?"

Rossiter backed down. "Yes, that's the place."

Morgan gave him a beaming smile. "Thank you for your help, sir. I'll be in touch if I need to speak to you again."

"Feel free."

As Rossiter walked back up into the portacabin and disappeared inside, Morgan and Innes climbed back into their car and closed the doors.

"What do you think?" he asked.

"Overly defensive and clearly uncomfortable with the questions."

"That's what I thought," he said.

"From barrister to minicab company owner," Innes said. "That's quite a comedown. There must be something more appropriate that pays better."

Morgan shrugged. "Depends what he did to get booted out. He might even have a record. We'll look into it and find out."

Innes's phone rang and she took the call, speaking with someone for a few moments. She hung up and said, "That was DS Mazurek, sir. She says she called you and left a message."

"Haven't checked messages since before lunch. What did she say?"

"She's called around the various jewellers in town and struck gold. You know Trelawney & Sons on Blue Boar Row?"

"I do indeed," he said wistfully. "Leanne wears many of their finest rings."

"Well, that's where the Saint got the Rolex. He bought it two weeks ago and paid cash."

Morgan looked at her, eyes wide. "Twenty grand cash? I like his style."

"I think we need to check out what's around that trout farm," Innes said. "A bit odd asking to be dropped off in the middle of nowhere like that."

Morgan gestured at the portacabin. "We only have *his* word for that."

"True. Shall we go there now?"

He looked at his watch and shook his head. "No time. It's getting late and we're meeting Richard Lyon over at the hospital in less than half an hour for the Saint's PM. Who knows what house of horrors that's going to turn into?"

# CHAPTER 14

Half an hour later, Morgan and Innes were walking through the white-painted corridors of Salisbury District Hospital on their way to the mortuary. The latest message from Richard Lyon was that the post-mortem was completed and he was ready for them. Pushing through the final set of double doors, they entered a space that was at once familiar and alien; stainless steel splashbacks behind a row of sinks and metal shelves carefully stacked with a host of ugly-looking instruments.

Stepping into the bright overhead light above one of the gurneys, Richard Lyon gave them a warm smile as they walked over to him. "Good afternoon, both."

"Afternoon, Richard." The Welshman glanced over at a compact stereo perched on a shelf through which classical music was gently playing. "I see you've made yourself at home."

Richard turned and switched the music off. He moved like a chef bustling about in his kitchen. "It helps pass the time. Believe it or not, corpses are not the best of company, although on occasion they are preferable to certain police officers."

"Blunt," Morgan said. "But I won't take it personally."

Innes gave a cautious smile. "Nor me."

"I might be blunt," Richard said, "but you have to admit I'm an improvement on the last guy."

"That you are," Morgan said. "That you are. Now, what have you got for us?"

"Here's your man." He pulled the disposable mortuary sheet away from the dead body with a theatrical flourish. "I haven't put him back together again yet though."

Morgan stared down at the rotting corpse with disgust and turned his head away. Richard's handiwork was there for all to see – open chest cavity, sawed bones and sliced flesh. Lifting a hand to hold back a wave of nausea, he cursed the senior pathologist. "Bloody hell, Richard! You could have warned me."

"And where's the fun in that?"

"Thanks."

Innes's eyes crawled over the dead man's horribly disfigured face. "God, that's even worse than I remember."

"Well, this is the real world," Richard boomed. "And the real world is awful, no? None of your surgical airbrushing for *hoi polloi* in here. Just the real thing."

Morgan had composed himself. "And what does the real thing tell you?"

"A long and weary tale of abuse, neglect, indulgence and violence."

The detectives exchanged a glance, and Richard continued his performance.

"He died from hypoxemia and irremediable cerebral anoxia, inducing acute drowning in the same water to be found in the River Avon in this fair city."

Innes leaned closer to the body, studying the rips and tears disfiguring his face. "So what did all this damage?"

"Put as succinctly as possible, this man was dinner for all the lovely pondlife floating about in the Avon," he said. "But that's not the fun part."

Morgan bristled at his use of the word fun, but taking a look around he forgave the old pathologist. If black humour was what it took to get through a day in here then he could use as much of it as he liked. "Fun part?"

"He was gripped from behind by a man with a large handspan. A strong man, I would say. The pattern of bruises on his neck tell a very clear story on this. Held under the water until dead."

"Murder, then." Morgan's words echoed in the metal mortuary.

"Doubtless."

"Any use of chloroform like the woman up in Avebury?" Innes asked.

Richard shook his head. "Not this time."

Morgan rubbed his nose. "And dead for how long?"

Richard sighed and scratched the back of his head. "This is a tough one because of the amount of decay, but I would say he was in the water for at least a week, maybe ten days."

"Which tallies up with some of the witness statements," Morgan said. "He was last seen alive last Saturday night which was nine days ago."

"God, I'm good," Richard said deadpan.

Innes rolled her eyes. "That's a long time to be floating around."

"He would have spent most of it submerged before the gasses inside him pushed him back up to the surface." Richard's smile faded as he stepped closer to the stainless steel gurney. "It was not a pleasant end," he said quietly. "But possibly better than the one he had coming."

Innes caught Morgan's eye before asking her question. "And what end was that?"

"I'm afraid to say that calling this man a heavy drinker and smoker would be a gross understatement. This man was also an intravenous drug user, and with the toxicology report back I can tell you that he used heroin and methamphetamine, also known as speed. I've rarely seen such damage to the internal organs. In my estimation this man couldn't have gone on much longer than another twelve months before coming to an abrupt and fatal stop."

Morgan winced. "Would he have known about his condition, Richard?"

He shrugged. "Possibly, but it's unlikely he was a regular visitor to any GP. I suspect he was too out of his mind most of the time to notice how far gone he was. At least this end was quick."

"How quick?" Morgan asked.

The pathologist pulled his surgical mask down over his face. "After he was forced under the surface he would have run out of air after around sixty seconds, probably less considering his overall health. He would have experienced an intense burning sensation as the water raced into his lungs and lost consciousness not long after. He would have been dead within five minutes, possibly less. Same for the woman in Avebury."

"Bloody hell," Innes said. "That's not the way to go."

"Quite." Richard leaned over the body and spoke from behind the surgical mask as he pulled the body over to expose the neck. "As you saw when you found him, this man was gripped with substantial force from behind and held underwater until he was dead by drowning. The bruise marks are caused by fingers pushing down deep into the flesh of his neck. I would say the killer is certainly a strong, fit man and judging by the handspan he is of above average size, but not enormous."

"So he just overpowered him?" Innes asked.

Richard shook his head. "Look here," he said, pointing a nitrile-gloved finger to the back of the man's head. "There's evidence here of a hefty whack to the back of the head. A rock, I'd say, but it wasn't hard enough to break the skull, and whether or not it was enough to knock him out I'd have to say the jury's still out."

"Come on, Richard!" Morgan said. "We're talking about a brutal murder here, and maybe even one linked to the death of a high-flying academic as well. I need answers."

The pathologist weighed it up again, looking almost in pain as he was forced to refine his answer to them. "Then *no*. I would say this blow was enough to knock him to the ground and disorient him but not to induce unconsciousness."

Innes crossed her arms. She was starting to look uncomfortable. "But you said the man who held him under the water was strong and fit."

"I did."

Innes frowned. "So the killer deliberately wanted him conscious?"

Morgan gave a nod. "I think so. I think the bastard wanted him to feel every minute he was being drowned."

Innes shuddered at the thought, made significantly worse by the stench of surgical antiseptic that washed up to her nose when Richard rolled the corpse back over and stood up to his full height. "Not nice."

"No," Richard said.

"And these injuries were the same as those on the body of the woman brought in from Avebury?" Morgan asked.

"Almost identical method, yes. The same pattern of bruises and the same handspan. The only difference is that the woman had no head injury and was rendered unconscious by the use of chloroform."

Morgan turned to Innes. "And the significance of that would be..?"

"It indicates premeditation for the Avebury killer – acquiring chloroform and taking it with him, but a rock indicates an improvised murder."

"Bang on the money," Morgan said, nodding his head.

Richard replaced the sheet and began to collect the various post-mortem tools – bone saw, rib cutter, scalpel, surgical scissors, enterotome and Hagedorn needle – and walk them over to the sink for cleaning. "So I would say you're looking for either the same killer, or two carefully coordinated murders."

"My gut says one killer," Morgan said.

Richard removed his nitrile gloves and turned to them with a smile. "And mine says it's time for dinner."

Innes looked at the body under the shroud sheet and up to the smiling Richard Lyon. "I think I'll pass tonight."

"Me too," Morgan said. "Besides, by the look of things, there's a seriously deranged nutcase on the loose and it's our job to find him."

Looking at her watch, Innes realised how late it was getting. "Couldn't drop me at home on your way back to Swindon could you, sir?"

"No probs, Laura."

*

Anna rubbed her eyes and wondered if she could get away with falling asleep. The chances were slim. Gareth was sitting right next to her and they were in the middle of Swindon's Wyvern Theatre watching what he had promised was the funniest man on earth.

She had seen plenty of stand-ups at the Comedy Store in London and she was fairly certain he wasn't even the funniest man in the theatre, never mind on the planet, but her boyfriend had insisted and so here she was. She suppressed a yawn and then flashed him a fake smile when he glanced at her.

Another gag and another embarrassing mix of laughter and groans from the audience. She glanced at her watch. She just knew tomorrow was going to be an even longer day than this one. Maybe she should have just told him she couldn't make it tonight, but she felt like she was growing apart from him and wanted to see if they could connect in some way again.

He sipped his lager. "This one's bloody hilarious!"

She doubted that, but dug deep and found another fake smile. She realised it was getting harder to do this. She didn't love him any longer and there was no point lying to herself about it. Time was running out on their relationship, and that meant big changes to her life. He was a nice bloke, and his property development company made more money than the entire top brass at the station earned in a year, but that wasn't what was important to her.

She was still young...*ish*, she added with a sigh. And pretty good-looking too, even if she did say it herself. She'd seen the way Bill Morgan had been looking at her recently and he wasn't the only one. There would be life after Gaz, she just knew it in her heart and yet something had made her stay with him. Fear, she guessed – being alone in a dark, cold world as she hit forty wasn't exactly the fairy tale she had dreamt of as a kid.

She yawned, this time audibly and Gareth and a few others in nearby seats turned and looked daggers at her.

Apparently, she was the only one in this place who'd rather be in bed right now.

# CHAPTER 15

Simon Marshall roared with laughter at the joke on the TV and cracked open another can of his favourite bitter. Still chuckling, he had to control himself to stop slopping it as he poured it slowly out into his dimpled glass beer stein.

Setting the empty can down on the side table, he stretched his legs up onto a black leather ottoman and sunk back down into his sofa. Working with so many homeless people and rough sleepers had given him an acute sense of gratitude for everything he had around him and he never took any of it for granted. Here, in the warmth of his fire and with the beer inside him, he started to slip away into the soft, welcoming sleep of home.

Until the window smashed.

Startled, he stumbled out of his chair and knocked his beer over. It spilled out over the carpet as he staggered to his feet and realised with horror that his front room was on fire. Flames spread out over the carpet and worked their way up the TV stand. Now, the frame around his plasma TV screen was bubbling and popping and noxious black smoke reeking of burnt plastic quickly filled the room.

He felt the cold, damp air of a March night blowing into his room, pushing his curtains in towards him like ghosts. He wanted to scream but for a moment he was lost for words and frozen to the spot like a statue. He heard wheels skidding outside but no way of seeing out through the burning window.

*You've got to get out of here!*

He scanned the room for his phone, snatched it from the arm of the chair and stumbled out with his hand to his mouth. Then, he raced down the hall, his head spinning with what had just happened to him, unlocked the front door and wrenched it open.

He tumbled out into the front garden enveloped by a thick cloud of smoke and heaved the clean, cool air into his lungs in between vicious coughing fits. Gripping the phone with a trembling hand, he dialled 999 emergency and tried to stay calm as he ordered the fire service and police to attend his house.

The woman on the other end of the line was trying to keep him calm, but he just stared up at the smoke pouring from his house and gasped. His chest heaved up and down with fear and shock. Orange and red light flickered through his windows in the dark night. Instinct forced him backwards now, taking short, unsure steps away from the lethal threat unfurling in the heart of his home.

*Who would do this?*

His mind crackled like a broken radio as he took in the sight of his burning home. An isolated barn conversion, he had no neighbours to run to, and could do nothing but collapse back on a garden bench and wait for the fire engine to arrive.

As the fire ripped through his house and burned his life to nothing, he buried his hands in his face and broke down in tears.

\*

Eighty miles west in Devon, the man in the baseball cap crossed his legs and turned the page of his Kindle novel. He'd been waiting here so long now he'd read more than half of *Dead Man's Folly* and Sophie Anderson was still sitting just inside the window of her third floor room. It looked like she was working on her computer, or maybe talking to someone on Skype. Hard to tell.

Seeing a couple walking towards him along the gravel path, he lowered his face back to the book and ignored them as they passed. As they made their way along the path beside the rose beds he lifted his gaze once again towards Reed Hall and watched his prey in the warm cosy amber of her room.

A cool breeze blew from the west, probably off the river. He shivered a little and pulled up the collar of his jacket. The Grade II listed building was just off the main campus of Exeter University and hidden safely in the middle of three hundred acres of beautifully maintained gardens. The Italianate mansion was used by the university as a venue for conferences and this week it was hosting a gathering of some of the world's greatest minds in criminal psychology and profiling.

He looked up. She was still sitting in the window, visible to the world and oblivious to the threat he posed.

He turned another page and followed Poirot into the next chapter before glancing at his watch. It had been dark for some time and the temperature was dropping. In another hour or so it would be too cold to sit here. For now, it was the best place to keep watch.

Looking up, she was tying her hair back now and closing the laptop down. He took out his iPhone and let his eyes crawl down the conference itinerary. According to this, dinner was being served in another hour or so and he guessed she'd want time to shower and get dressed and then maybe meet friends and colleagues in the bar for an aperitif before eating.

She got up from the desk and walked out of sight. The blue-eyed girl in the inner sanctum, safe but not for long because *here I am*, watching you with something terrible in my mind. She came back into view, clothes gone and wrapped in a towel. Steam formed on the inside of the window. She was going into the shower now.

He thought about ending all this and walking away. But it was too late. He had no choice. He had to go on with it, no matter how wicked it was.

No matter how terrible.

*

By the time Jacob arrived at Grange Court the fire service were already hard at work. Thick red hoses fixed to the back of the engine snaked across the lawn, gripped at the other ends by firefighters as they doused the barn conversion with a high-pressure jet of cold water.

Tony Wright, the crew manager padded over to Jacob and lifted the visor on his safety helmet.

"Jacob."

"Tony."

"Nasty business, but it's all under control. I'd say he's lost around twenty percent of the building and he has a lot of hard work ahead of him."

Jacob nodded, but said nothing in response. Instead, he was looking up at the wrecked barn, its wooden beams and support columns like the ribs of some dead animal sticking up at grotesque angles in the damp night.

"What are you doing here, anyway?" Tony asked. "Didn't expect to see a senior chap such as yourself out on a regular call out like this."

"He's involved in a case I'm investigating," Jacob said. "He talked to Bill Morgan earlier today and I think this might be connected."

"I can see you're very happy to be here."

He shrugged. "Like I say, what happened here tonight may very well have something to do with the case we're working on."

"You mean witness intimidation?"

He gave an absent-minded nod of his head, eyes fixed on the smoking heap. "Maybe."

"I don't know how you can spend your life with all that low life. Give me fire any day of the week."

Jacob turned to him, eyes straight and level. "Give me crime over working with fire."

Tony Wright looked away and pretended to assess the fire damage once again. "I'm sorry, Jacob. I didn't think."

"Forget it, Tony. I presume that's him over there in the back of the ambulance?"

Tony nodded. "Treated for smoke inhalation. I think they must be about done by now."

Jacob thanked him and wandered over to the ambulance with his hands in his pockets, working hard not to think about the burning embers in the barn to his right.

"Mr Marshall?"

A sad, frightened man holding an oxygen face mask in one hand looked up at him. "That's me."

"I'm DCI Jacob from Wiltshire CID. You spoke with one of my colleagues earlier today down in the shelter in Salisbury."

"That's right — a Welsh bloke and a young redheaded girl."

"DI Morgan and DC Innes."

He sucked on the mask a few times and coughed. "They were very good."

Jacob nodded. "They're among the best I've ever worked with."

The two men sat in silence for a few moments while the paramedics fussed around with blankets making sure he was warm. Beyond them, Tony Wright and his crew were cautiously going inside the barn and making a more detailed note of the damage.

"You think this is about the Saint's murder, don't you?"

Jacob sighed, considering the line between keeping the man informed and panicking him. "I won't lie, my instinct says this is connected."

"Oh, *God*... I just want to help people. Who would do something like this?"

"Tell me, have you always worked with the Samaritans, Mr Marshall?"

"No, it's a new calling. In a former life I was a barrister but wanted to do something with more meaning so I left the Law Society a long time ago and devoted my life to the homeless."

"That's very noble of you, I..."

Jacob's reply was interrupted by Tony Wright who had approached them with something in his gloved hand.

"What have you got, Tony?"

The crew manager sighed. "They'll be a full report on your desk within twenty-four hours, but I've been doing this a long time and I can tell you now, informally, that this was arson.

"I already told you that!" Simon said.

"We can't take your word for it, sir," Jacob said. "Go on, Tony."

"This is the base of a bottle one of my men found behind the TV set, and there are other fragments as well.

All my experience tells me this fire was caused by a Molotov cocktail coming in through the front window."

Simon's eyes widened with terror. "Then it *was* a deliberate attempt to murder me!"

"Just calm down, sir," Jacob said. "We don't know anything for certain yet. What I will say is that there is enough evidence in my mind to advise you to stay somewhere safe tonight – somewhere you trust. Do you have anywhere?"

"I'd rather check into a hotel," he said, visibly shocked. "Whoever did this can't possibly know where I am if I check into a hotel, can they?"

Jacob considered it. "It's not a bad idea, no."

Simon turned two hopeful, desperate eyes up to the tall detective's face. "I mean, that's what most people would do, isn't it?"

Simon Marshall and Tony Wright waited in the solemn silence a long time for Jacob's reply.

"I wouldn't know, sir," he said at last, darkly contemplating the wreckage. "I don't run with the crowd."

# CHAPTER 16

*Tuesday, 12<sup>th</sup> March*

In the dawn's pale, fragile light, Hannah Wilson pulled her Citroën C1 off the main road and cruised slowly around the sweeping driveway leading to Avebury Manor. Passing the National Trust Museum on her left, she drove the small car along a narrow lane until pulling up in the car park she liked to use beside the manor's walled garden. She wanted to get in early this morning to get some extra work done and the car park was empty.

She switched off the headlights and engine and opened the door. As the heat from the car gushed outside, she felt a cold breeze blowing on her face and neck. Shivering as she climbed out of the car, she locked the door and made her way over to the manor house. She had worked here for the National Trust for over a year now and was beginning to feel like she was finally getting on top of the job.

Her thoughts were stopped by the sound of footsteps behind her. She was still on the dark lane when she heard them and now she swung around and peered into the gloom between the north wall of the garden and an old potting shed.

"Is there anyone there?"

She gasped when she saw him, and took a step back into the middle of the lane. "How…"

"Hello, Hannah."

She felt her blood freeze in her veins. "I don't understand how…"

He took a step towards her, gloved hands hanging limply at his sides. "You don't need to understand a thing. All you need to know is that your torment is over now."

She shook her head dumbly and raised a hand in warning. "You get away from me."

He struck fast, closing the small gap between them in a heartbeat. Before she could scream, he brought his right hand up, curled into a fist, and punched her on the side of the head. She fell backwards like a straw doll, landing on her backside in a daze as he grabbed her arms and pulled her away. She felt herself slipping in and out of consciousness from the power of the blow to her head and she was only dimly aware of being dragged through one of the gates leading into the walled garden.

Then, a wave of ice-cold water crashed into her face and brought her back to reality.

They were in the ornamental pond now and she felt his hands on her neck. The grip was as strong as iron and painful, and then she felt him thrust her forward into the water once again. She gasped with terror as she went in a second time and swallowed a mouthful of the cold water.

The water swam in her ears as he held her head under the surface. She wanted to scream for help but he was still holding her under. She had presumed he was going to pull her out again before thrusting her back down into the water. Then she would scream for help, but who would hear her at this time in the morning?

The grip of the gloved fingers on her neck.

The icy sting of the pond water in her eyes.

The blackness.

The fear when she realised he wasn't going to pull her out again.

She thrashed around, desperately trying to hit him with her arms but there was no hope. No way to reach the man who was slowly drowning her in the freezing water. She felt the water flood down inside her now and her eyes bulged so hard with the fear and the fight she thought they might burst out of her head. Her ears started to whistle and whine and then everything went silent.

And black.

\*

Sophie Anderson held a moment of hope in her heart as a ray of Devon sunshine broke through the tempestuous spring clouds and sparkled on the River Exe. It lingered for a few moments before disappearing once again inside the belly of the rainstorm raging over the ancient city. Turning away from her hotel window, she mumbled a complaint about the length of the British winter and switched on her laptop.

Activating Skype, she saw Jacob was not online yet. Sighing, she walked over to her notes from yesterday evening's lecture and started to read through them again. Dr Kit Bailey, one of the world's most celebrated and accomplished criminal psychologists, had spoken at the conference she was attending in Exeter and she wanted to go over some of his lecture.

To call Bailey experienced was a wild understatement. He had started his life as a psychologist working for the Devon Health Authority and soon progressed to the senior clinical psychologist working in various mental illness units across the county. After that, a lengthy spell in a number of London hospitals followed before working in the United States for many years. His return home to Devon was designed to give him time to start a family before it was too late, but he had told last night's conference he still struggled to find the time to have a personal life.

She glanced at the Skype screen but still no sign of Jacob.

She really had to stop doing that. He had a busy, important job and he'd probably been called away at the last minute. She checked online for any Wiltshire news but there was nothing of note. No more murders and no other serious crimes. The world was safe, or at least their little part of it. She realised she felt safe too – safer than she did in her own home.

She hadn't felt secure there since she'd found the coin. To anyone else it was just a tiny, silver coin, sent to her in a harmless jewellery box. But to her it meant much more than that. The object was an *obol*, an old coin used by the ancient Greeks and Romans to pay for the passage of their deceased loved ones when it was time to cross the River Styx and enter the afterlife. The coins were left either on the forehead of the dead or in their mouths, and they believed Charon took this money and sailed the dead across the river on his ferry. The ferryman always had to be paid if the soul was to reach the afterlife.

The myth had inspired a polymath genius university scholar by the name of Professor Alistair Keeley to go on the country's most notorious killing spree, murdering women and leaving obols in their mouths as his calling card. He had struck so many times across London that the Metropolitan Police had wondered if the killing was ever going to stop. After the third death they had tried to bring Kit Bailey into the case but he was hunting a serial killer in Chicago. They then turned to his protégé, Dr Theo Miles, and he had brought in his PhD student, Sophie Anderson.

They worked together, hand in hand with the Met's best CID detectives and she had risked her life to catch Keeley by posing as one of his students. After a long and bloody hunt culminating in an abandoned meat packing warehouse in London's East End, he had nearly killed her.

She still saw his face in her nightmares.

The way he forced the coin in her mouth. The sensation of his gloved hands around her throat. His breath on her neck when he whispered into her hear... *I do this because I love you...*

The smile on his face when he turned to her in court and the last thing he said to her before being dragged away from the dock.

*I'll send you over the river, Sophie, if it's the last thing I ever do.*

The river. In his deranged, psychopathic mind that meant the Styx or the Acheron. It was a clear death threat made in public for all to hear. It sent a shiver down her spine, but Theo and her friends comforted her with soft words of reassurance.

His sentence was a whole life tariff without parole.

They'd throw away the key.

He'd never see the light of day again.

But that smile…

She was startled by the sound of her computer alerting her to an incoming Skype. She shook herself free of the past and saw it was Jacob.

"Hey." She was glad to see his face. If the grim, hateful smirk of the Ferryman in the Old Bailey was the past, then the warm, humorous smile of Tom Jacob was the future. Except his smile quickly faded and she saw he looked troubled. "Anything wrong?"

"I'm afraid so," he said. "We found a dead man in Salisbury yesterday morning and there's a strong chance his murder is linked to the killing up at Avebury. Same M.O."

"I'm so sorry."

"And there's something I didn't tell you."

Sophie paused briefly as she stopped to consider what was coming next. "What's that?"

"The killer left a calling card on both bodies."

"A signature?"

He nodded. "A homemade wooden crucifix."

She narrowed her eyes in confusion. "A crucifix?"

"Uh-huh. With a Latin inscription carved onto them – *Angelus mortis venturus test.* It means the Angel of Death is coming."

A long, thoughtful silence stretched between them, and then she said, "That changes everything, Jacob. You know that."

"I know, but I want to know your thoughts."

"In criminal psychology, an Angel of Death, sometimes called an Angel of Mercy is a specific category of offender who murders people in the belief he is helping them. They're often care home workers or nurses and so on, but absolutely not restricted to those professions."

Jacob furrowed his brow. "Wait, you're saying this guy thinks he's helping these people?"

She shrugged. "I'm just telling you what the Angel of Death reference could be about."

"But aren't mercy killings usually relatively painless, almost like euthanasia?"

"They don't have to be, Jacob. Mercy is one category, but so is sadism and then a sort of anti-hero who puts people in danger just so he or she can save them again."

"Bloody hell. We've got to work hard to keep this out of the press. After what happened before with Grovely, Kent is desperate to avoid another panic but it's like the killer's always one step ahead of us. We've only just put Spargo behind us, Soph."

"I know. I understand. You'll catch him."

"We've got next to nothing to go on except for the wooden crucifixes." He blew out a breath. "We're on day three of the investigation and we have no leads and now we have two victims. Any pointers on the profiling front?"

"I think you're looking for a man."

"So do we, but probably for different reasons."

"Like?"

"The handspan and the strength involved in the method of killing. What makes *you* say it's a man?"

"The main motive for homicides changes very strongly depending on whether the killer is a man or a woman," she began. "For women, the main motive driving them to kill is domestic arguments, which at nearly half of all female killings is big motive, and after that it's no obvious motive at all. Then it's other arguments, money and drugs, revenge and finally drunken behaviour."

"That fits in with my experience," Jacob said sadly.

"Men are different," she said. "The main motive is regular arguments with people and grudges, then no obvious motive, then revenge, money and drugs or domestic arguments, which are all at the same rate. Finally it's drunken behaviour. In my opinion, the crucifix suggests this is about revenge so it's much more likely to be a man."

He nodded. "Plus we have the handspan and the strength involved in the drowning, as I say. There's no doubt in my mind we're looking for a man, but what type of man?"

"I think we can get a lot from looking at the method of killing. Strangulation and asphyxiation are actually the second most common cause of homicide for male victims, and the third most common for females, but I think this is more than that."

"I agree, but go on."

"Drowning and asphyxia are linked very closely, but the fact both of these victims were drowned so specifically and in exactly the same way suggests to me that the water has some sort of significance to the killer."

"And what about the crucifix?" he asked.

A shake of the head. "On its own, it could mean anything. It could be a very personal symbol for the killer, either something of great importance to him personally or something he connects with the victim. I just can't go any further than that unless I have more to work on. Have you thought about the locations?"

He gave a shallow nod and blew out a deep breath. "Yes, of course. Fact is, they have nothing in common. One is a prehistoric site in the north of the county and the other is in Salisbury in the south."

"But they both have religious significance?"

"That's a bit of a stretch though, don't you think? I'm struggling to think what links the religions of prehistoric England with an Anglican cathedral twenty-fives miles away."

"Just an idea."

"Sorry, and thanks. It really helps to have someone away from the team to speak to about it all."

"Even though it's completely illegal?"

He shrugged. "I have a somewhat baroque relationship to rules, Soph."

She gave him a hopeless smile. "So I presume Marcus Kent is not aware of this conversation?"

"This is a private conversation between you and me. It has nothing to do with him at all. I haven't told you anything confidential."

"Apart from the fact the neither murder is in the public sphere yet."

He grinned. "Apart from that."

"And the crucifix calling cards?"

"And also that."

She shook her head. "You really like skating on thin ice, don't you?"

"I wouldn't say that, exactly."

"What would you say then?"

He thought for a moment. "I'd say if there's one thing that pisses me off more than anything else, it's incompetent people abusing their authority. Kent is a mover and shaker. He knows that it's the squeaky wheel that gets the grease and he works the system. I don't like that and I prefer and trust my judgement over his."

She laughed.

"What?"

"Nothing, it's just the way your face starts to turn red when you get angry."

"Doesn't everyone's?"

"Yes," she said breezily. "But I only smile when I see yours doing it."

Jacob sat back in his chair and worked hard to keep the smile from his face. "Thanks, I think."

# CHAPTER 17

Anna removed the spark plug wire boot and slotted the spanner over the plug. Turning counter-clockwise once, she removed the spanner and turned the socket until the plug was free. She held it in the light for a moment and studied it. The last one was black and she had leaned the mixture out and rebuilt her carburettor to fix the problem. This one was tan. She considered cleaning the gap and replacing it, but decided to put in a new plug.

Then, she stood up and wiped the oil from her hands onto an old rag. She wondered how Jacob was going with the Alvis. How anyone could do this for pleasure was something she would never understand. As far as she was concerned a car, or in this case a motorbike, was a tool to be used. Fixing them was not something to look forward to.

Staring at the old Ducati, she wondered if she should get rid of it. Riding bikes was something she had got into as a much younger woman when she had the time to go to racing circuits and have some fun. These days she seemed to be too tired to attend race meets and she rarely seemed to get the time even to ride the thing to the shops. She had the Audi, she told herself. Maybe it was time to let go of her wayward past, and sell the bike.

If only she could get rid of the memories so easily. When she looked at the Ducati, she saw not just a superbike in need of some desperate TLC, but Declan Taylor, her ex-husband. If she closed her eyes she could see him. He was sitting on it now, with a cigarette hanging off his lip and a lock of hair over his forehead, aiming for the Jimmy Dean look and not missing by much. He winked at her, and she felt a shiver go down her spine.

Back to reality, she tossed the oily rag onto the workbench and decided to give herself a break before grabbing a shower and heading into work. Unable to sleep because of the case, she'd got up at the crack of dawn and killed some time on the bike, but now Declan had crept into her day it was time to move on and get things going. That way she could fool herself into believing she was staying ahead of him, that he would never catch up with her.

But she knew he would. He was out of prison now and had already kept good his promise of getting back at her. He'd been sending texts to her phone, presumably from a burner. She knew him well enough to know he'd never leave a trail of breadcrumbs for the police to follow. Even more worrying was the fear he would escalate the stalking and move up from threatening texts to physical contact. She'd already found herself getting jumpy when she heard something around the house.

She checked her watch and saw it was time to go into work. She felt confused and insecure about Declan's stalking and knew the best thing to do was blow the old cobwebs out of her mind and try and see things from a fresh perspective.

And maybe that meant the superbike after all.

After changing into her leathers she straddled the powerful machine and wheeled it back out of the garage. She kick-started it and it turned over first time and before she knew it she was racing down the A361 on her way to Devizes.

*

When she pulled up in the station car park and climbed off the bike she felt much better, but still found it hard to shake off the fear that her ex-husband might escalate the stalking. Taking off her helmet she marched through the double doors at the front of the building and made her way through HQ to the open plan office she called her home for so much of her working week.

Jacob was already at his desk, and when she set her helmet down on top of her filing cabinet he walked over to her and smiled.

"Everything OK?" he asked.

"Sure, why wouldn't it be?"

He shrugged. "You just look a bit unsettled."

"Do I?"

"I think so. Do you want to talk about anything?"

She thought about the offer. He was a good man, and a brave one too. If she told him, he would know what to do. He would start talking about cautions and restraining orders. But was that overkill? Maybe all she needed to do was meet with Declan and have a quiet word with him. Tell him her life had moved on since they had separated. Maybe he would understand. Maybe he would keep what had happened to himself and let her get on with her new life.

Or was he just too possessive?

She opened her mouth to reply when PC Priest put his head around the door.

"Sir, we've just had a call from a woman working for the National Trust. She thinks she might have found a dead body."

Jacob and Anna  exchanged a grim look. "Where?"

"Up at Avebury again."

"Not in the stone circle?" Jacob said. "It's still a crime scene!"

"Not this time, sir, no. This time the killer left the body up at Avebury Manor."

*

The drive from Devizes across to Avebury was marked by constant rainfall. Jacob's headlights formed two white arcs in the dreary, wet day as they made their way across the North Wessex Downs. Cutting a neat line across endless miles of rolling fields, he peered through the rain-streaked windows of the Alvis at a landscape of isolated farm buildings. Telegraph poles receded across the fields until dropping out of sight in the grey drizzle.

Sitting beside him, Anna Mazurek still seemed unsettled. She was normally very cool and focussed but lately he'd noticed her growing more introspective and distracted. He'd asked her back at the office if she was OK and she'd declined to talk about it, and he knew her well enough to leave it at that. If she wanted to talk about it she'd go ahead and talk about it with him so he decided to change tack and go back to business.

"What do we know about this place?"

Anna, who had been scrolling through some screens on her phone sighed and said, "According to this website, the manor was built on the site of a Benedictine priory which was founded in 1114. After that it was owned by various families but was eventually bought by the National Trust. It was featured on a BBC programme a few years ago and some say it's haunted."

"Why do you say that with the ghost of a smile on your lips?"

Anna put her phone away and fiddled with her silver lighter as they pulled off the High Street and turned into the grounds of Avebury Manor. "Because the last thing we need is a bloody... ah, I see what you did there."

"Just trying to cheer you up."

She rolled her eyes. "I'm fine, I told you that back at the station."

"Saved by the bell," he said. "We're here – look."

He raised a finger off the steering wheel and pointed through the windscreen at the impressive outline of the manor house, just visible now behind a line of oak and ash trees. Thinking about what Anna had just told him about the long history of the place, he tried to imagine all the people who had lived on the site over at least the last thousand years.

As manor houses went, this one was beautiful but modest, nestling in an oasis of mature black poplars and chestnut trees. Closer in, formal gardens created an atmosphere of carefully maintained peace and prosperity but already his mind was focussing on the detail that this place had religious significance.

Driving past a National Trust Museum he parked up beside St James's Church and they made their way along the path to the manor's main entrance. Lined with lavender bushes, the path would have been a striking purple in the summer, but like everywhere else today, the gardens were soaking wet and muted. Reaching a uniformed constable outside the main entrance, he asked where to go.

"Just around the back of the house, sir."

They turned the corner of the manor house and saw the forensics team was already hard at work, led by the indefatigable Mia Francis.

"Mia."

She turned and gave him a private smile. "We really have to stop meeting like this, Jacob. What would our grandchildren say? Their eyes met over a corpse?"

Jacob raised an eyebrow. "How's the internet dating working out?"

"Not good," she said. "Most of the men recommended to me look like the ones on our mugshot database."

"Now, now," he replied. "You mustn't judge a book by its cover."

The rain dappled on the plastic roof of the forensic tent as she cocked her head. "One of them listed collecting post-mortem photography as his hobby."

He looked at her sympathetically. "Ah."

"Yeah, exactly – how do you like that book cover?"

After a short pause, he said, "At least you have something in common."

"I'll pretend you never said that."

He smiled. "Shall we get on?"

"I thought you'd never ask," she said, handing them two plastic packs. "Your forensic suits, and don't forget the lovely disposable shoes."

Jacob and Anna quickly slipped on the paper suits and shoes and followed Mia inside the tent. He was surprised to see the enormous tent had been erected at the side of the formal pond to the west of the manor house. The tent had obscured it from his sight when he had stepped around the side of the house and this was the first he'd seen of it.

"Another drowning?"

"Seems that way, yes."

Anna took out her pocketbook and pen. "Three murders, exactly the same MO with two here in Avebury and one down in Salisbury. Two were women in their early forties and one was a slightly older homeless man. I don't know about you but I'm struggling to connect it all, guv."

Jacob gave a simple nod and tucked his head lower into his collar to escape the breeze blowing in through the tent door. "Our killer certainly gets around. I'll give him that. Who found her?"

"One of the office clerks, apparently," Mia said. "She'd come in early to get a head start. The staff car park is just down there."

He followed where she had indicated and saw a line of cars parked up on a gravelled car park under a line of dark, towering trees.

"First in, then?"

"The clerk says hers was the only one car in the car park when she arrived."

He looked at her. "Not quite the same thing though, is it?"

"That's your department, Jacob."

He took a step closer to the body and crouched down, careful not to topple into the pond as he craned his neck to get a better look at it. "You think she was killed here?"

Mia nodded her head. "Looks like she was knocked unconscious in the car park and dragged over here to the pond before being drowned. There are clear struggle marks in the gravel and scuff marks with matching rock samples on the heels of her shoes."

"He could have killed her in the car park," Anna said. "Drawn less attention to himself, but instead he dragged her out here and drowned her."

"They have to drown," Jacob said darkly. "He's compelled to drown his victims and he's taking risks to kill them that way."

Mia raised her eyebrows. "And they all have to have a cross in their hands, as well."

His eyes darted over to her. "What did you say?"

She held out her blue nitrile-gloved hand. "I found this clasped in her right hand."

He got back up to his full height in a hurry. "Another crucifix?"

"Sorry, but yes."

He looked down at the wooden cross and frowned. Taking it from her, he held it up to the light and turned it in his hands. "This message is different," he muttered. "Hic Est Angelus Mortis. The Angel of Death is Here. Anna, I want all her co-workers interviewed right away, and a list of everyone who has visited the manor over the course of the last week."

"Guv."

"Has anyone spoken to the woman who found her?"

"PC Cook took a full statement from her when he arrived," Mia said. "He was first on scene."

"All right, thanks Mia," he said. "And make sure that statement gets to my desk, Anna."

"Yes, guv."

He turned to Mia. "What time are you going over to that arson attack?"

"Straight after this."

Staring down at the dead, broken woman Jacob realised he was grinding his teeth with anger and he blew out a long, slow breath to calm himself down. Running a hand through his hair, he turned on the spot and stared through the open tent flap at the expansive manor house. "What the hell's going on, Anna?"

"Boss?"

"Look at the timeline of our killer. First, he drowns a homeless man in the Avon and dumps his body in the river to float downstream, then he kills a woman in a ditch at the Avebury stone circle and drags her body to the Devil's Chair sarsen, and now he drowns a woman in an ornamental pond at Avebury Manor."

"And he leaves the crosses."

He turned and took another look at the dead woman. He nodded absent-mindedly and brushed the back of his hand against the stubble on his chin. "And he leaves the crosses."

"And he wants us to find them."

"Not the Saint – he was just dumped in the river. The two women were deliberately left in public places where they'd be found, but leaving the body in the river meant leaving his discovery to chance. There was no way for the killer to know where he would be found or even *if* he would be found. If he'd not resurfaced until a quiet stretch of the water or got snagged in the reeds he might have never been found, and yet the women were laid out for us like sacrifices."

"Don't use that word, please guv."

"A place like this must be covered in CCTV," he said sharply. "I want every camera's footage checked in and out by at least two people. He must have left a clue somewhere, and I want to know what it is."

She made a note on her pad and then lifted her eyes. Looking at something over his shoulder through the tent's opening she sighed. "Looks like we're about to go public as well."

Jacob turned to look over his shoulder and saw a van. It had BBC WILTSHIRE written on the door and a colourful pattern of county town names printed on the side: Warminster, Royal Wootton Bassett, Chippenham.

"Bloody hell," he mumbled. "That's all we need. Get them out of here and tell them to keep away. No one broadcasts a thing until we've spoken to the next of kin. After that I want the whole team assembled for a full briefing. We have another victim and we need to speed up our response."

"Leave it to me."

# CHAPTER 18

J acob hit the brakes and steered around the hairpin bend. The hedges either side of the lane were at least twice the height of the car and totally blocked the view of any oncoming traffic. He sighed as he made the corner and shook his head. "These bloody roads always were lethal."

Anna turned away to disguise her monumental eye-roll. "Maybe if you drove a newer car, guv, it might be an easier ride?"

He looked at her, genuine confusion on his face. "Independent front suspension with coil springs and leaf springs at the rear," he said proudly, pulling into the tiny village of Winterbourne Monkton. "Like sailing on a millpond."

He parked up outside the house and killed the engine.

"Ready?"

"Never."

"I know how you feel."

They walked up the path and Jacob rang the bell. Moments later a man in his forties came to the door and swung it open. "Hello?" He was holding a cup of coffee in his hands and had large purple bags under his eyes.

"Mr Keith Wilson?"

The man's eyes immediately narrowed. "Yes, what is this?"

Jacob showed him his ID and gestured to the woman standing at his side. "And this is Detective Sergeant Mazurek. We're from Wiltshire CID."

The confusion grew stronger. "What's this about?" He had set his coffee cup down on a little hallway table now and was fiddling with his hands. A young woman's voice called down from upstairs, but he ignored it. "You'd better come in."

He led the two detectives into the kitchen at the back of the house. The kettle was still steaming, and some freshly buttered toast was getting cold on a plate beside a newspaper on the table. Jacob had already seen the degree certificate hanging on the wall beside the mirror and exchanged a knowing look with his sergeant. *This*, he had thought painfully. *How much I hate it.*

The young woman bustled into the kitchen. In her early twenties, he guessed she was their daughter. She was still tying a knot in her dressing gown and her hair was all over the place. She looked first to her father, and then to the two strange people who seemed to be taking up a very large space in the centre of the room.

"What's this about?" she said.

"They're from the police," the man said.

Jacob lowered his voice. "I'm sorry to have to tell you that your wife Hannah was found dead earlier today."

They exchanged a glance, confused and scared.

"That can't be right," Keith said. "Hannah's at work."

"No, sir," Jacob said quietly. "She's not at work."

"You can't mean Mum?" said the young woman.

"I'm afraid so…"

Without warning, Madeleine Wilson began sobbing and her father had to help her into one of the wooden chairs at the table. Jacob looked at Anna. The younger woman scratched behind her ear and clenched her jaw. Like him, she wanted to be anywhere else on earth than here, now.

When he had calmed his daughter, Keith Wilson turned two tear-stained eyes to Jacob and said one word. "How?"

"We're waiting for the official report from the police pathologist, but it looks like she was drowned."

Keith's gaunt face registered the news with total horror. "You can't mean she was *murdered?*"

"I'm sorry, but we believe so, yes."

Maddy Wilson moaned like she had been stabbed in the chest and Anna shifted uncomfortably on the spot. Through the pained, horrified anguish, Jacob heard a trembling voice say, "Are you sure someone hasn't made some kind of mistake?"

"No mistake. She was found this morning at her workplace by a colleague who immediately called us to attend. Upon arrival our CSI team found her in the ornamental pond at the manor and pronounced her dead. I'm very sorry for your loss, but we will of course require a formal identification."

"Drowned?" Maddy repeated the word in a horrified whisper.

"We think so. I'm very sorry."

Keith Wilson brought himself up to his full height. The shock on his face was turning into something else now. His eyes had dried, and his face had hardened into a rictus of growing rage. "Who did this?"

"We've only just opened our investigation," Jacob said. "It's very early days and we think there may be a connection with two other murders in the area this week."

"Other murders?" Keith said. "We've heard nothing on the news about any murders."

"We tried to keep them from the press but unfortunately there were some reporters at Avebury Manor this morning. We think someone who works at the manor may have called them. We're not sure, but it will be public now which is why I wanted to speak with you as soon as possible. I can assure you both that we'll be doing everything in our power to track down the person responsible."

"Person?" Keith locked his eyes on the senior detective. "You think this was done by a person? This was done by an animal, Chief Inspector."

"I understand how you feel, Mr Wilson."

"How do you? Has this happened to you? Has some kind of animal killed your wife?"

Jacob said nothing. He felt the anguish emanating from Keith Wilson like heat from a radiator. Red face, clenched jaw and hands bundled up into meaty fists ready to smash the first thing he saw. Not even telling him about how he understood his pain, about what he had gone through after his fiancée's death, would be enough to quell the hatred burning in this man's heart. He knew only time could do that.

Anna had already taken out her notebook, and Jacob did the same. His was a brand new Alwych with an all-weather cover. Jess had bought him his first one the day he'd graduated from Hendon Police College, and he'd kept every single one of them. Now, they resided somewhere at the bottom of one of the unpacked boxes stuffed in the back room of the Old Watermill. Lost somewhere in a jumble of old memories and forgotten moments.

"Could you tell me when was the last time that you spoke to Hannah?"

"This morning," Maddy said. She was clutching a wad of tear-streaked kitchen roll to her face and it muffled her words. "We ate breakfast together at this table."

"Did she have many friends?" Anna asked.

The past tense reduced her to a sobbing wreck once more, and her father stepped in and gave the information to the police. Anna carefully wrote down a list of all her friends.

"It's not easy to ask this," Jacob began, "but is it possible your wife was seeing anyone else?"

Keith Wilson's face reddened further. "Absolutely not."

"Miss Wilson?"

Maddy shrugged. Already, the confident, happy woman who had existed up until a few moments ago was now a broken, gutted shell. When she spoke, she stared with a vacant wide-eyes stare at the kitchen carpet tiles. "Of course not. Mum was a good woman. A kind mother."

Keith Wilson held a hand to his mouth and shook his head. His bulging, bloodshot eyes stared out at nothing as he struggled to accept the nightmare that was unfolding around him. "If I find who did this before you do, I *will* kill him. I'll take his damned life like that!" He clicked his fingers to emphasise just how easily he would do it.

Jacob and Anna shared a glance. It wasn't unusual for someone in this position to make threats like this and they both knew he wasn't thinking straight.

"Please, sir," Jacob said. "You have to let us do our job. We'll find him and we'll put him in prison."

"Not if I get to him."

"I want to see her," Maddy said.

"We'll be arranging that as soon as possible. We'll need a formal identification."

Keith squeezed his hands into even tighter fists. "Find him, Mr Jacob. Find him before I do."

Jacob put his notebook away and caught Anna's eye.

"We'll see ourselves out."

*

Back at HQ, Anna had finished organising the team briefing and was just getting herself a quick cup of coffee when Marcus Kent called her into his office. Swallowing her sigh, she took her coffee cup into the office and he

185

closed the door behind her with a gentle click. He gestured to a chair as he took up position behind his desk, lacing his fingers behind his head and leaning back in his padded leather captain's chair.

"I'm glad I caught you sergeant."

"Yes, sir."

"How's the case going?"

"The Chief Inspector has a major team briefing in a few minutes."

"I see." A long pause. "The bottom line is that once again we have another killer running rings around us and it's starting to look like moving to Wiltshire might be very bad for your health."

"With all due respect, sir..."

Before she could finish her sentence, the Detective Chief Superintendent glared at her and said, "With all *due respect*, DS Mazurek the only thing I want to hear from you now is that either you or DCI Jacob here have a solid lead on Operation Avebury." He uncrossed his hands and leaned on the desk, fixing her in the eye. "Well, do you?"

"Not exactly," she said.

"No, I didn't think so. Jacob staying on top of things?"

"Of course."

He nodded and picked up his phone to speak to his personal assistant. "Send DCI Jacob into my office immediately, please."

They waited in silence for a few moments until there was a firm knock on the door.

"Come!"

Jacob entered and caught Anna's eye.

"Take a seat, please."

Jacob sat beside his sergeant, smelling her coffee as it drifted on the warm, heated air of the Chief Super's comfortable office.

"Right," Kent said. "Better start with what you *do* have."

Jacob spoke first. "We have the same MO across all three deaths – victims are drowned and a calling card consisting of a small, handmade wooden crucifix is left behind. Two of the crosses have said the Angel of Death is coming and one has said the Angel of Death is here. I'm not sure if the differing messages are significant. We also know the Saint had come into some money – a lot of money."

"And?" Kent's eyes narrowed. "Please don't tell me that's it."

"Not exactly," Jacob said. "There was an arson attack against the man who runs one of the homeless shelters in Salisbury. He was spoken to in connection with the death of the man known as the Saint."

"I heard about that. You think someone was trying to kill him or warn him away from something?"

"According to the fire crew manager I spoke with at the scene, they meant business."

"Any idea who did it?"

Jacob shrugged. "Not yet. Mia is sending some of her team over later today."

"And that's all you've got?"

"That's it."

"It's not good enough. These are not serious leads. The press have already been on the phone. BBC Wiltshire are all over it – it's on their website now, for pity's sake. Unconfirmed, they say. Next thing you know it'll be all over social media and then Chinese Whispers will kick in and we'll have a panic on our hands. Bennett's murder was one thing, but with the body discovered in the Avon and this poor woman found floating in the pond over in Avebury Manor we're starting to look downright bloody incompetent."

Jacob looked up at the clock and then allowed his eyes to walk over to the window. A typical March day outside, with high winds and a lot of water in the air, and yet he would rather be walking out on the Downs than sitting in here listening to this.

At least out there he would be able to think, and then he realised that something was bothering him. It was something someone had told him but he couldn't remember when. It nagged at him like an itch but he just could not get a hold of it in his mind. It had something to do with *fire*, he thought with a shudder.

"Did you hear what I just said, Jacob?" Kent said, pursing his lips and glowering at him. "Or are you composing a watercolour landscape from the view outside my window?"

"I think these are revenge murders, sir," Jacob said out of nowhere. "Not random spree killings."

"And what makes you think that?"

Jacob paused and sensed Anna turning to look at him. "The victims are too different to fit the usual profile of most serial killers. Something links the victims but I just cannot work out what it is. All our trace and eliminate work has turned up nothing at all and I can't even prove they knew each other."

"Get to the bottom of it, Jacob. Whatever it is."

"Sir."

"I presume you have informed Hannah Wilson's next of kin?"

Jacob nodded. "They took it very badly, as you can imagine."

"Naturally. What's your next move?"

"I need to brief the team on Hannah Wilson's murder and then I've got a meeting with Sarah Bennett's employers at the university. Morgan and Innes are still making enquiries about the Saint. Also, sir, I think it's time we gave a press conference. The original idea of not giving the killer the publicity was a good one, but now the press have got hold of it, that cat is well and truly out of the bag. I think it's important we set out the facts."

Kent clenched his jaw. "Agreed and authorised. Set it up for after your briefing and pray to God no one else gets killed before the day is out."

"Sir."

# CHAPTER 19

The murder of Hannah Wilson had changed everything. With the deaths of all three victims bearing the same modus operandi of being held underwater until drowned, Jacob accepted Sophie's theory about the murders being about revenge. Others disagreed, and Kent and the upper echelons were grimly leaning towards the idea they were dealing with a spree killer. The murders were too close together in time to fulfil the traditional definition of serial killer, but that was just a matter of terminology as far as any potential future victims were concerned.

Whoever was right, the bottom line was that three people had been brutally murdered in less than two weeks and now the top brass were pouring ever more resources into the investigation in a bid to catch the killer. Now, the murder room was even busier with supplemental personnel on telephones and computers and members of the IT staff walking through the door with extra monitors and boxes of paper for the printers.

Progress, or that's what it looked like, at least. Jacob walked through the busy room and stepped into a quieter briefing room at the far end. Waiting until the last few stragglers had entered, he called everyone to order. "All right, let's bring it down a bit. We've got a lot to get through."

When everyone had taken their seats and calmed down to a gentle hush, he walked around to the white board at the front of the room and wrote OPERATION AVEBURY in large black letters.

"As most of you will know, because of the intrusion we faced during the Grovely murders, the top brass wanted to keep the press out of our hair for as long as possible on this one. Unfortunately, that is no longer an option since a member of the National Trust working at Avebury Manor alerted BBC Wiltshire to the discovery of the body at the site this morning."

"Very helpful," someone shouted.

"It is what it is, and we have to deal with it. The important thing is the BBC kept it off their website until the next of kin had been informed, just as we requested."

"But it just makes everything so much harder," Holloway said.

Morgan swivelled in his seat. "But they can help too, don't forget. Especially with appeals and so on."

"Talking of Grovely," PC Cook said from the back. "Is it possible there's a connection between that and these murders, sir?"

Jacob looked sceptical. "Since the news broke we've been inundated with calls from both the public and the broader press demanding to know if these murders have any ritual significance. There's a special interest in whether or not they're connected in some way to Ethan Spargo and the Witch-Hunt murders we handled back at Christmas time. This is only to be expected after the enormity of that case, but I'm ninety-nine percent certain they have nothing to do with it."

"What about the one percent?" Anna said. "That's the bit that bothers me."

Jacob understood what she meant and knew what the rest of the team would be thinking. "The fact is that Spargo died up at Stonehenge. I saw it with my own eyes. The rest of the *Lucus*, or his Sacred Druidic Grove, is either dead, in the cases of Lucinda Beecham and Hugo Winter, or in the cases of Richard Everett and Miranda Dunn, they're in prison awaiting trial for a range of serious offences."

"But how do we know there aren't other members of the Grove out there, getting some kind of weird and twisted revenge?" Innes asked.

Holloway agreed. "Exactly – maybe that's what these weird crosses are all about that he's leaving behind on the victims?"

Jacob took a deep breath. "I understand, but the crucifix is obviously a Christian symbol, and the Witch-Hunt murders were based on a druidic, pagan cult. What we're facing now is a quite different kettle of fish. We need to ask other questions now and forget about Grovely."

"Do we have an ID on the homeless chap yet?" Holloway asked.

Morgan said, "Not yet. For now he's still just *The Saint*, I'm afraid. We're waiting for anything that can ID him and then we'll use dental records for a confirmation. As soon as I know, you'll all know."

Jacob nodded. "In the meantime, the official line is that these murders have nothing to do with the Witch-Hunt case at all and are an entirely separate case," he said firmly. "Which I genuinely believe to be the case. Laura, I asked you to run the names Sarah Bennett and Sarah Taylor through our records. I'm guessing nothing came up?"

"Nothing at all for Dr Sarah Bennett, sir," she said. "But it's the opposite problem for Sarah Taylor. Even when I cross reference with her birthday there are a lot of results because I'm checking over a quarter of a century of records. I've narrowed it down to nineteen and I'm going through them and crossing them off one by one."

"Anything interesting?" Jacob asked.

"Mostly drugs cautions and convictions, shoplifting, one ABH, a few of them were witnesses at various trials and one was a blackmail case, among many others. Unfortunately, her husband couldn't give me the addresses she grew up in and I'm having trouble getting hold of her parents, which makes narrowing them down any further much harder."

"Now you've got Hannah Wilson to help you cross-reference, too. Remember to check her maiden name, Smith."

"Will do, sir."

"Keep on it," he said with a smile. "I know you'll crack it in the end. And Anna – anything from the CCTV at the National Trust?"

She shook her head. "Not a sausage, boss. All we have is the shadow of a man in the car park, deliberately standing out of sight. You can't see the murder because there's no direct coverage of the ornamental pond."

"All right, at least we tried."

"Her colleagues?"

"They've all been interviewed but everyone has an alibi. It's a small team and all of them were at home with their families."

"Damn it all."

He turned and looked into the faces of Sarah Bennett, the Saint and Hannah Wilson. Each of them stared back from the confines of their photographs. Along with the memories of their loved ones, these images were the only place they existed in the world.

"These people were all alive ten days ago, and now they're all dead. Each one of them brutally murdered and snatched from their loved ones and friends. Take a good look at them. Try and get a sense of what sort of people they were, and understand that it's your job to catch the person who did this and bring him to justice."

Innes raised a hand. "Any idea about motive, sir?"

"I've spoken informally with Sophie Anderson about the motive for these murders and we shared the view that the carefully reproduced killing method and calling cards are indicative of a man dealing out some sort of revenge."

"Please don't tell me Dr Anderson's officially on the case, sir?" Holloway asked. "Not after all the trouble the last time, surely."

"No, she's not involved at all. It was a private conversation and nothing confidential from the case was passed to her. Everything we discussed is already out in the public sphere." It was a lie, but he was happy with it. In his judgement, Sophie could be trusted as much as anyone on the case and he wasn't going to start holding information back from a woman he was seriously thinking about sharing the rest of his life with.

"Thank god for that," Morgan said. "Or I might be working directly for Kent instead of you."

Jacob managed half a smile. "You can relax – for now. I'm still the SIO and no rules have been bent or broken."

"So why do you think this is about revenge, sir?" Innes asked.

"I'd like to say copper's nose, but it's more than that," he began. "If these were murders intended to silence witnesses, for example, then why go to the lengths of drowning them all in exactly the same way? If they were a spree killer…"

"Like the Chief Super thinks," Anna said.

"Like the Chief Super thinks," Jacob continued, "then what links them? Why kill one man and two women? What's his MO? And this is not an easy way to kill someone. It's noisy and messy and takes a lot of strength. Anyone killing people to silence them can choose many easier and quieter methods."

"I agree," Morgan said. "Could still be plain old ritual killings though."

Jacob nodded. "Possible, but there's no link between the locations where the bodies were found, either."

"Religious sites?" Holloway asked.

Jacob shook his head. "That's too much of a stretch. The first was found on an ancient English Heritage site, the second, which we now know was the first victim, was found in the Avon just outside Salisbury and the third victim was up at Avebury Manor which is National Trust property. If they are ritual killings, it's hard to see what significance the locations have."

"Agreed," Morgan said.

"If the killer knew the first victim, then he must have been waiting outside The Crowne Inn," Anna said. "So how did he know she was going to be there, or what it just opportunistic?"

"I don't think so," Jacob said. "He wanted Sarah Bennett. All of this is very premeditated. I believe the killer followed her from her home in Marlborough all the way out to Avebury and then snatched her when she was alone in the pub car park. Same with Hannah Wilson. I believe he followed her from her home and pounced when she was on her own in the car park. Same maybe goes for the Saint – following him through Salisbury until he was alone and then killing him, in each case improvising a drowning with whatever water source he could find."

One of the uniformed constables caught Jacob's eye. "So when was the homeless man killed, exactly, sir?"

"We're not one hundred percent on that because it's hard to date a corpse that's been underwater for a long period of time. The expert assessment from the doctor is that he'd been dead around ten days before the body was found."

"So around the first weekend of March, sir?"

"That's right," Jacob said. "And if anyone wants any basic addition or subtraction done then PC Fisher here is your man."

A low rumble of laughter but Holloway brought the room back to business. "Maybe this is someone at the university?"

"I've considered it," Jacob said. "Go on."

He shrugged. "I'm just pointing out the timing, sir. An academic at Oxford University is murdered a week after a homeless man is drowned and all that happened around the same time that one of their terms is about to finish. It could be someone from the university. It's something that links the bodies besides the drowning method."

"Not Hannah Wilson," Anna said. "There's nothing to link her to the university and besides, I think trying to link the Saint's death to the uni just because he was killed during term time is a bit of a stretch."

Holloway twirled his pen and tried to save face. "Just saying, the uni seems to be popping up a bit, that and the weird signatures. All seems a bit *academic*."

"Wait," Innes said. "That's not true about there being nothing to link her to the university. She went to St Hilda's College to study history. Got a first."

Jacob's eyes flicked over to her. "Did she now? That's a good link. A good connection. They're the same age and both went to Oxford."

"Different colleges, though," Innes said.

"And different schools," Anna added.

"All right, keep digging." Jacob took a deep breath and blew it out slowly. "I need to mention something that was passed to me by Sophie, and that concerns the crucifixes."

"The creepiest part of this case, if you ask me," Morgan said.

Jacob made no comment and moved along. "She told me that there is a specific category of offender in criminal psychology called the Angel of Death, or Angel of Mercy. This is a person who kills in the belief they are helping their victim, although sometimes their motivation can be pure sadism."

"So not revenge or spree killing?" Anna asked.

"No it's a third possibility. Kent and the Brass think this is a spree killer, as you know. My money's on revenge and for what it's worth, Sophie thinks that is a possibility, too. She's just trying to offer some light on the inscriptions carved into the crosses. I think an Angel of Death is more than capable of revenge killings as well. Maybe he feels the people he's killing deserve to die, and that he is helping them in doing so."

"Bloody hell," Morgan said. "The last murder case was a bunch of nutcases who thought they were ancient Celtic gods and now you're telling me this one is about a psycho who thinks he's helping people out by drowning them?"

"Maybe," Innes said. "Maybe he's had his revenge and all this is over."

"Or maybe a fourth victim is on the way," came a low Welsh grumble.

A hush fell over the room as everyone considered Morgan's words.

"Exactly," said Jacob. "Something for us all to think about, but finding a link between the victims is the critical part right now. The only thing we have is that both women were of a similar age – forty-three and forty-two and went to Oxford – but it's weak."

"Oh, happy day," Anna said.

Jacob raised an eyebrow at her but ignored her comment. "As for the orders today, they're simple enough. Bill, you take DC Innes and continue working on the Saint's murder down in Salisbury. Try and get something out of the homeless community down there. I know it can be hard but it could give us the lead we're looking for."

"Leave it with me, boss."

He turned to Holloway who was staring up at him, expectant. "On the same subject, there's still a lot of CCTV footage to go through from Salisbury and someone's got to go through it all."

"And that lucky person is me, sir?"

"Keep making deductions like that and you've got a long and illustrious career ahead of you as a detective."

"Thank you, sir."

"Listen everyone." Jacob's tone grew more serious. "I know Operation Grovely left a mark on us all, but it looks like this could turn into something much worse. We've already got three dead bodies on our hands and with no real leads or suspects. Whoever is behind these murders is ruthless, clever and violent and they need to be taken off the streets in a hurry. We all need to up our game. I want a link between these victims. Let's get on it."

"Yes, sir," said a chorus of voices.

He glanced at his watch and sighed. "And lucky old me now has a press conference to give."

*

Jacob sat behind the trestle table at the top of the room and stared out at dozens of faces. They stared back, most holding phones set to record and others with notepads and pens. Behind them was a row of TV cameras from various national and local news corporations including the BBC, Sky and ITV and he even saw the faces of one or two famous national news reporters in the front row.

Under strict instructions to keep his mouth shut unless invited to speak by Kent, he sat beside the head of the CID and listened calmly as the Chief Superintendent explained the situation to the world. When he'd finished, he invited questions from the press pack but the very first one put an instant frown on his face.

"A question for Chief Inspector Jacob, please. Isn't it possible that this is another member of the Sacred Grove dealing out some sort of crazy revenge?"

Kent's frown grew worse as he gave way to his junior.

"It's possible," Jacob said. "But highly unlikely."

"How unlikely?"

"It's not a serious consideration as far as I'm concerned. Grovely was pagan, and for this reason we're ruling out a link at this stage."

"For what reason? Is there something you're withholding from the public?"

Kent pointed at another journalist, ignoring the last question completely. "Yes?"

"How is it possible that the Drowning Man has killed three times in less than two weeks and yet the police have no serious leads?"

Jacob and Kent exchanged a subtle glance.

"The Drowning Man?" Kent asked.

"The man drowning his victims, Chief Superintendent," the journalist said. "It's already trending right across social media."

"Is it now?" Jacob said, lowering his voice to a mumble heard only by his boss. "*Better than the Angel of Death.*"

Kent lowered his voice. "Easy."

"How many more people must die before you catch him, Chief Inspector?" another shouted.

And then from another, "And will this end in chaos like your last investigation?"

Jacob said, "The last investigation was…"

"Was a total success," Kent said, speaking over the top of him. "DCI Jacob worked tirelessly around the clock to end the murders and apprehended the suspect before he could kill one of his colleagues in cold blood. The suspect was shot because he failed to obey a police order and moved to attack DCI Jacob with a knife."

"Sounds like chaos to me."

Grim laughter rippled around the room.

"This is no laughing matter," Jacob said abruptly, his eyes fixed like lasers on the reporter who had made the comment. "Three people have been murdered and others may be at risk. Your job is to inform members of the public to be on their guard for a suspicious man, a strong man, and to stay away from secluded areas, particularly around water."

"And we aim to have the man in custody by the end of the week," Kent said bringing the conference to an end. "Without any further killing."

But something told Jacob that was not how this was going to end.

*

Hold the neck, grip the flesh. Push them under and hold them down. Watch them kick and flail. Hear their screams and gasps muffled and muted by the freezing water. By the dirty ditch. Feel their lives drain away into the water, all the evil washed away by the rushing rivers or the silent ponds. All the darkness cleansed by the cool water. Wash away their sin and clean their souls.

The man was pleased they had found the body up at the manor, especially after the disappointment following the homeless drunk. He'd been bobbing about in the Avon for some time now. The discovery of Hannah Wilson in the pond was a thing of beauty, and he prayed to God the others would see it on the news, terrified and hopeless.

But why had it only just got on the news? And why were they not reporting his calling card? Those crosses were an important part of the torture.

He knew from the now-famous Witch-Hunt Murders that DCI Jacob wasn't exactly camera shy. He was in front of the press every five minutes for a week during the notorious killing spree earlier in the year, but this time not a word of what he was doing until this very moment. All his hard work, all his planning gone to waste.

Squeeze their throats and choke out the sin.

He watched Jacob on the tiny iPhone screen as he spoke quietly to the press. He looked dangerous, and even more menacing than he remembered him from the Witch-Hunt Murders, and yet... he was sure he could outwit him and deal out the death he had to do to make them all clean again.

He cracked open another can and gulped down some of the cold lager. His mind buzzed fitfully with the next part of the plan, the next scene in the final act. There would be no keeping that from the press and then they would all know.

Feel the body go limp in the water and know the hand of fate has struck again.

He watched the clouds skipping over the landscape from behind the wheel of the old van. Looking over his shoulder he considered if there was enough room in the back for what came next. Yes, he thought, but he'd need to buy some duct tape first. And some cable ties, too.

*The instruments of darkness tell us truths*, he thought with a grim smile. All that time, all that life, all for nothing if not for this. He drank hurriedly from the can and tossed it into the passenger's footwell before belching loudly. He switched on the van's engine and pulled out of the layby. He had somewhere to be and someone to meet.

Even if they didn't know it yet.

# CHAPTER 20

After driving to Oxford, Jacob and Anna emerged from the cosy interior of the Alvis into yet more cold rain. He stared into the sky and then gave his sergeant a philosophical look before opening his umbrella. Huddled beneath the black canopy, they made their way along the street until reaching a coffee shop. Anna walked in and bought a latte, and after another short walk with the wind buffeting them all the way, they were both very glad to get back to his car.

Jacob turned the ignition and switched the old heater on. "March winds, April showers."

"If that means another seven weeks of this, then thanks for reminding me."

They laughed, but the smile quickly faded from Anna's face when her eyes started to move around the inside of the car. As he pulled out of the car park, he turned to her. "Something wrong?"

Her eyes narrowed as she opened the walnut veneer glove compartment and peered inside. "Any cup holders?"

He stifled a laugh. "Are you kidding? This was made in 1962, long before people couldn't go ten minutes without a cup of takeaway coffee."

"Ouch." Her voice dripped with sarcasm. "That cut me deep."

He gave an innocent shrug. "Just saying."

"But you could buy one and fit it, right?"

"And ruin the ambience?" he said. "Never."

"Sometimes I can't tell if you're joking or not."

"Yes, you can."

"You're right, I can."

He smiled, but said nothing.

"What?" she said, leaning into him. "What's so funny?"

"Nothing," he said at last. "Nothing at all. Come on, let's drive up to St Giles and get on with it."

Moving deeper into Oxford, they cruised past the Martyrs' Memorial and then slowed and indicated right before pulling into a rare empty bay on one of the street's pay and display car parks. Jacob knew the city well not only from his days working out of St Aldates, but also from much longer ago when he came here drinking as a younger man with his old friends. He had a love-hate relationship with the city, but today the cold and rain were pushing things very much over to the latter.

He slid a sign up onto his dashboard stating he was police and they climbed out of the car, looking up at the building in front of them. Originally founded as a men's college in 1555, the façade of St John's College was modest compared to some of the other colleges, but it concealed behind it the city's wealthiest college and a sprawling campus with several quads and sumptuous private gardens. Today, the low light seemed to reduce its stature even more as they approached the porter's lodge and pulled out their warrant cards.

The man peered down at the identification and then gave an appreciative nod. "Yes?"

"We have an appointment with one of the academics here," Jacob said. "Professor Seward."

"Oh right," he said, pushing his glasses up the bridge of his nose and fiddling with his right ear. "You'll find him on the other side of this first quad, up on the second floor."

"Thanks."

Walking around the peaceful quad, Anna caught the aroma of cigarette smoke drifting on the breeze and just above the spires she watched a helicopter skimming along beneath the cloud ceiling. With Hilary Term reaching its end, the city was slowly emptying of undergraduate students and an unusual hush had settled over the college grounds. A few hundred yards to the north, the famous bells of St Giles's Church rang out midday.

They entered the far side of the old building and followed the porter's instructions up a narrow staircase before reaching their destination.

"It's here," Jacob said, pointing at a half-open heavy oak door.

He peered through the gap in the doorway and saw a young man sitting behind a desk. He was in his twenties with a full beard and wearing wayfarer-style reading glasses. He looked up and frowned. "Yes?"

"I have an appointment with Professor Seward," Jacob said.

"And you are?"

They now walked into the office and showed him their warrant cards. "I'm DCI Jacob and this is DS Mazurek," he said with a polite smile. "Is he around?"

"Of course he's around," he said. "He has an appointment with you and you're late."

"And what's your name?" Jacob said with a broad smile.

"I'm Toby Barnett," he said. "I'm Professor Seward's personal assistant."

Anna slipped her ID back into her suit jacket. "How very nice to meet you, Toby."

He got up from his desk and tapped on the door. "Your quarter to twelve appointment, Professor."

"Send them in, thanks."

Toby showed them into the office and then made himself scarce. It was a cosy space of hardwood panels and houseplants in colourful ceramic pots. An expansive daulatabad rug occupied pride of place in the centre of the floor and every wall was a bookshelf, filled to bursting with hardbacks, journals and magazines.

Behind a desk in front of a lead-lined window was a man in his fifties who now looked up from his work and peered at them over the top of a pair of tortoiseshell glasses. "Hello, and do come in. I'm Iain Seward. Please take a seat."

"Thank you," Jacob said, taking him up on his offer. "And thanks for finding the time to see us today."

"Not at all."

"I'm DCI Jacob and this is DS Mazurek. We're with Wiltshire CID, here in connection with the death of Dr Sarah Bennett."

He turned to look at each of them, his head moving in sharp, birdlike movements. "Absolutely dreadful business. We're all in shock. Tell me, do you want coffee? Did Toby offer you coffee?"

"No, I'm fine," Jacob said.

Anna waved the offer politely away. "No, but thank you."

"He should have offered you coffee. Please don't mind Toby," he said. "He's got a wonderful mind but his personal skills are lacking finesse."

"He said he was your personal assistant?" Jacob asked.

"He's just being modest," he said. "He *is* my PA, but he's also a brilliant academic. He's writing a doctorate here at the college. I'm his supervisor."

"So he's an academic like you?"

"He has many years of gruelling research and publications to go before he's guilty of that charge, but at the moment he's technically a student. So no, he's not a full-time member of the academic faculty."

Jacob smiled. "Now I understand. Tell me, what's your specialist field?"

"Roman historiography."

Seward looked at their blank expressions.

"I spend my life researching Latin prose literature, Chief Inspector. Mostly Tacitus and the imperial era. I'm particularly interested in matters surrounding the use of syntax."

"And what about Dr Bennett?" he asked.

"We're all crushed. Sarah was new to the department, having spent several years at the University of Chicago, but her murder has hit us hard. We weren't personally close and most of our communication was by email, but I shall miss her terribly. She spends all those years in a city like Chicago and then gets murdered in a sleepy English hamlet. Makes you think."

"It certainly does," Jacob said. "What was her specialist subject?"

"Christianity in the Roman Empire."

"I'm presuming that this would include a fairly comprehensive study of the Bible?"

"Of course. She was familiar with most of the ancient texts of the Biblical canon. What has this got to do with her murder?"

Without warning, Jacob reached into his pocket and pulled out his phone. "I have here some photos of an object that was left on her body."

Iain Seward started to pale. "Really?"

Jacob nodded. "I was wondering if you could tell me what you make of them."

The professor frowned as he stared at the photos. "And this was found on her body?"

Jacob nodded. "And on the bodies of two other murder victims recently killed in the county. These crosses were either clasped in their hands or placed in a pocket."

He puffed out his cheeks. "I'd say your killer is an educated man with a reasonable knowledge of Latin, but as for the motive to leave such a horrible thing on their bodies, I can't help you. Perhaps the killer feels he is helping them in some way, that there is some virtue in his vice, so to speak."

Anna shifted in her seat. "Virtue in his vice? This is plain murder, sir. A depraved killing."

Iain Seward smiled broadly. "Forgive me, sergeant. I spend so long living in the ancient world I forget sometimes how different our *mores* are today. In the ancient world, the consequences of one's actions were decided in accordance with the gods' judgement. Not much different from ideas of Christian morality, except perhaps they placed a higher value on ideas like fate, destiny. It was a very *male* time," he said. "Thankfully these days we are somewhat more enlightened. Even here in Oxford. They finally let women into this college in 1979, you realise."

Anna crossed her legs and leaned back in her seat. "They only let men into St Hilda's in 2008."

He gave her a patronising smile. "That's quite different, sergeant."

Jacob decided to step in. "Would you mind telling me your whereabouts between ten and midnight on Saturday night, sir?"

"At home with Rufus."

"Rufus?"

"My French bulldog."

"And no one can corroborate that?"

"Rufus, but he only speaks French."

Jacob's smile was thin. "Well, thank you for your time, Professor Seward."

"Not at all, and please do pass on our condolences to Sarah's family."

Walking back into the antechamber outside his office they saw Toby Barnett was no longer at his desk, but when they walked down the steps and turned to go back into the quad, they nearly collided with him.

"We meet again," Jacob said.

The man shuffled backwards nervously. "Was the professor able to help you?"

"He's a very knowledgeable person. He tells me you're also an academic."

"For my sins."

"But you never mentioned that to us."

"I fail to see the relevance."

"What's your specialist subject, Mr Barnett?"

"Old Latin poetry, of course."

Jacob gave him a cold smile. "Of course. Tell me, sir – where were you between ten and midnight on Saturday night?"

"Me? You have to be joking! I got on really well with Sarah! I would never kill her."

"Where were you?" Jacob pressed him.

"In my flat reading, no alibis, no witnesses." He gave a smug smile. "Sorry about that."

"Nothing to be sorry about, Mr Barnett," Jacob said. "Tell me, do you like Shakespeare?"

Toby looked confused. "Why?"

"I saw a copy of one of his plays on your desk."

"Ah, that wasn't mine. You need to talk to Professor Seward about all that. He even goes up to the Globe Theatre sometimes to watch productions."

"I see," Jacob said. "Well, thank you, sir. Try and stay in Oxford for the next few days."

And with that they walked back to the car.

# CHAPTER 21

Back at HQ and the team had worked through lunch on their various jobs, all desperate to find anything that might lead them to the identity of who the press were now calling *The Angel of Death*. No one knew how, but somehow a journalist for the Oxford Times had got hold of the information about the crucifixes

and the story had injected an even greater sense of panic into the case.

A furious Marcus Kent had broken the development to the team and ranted about the need to pick things up and gets results. Freshly back from his interview with Professor Seward, Jacob couldn't disagree.

"And we thought the press calling him the Drowning Man was bad," Anna said.

"Tell me about it," Holloway called over as he walked out of the office.

But Jacob was quiet at his desk, struggling to work out where to put the handful of pieces in one of the worst jigsaw puzzles he had ever known. He had no idea what it all meant. He tried to think like the murderer but getting inside the mind of a man who had brutally drowned a man and two women was almost impossible. Whoever was behind these deaths was dangerous, violent and cunning. Maybe even deranged, but he had no way of knowing.

Some killers were able to murder people in the most terrifying of circumstances and then turn up for work on Monday morning with a friendly smile and a joke on their lips.

If only he could find a way to link the victims he might be able to warn people about any future threat from the killer, but there was none. There was nothing to suggest the victims knew each other and they all came from radically different walks of life. One was a tragic down-and-out junkie, the other a highly educated classics scholar and the final victim was a middle-management bureaucrat for the National Trust.

No link.

No connection.

No way to predict who was the Angel of Death's next victim.

He was brought back to reality by the sight of Bill Morgan wandering over to his desk, a greasy paper bag in each hand.

"Now this is the kind of news I like to get out of nowhere," he said smiling.

"No good can ever come from skipping lunch, boss." He handed Jacob one of the bags. "So I was a bit naughty and bought two steak bakes."

"You read my mind."

"I thought I might have."

Jacob opened the paper bag and took a chunky bite from the steaming bake. Hot, flaky pastry and delicious beef melted in his mouth. "This is more like it. How's the investigation into the homeless man's murder going?"

Morgan pulled up a chair and unwrapped his late lunch. "I'm meeting Matt after this. He's been going through the CCTV like you ordered, so fingers crossed."

Jacob nodded. "It feels a bit like that, doesn't it?"

"Like what, boss?"

"Like we need some luck."

"We'll get there." Morgan's tone was quiet but reassuring. "These things take time, especially if the killer is a clever little bastard, like this one obviously is."

"Soph says he is."

"She's a clever sod too, that one."

Jacob smiled, but Morgan spoke next.

"I know you too well, Jacob. Things getting serious between you two?"

Jacob ignored the question and ate more of the bake. Changing the subject, he said, "She says a lot of murders attributed to serial killers are really spree killings but because the press just aren't as familiar with the term they don't use it."

"Always looking for the big headlines, I suppose."

"Exactly. Revenge is also a strong possibility though. My copper's nose says revenge."

"Have you seen much of her this week, then?"

Jacob shook his head. "She's at a conference in Exeter. The brightest and the best in the world of criminal psychology from all over the world are there."

"I can see why she's there then," he said. "She's a hell of a girl, boss."

"She is that," He said. "What about Leanne?"

Morgan visibly deflated. "Same old shit. Still arguing the toss over every last penny. My solicitor tells me this could go on for months, or maybe even years. Funny thing is, the longer we spend apart the more I miss her. I know it sounds nuts but we were together a very long time. All through my years in the Marines and everything. Life's odd without her."

Jacob nodded and took another bite. "So you want to get back together?"

Morgan stopped chewing. "Are you crazy?"

After a short pause, both men laughed. Then, Morgan said, "You think we're not going to get him."

"Oh, we'll get the bastard," Jacob said.

Morgan sighed. "And what then?"

Jacob took a bite of the hot, flaky pastry and looked up at his old friend. "How do you mean?"

"The problem is," he grumbled, "the bloody lawyers are letting them out faster than we can catch them."

"It can be frustrating, I realise that," Jacob said. "But there's not much we can do about it. Our job is to find them and bring them to justice. What justice does to them afterwards is out of our hands."

Morgan gave a low growl but seemed to accept the point. "I'll be retiring out of all this crap soon enough," he said. "After that it'll all be your problem, boss."

"Thanks."

He raised his palms. "Just laying out the facts. Oh, and by the way. Innes got some info on a Mr James Cowan."

"Owner of The Crowne Inn in Avebury?"

"The very same. He's got a record. Domestic abuse. Turns out he likes hitting women."

"Does he now? Violence against women?"

The Welshman nodded. "It's weak, I know. But better than nothing."

"Plus his alibi was a joke, too. I'll give him a visit tomorrow."

Jacob loosened his tie and took another look at the map on the wall of his office. Three neat little red pins marked the locations of the three brutal murders.

"And where do you plan on spending that retirement?"

"I was thinking Barbados," Morgan said with a dreamy smile.

"You mean after you've knocked off a couple of post offices?"

Morgan got up and placed a heavy, nicotine-stained hand down on Jacob's shoulder. "If I do," he said deadpan, "you'll never find me."

\*

After lunch, Bill Morgan walked back down the corridor to the office that he and Matt Holloway had been using to direct the investigation into the Saint's murder. His own workspace was carefully hidden away from the chaos of

218

the main office by several strategically-placed office partitions, but this new space was totally isolated.

Focussing on the Saint, he had instructed him to go through everything they had gathered on his death so far. Witness statements, interview notes, CSI reports and the post-mortem files were all studied and analysed in search of anything that might give them a clue leading to his killer. So far, things had been lean, to say the least.

"Anything to report on the CCTV, Matt?"

"I think so, sir."

He turned sharply, surprised by the good news. "You're kidding?"

"No, sir – not at all. Most of the cameras were of no use at all. They were either pointing in the wrong direction or not even functioning."

"Dummies?"

"In some cases. Others were real enough but just not working. However, the camera fitted on the side of the charity shop is another story, as is the footage from the camera on the New Street car park."

"I almost wish I'd bought you a steak bake now as well," Morgan muttered to himself.

"Sir?"

"Nothing – what have you got then?"

"Isolating the only cameras with any footage on them was soul-destroying work, sir, but worth it in the end."

"If you got us a result, then I'd say so."

"Look here, sir."

Holloway froze the grainy black and white image and zoomed in on a crowd of people outside one of the shops. They were standing on the pavement smoking cigarettes, and one was holding a beer. "I think that's our man, right there."

Morgan peered in closer to the screen and studied the vague image. "I can see what you mean, but all we can really say is that the clothes are the same as those found on the dead man."

"And the hat."

"And the hat, sure. I think for now we have to presume it's the Saint but bear in mind it could be someone else wearing his clothes."

"He has the same beard."

"Beards are easy to grow and even easier to fake."

"As part of some sort of deception, sir?"

"Maybe, or maybe he just loaned someone else his gear to keep warm outside while he was in a shelter. Looking at the time stamp it says this was after ten at night just over a week ago. If it's him then it's likely to be the last few hours of his life."

"It's him, sir, I just know it."

Morgan gave the young detective a silent look of approval. "Let's say it is. Where does he go next?"

"He and one other go into The Mitre."

"The other one is Denny Marks," Morgan said. "Another homeless lad."

"They're in the pub for half an hour and when they come out, Marks wanders off, obviously drunk, and the Saint gets into a cab."

Morgan gave a knowing nod. "Preston Rossiter. Innes and I had the misfortune of speaking with him this morning. Where does he go?"

"Unfortunately we don't know. Using the city's CCTV network we can follow the cab journey from New Street down Exeter Street and then south into East Harnham. After that they drive down Downton Road and then leave the bright lights of the city behind."

"They drive into the countryside?"

Holloway nodded. "They return around twenty minutes later."

"Just as Rossiter told us," Morgan said with a sigh. "Don't tell me, he gets out of the cab on Exeter Street?"

"That's right, sir," Holloway said, twisting his neck to look up at the Welshman. "When he gets out of the cab, he walks over the street to the cathedral."

"The cathedral?"

"Yes, sir. He enters the grounds from the Bishop's Walk entrance just after eleven."

"A bit late for a regular service wouldn't you say?"

"And there's more." Holloway leaned in and tapped his pen on the screen. "If I'm not very much mistaken, that car parked up right there behind him is Preston Rossiter's minicab."

Morgan leaned in further and squinted his eyes. "Bugger me, so it is."

"After he dropped the Saint off he turned around and followed him along the road to the cathedral."

"Run it forward."

"Already done it, sir. Rossiter's car pulls away fifteen minutes later and drives home, no passengers."

"And the Saint?"

"No more sight of him. He must have left the cathedral by another exit because this image right here is the last picture of him when he's still alive. He was found dead a week later in the river running just south of the cathedral."

Morgan leaned in now and looked at the black and white image of the homeless man walking up the path to the cathedral's famous Chapter House.

"Looks like I need to have a chat with someone in the cathedral, Holloway."

"Just what I was thinking, sir."

"In the meantime, we can start building a list of people who saw him last using the CCTV footage here, focussing on the people he was hanging around with near the car park. If we disregard a random nutcase, then it's also possible the Angel of Death knew him."

Holloway nodded. "A solid assumption – at least to start with."

"So taking that assumption, we can refine things further by looking at people we know he had some sort of relationship with, and which of them saw him in the twenty-four hours up to his death. He'd got hold of money, remember, Matt. Where there's money there's muck."

When Innes walked into the room, Morgan gave her a smile. "Have you seen this footage?"

"Yes, sir. I thought it looked encouraging."

"Indeed it does. I know you're working on the other victims to see if they're on our records, but did you get around to looking into the Saint's friends from the shelters - do any of them know Sarah Bennett or Hannah Wilson?"

"I can't find any link yet, sir," Innes said. "I'm still looking into it but it's like finding a needle in a haystack."

"That's what detective work is like," he said firmly. "It's not like on the TV where everything just presents itself exactly when needed to move the story on. In the real world we have to do a lot of very boring donkey work to get the results, and we face failure every day."

"I suppose so, sir," she said sullenly.

Morgan pursed his lips as he watched her frown. "Listen, you did some bloody amazing work on Operation Grovely, and we were all very proud of you, but you still have a lot to learn. You're very new to all this. I've been in this job for nearly thirty years and I still have a lot to learn, yeah?"

She looked up at him and nodded. "I'm just running out of ideas. We've interviewed everyone who knew the three victims and none of them seem to know each other, that's all. I can't find the link."

"If there even *is* a link," Holloway said.

Morgan weighed his words. "The boss is pretty sure there's a link, and frankly he's got the best copper's nose I've ever known. If he says there's a link between the three murders, then there's a link – besides, that's my view as well. Despite Grovely, this is a pretty peaceful and safe county. No way are three murders going down in such a short time with no connection. Keep going – you'll get there."

Innes smiled. "Thanks, sir."

He paused a moment and then raised an eyebrow. "In the meantime, fancy a trip to Salisbury Cathedral?"

\*

High on the top floor, Chief Constable Bernard Portman sat in his leather swivel chair and caught a glance of himself in the small mirror on the far wall of his office. For a moment he wondered who the old man looking back at him was. Grey, thinning hair, slightly too much chub around the chops and a barely concealable gut held in place by a leather belt that was expanding at the same rate as the rest of the universe. What had happened?

Age had happened, and he realised it was now time to go. His long-suffering wife Angela had been begging him to take retirement for two years now and he had finally relented. He might be getting on a bit but he was still young enough to enjoy whatever life he had left. The two of them had even talked about buying a cottage in Cornwall and getting a couple of rescue dogs to walk on the beach. After a life processing perps, the very idea seemed almost like heaven.

But he had to close down Operation Avebury first. He had an exemplary success rate right across his career and he wasn't about to walk away from an unsolved triple murder right on his doorstep. *Not a bit of it, chum*, he said to himself.

The intercom buzzer on his desk startled him out of his daydream

"It's DCI Jacob, sir."

"Send him in."

He watched his old friend walk into the room. His height still commanded attention, and he still possessed an almost aristocratic authority with the easy, unhurried way he moved, but there was a sadness in his face, a permanent anguish branded on his mood by the fire that killed his fiancée.

"Take a seat, Jacob."

"Thank you, sir."

Portman sighed again but managed to find a smile from somewhere. "This is all going a bit pear-shaped, wouldn't you say?"

A long pause. "Whoever's behind this is no ordinary killer, sir. He's clever."

He gave Jacob a weary look. "Three murders in less than two weeks and no leads would suggest exactly that, Jacob, but the reason you're here being paid by the county is to be even cleverer, isn't it?"

"Sir."

"Kent tells me you're still thinking this is about revenge and not just some insane spree killer."

"We don't get a lot of insane spree killers in England, sir, but revenge is much easier to come by."

Portman reflected. "I'm inclined to agree with you. What about this mercy killing theory?"

Jacob shrugged. "It's just that, a theory. There could be something to it, but I'm focussed on trying to find a link between the victims. If we get that we crack the case. I'm certain of it."

"And what if there is no link?"

"We're back to spree killers, and my instinct tells me that is not what's going on here. These people are being killed for a reason."

Portman drummed his fingers on the desk. "Local BBC have got hold of the Angel of Death detail from The Oxford Times. It's all over the internet now. People are scared. They think this is a serial killer with some sort of religious obsession ritually murdering people. Frankly, you can't blame them – a good part of me thinks they might just be right."

"Sir."

"I want you to issue another press statement clarifying this to calm the public."

"For that, we'd have to emphasise our belief it's a revenge killer targeting specific people."

"And?"

"I could be wrong."

"I think you should go with your gut Jacob. Another press statement will clarify precisely what is going on and reassure the public that everything is under control." He paused and narrowed his eyes. "It *is* under control, isn't it, Jacob?"

"Yes, sir."

"Hmm. To other business, and I want you to know I'm considering throwing the towel in."

"You're retiring, sir?"

He nodded his head. "Angela wants to move down to Cornwall. See out her days in a little cottage somewhere on the coast. Long beach walks. Cosy, crackling fire. Of course, this means there will be a bit of a shake up around here. From your point of view, there's bad news and good news."

Jacob said nothing.

"The bad news is that Marcus is the front-runner for my job. The good news is I'll recommend you for promotion to Chief Super. You deserve and you can do it."

"I'm not so sure, sir."

"This is one of the oldest police forces in the country, Jacob. It's an honour to be part of something with so much heritage. Being a Chief Superintendent will be quite a feather in your cap. Go away and think about it."

Jacob had already thought about it, but he humoured his old friend. "Yes, sir."

"Good work, now go and catch that killer."

"I'm getting closer, sir."

"Don't let me down."

Jacob closed the door behind him and took a deep breath. Something was still bothering him, something he had heard. Something someone had told him. Something about a fire.

# CHAPTER 22

In his home outside of Bradford-on-Avon in Wiltshire's west, Jacob was sitting in the Old Watermill watching the river rush along through his garden. Spring was on the way and some of the trees were beginning to come into blossom, but mostly the garden still resembled trench warfare with mud and waterlogged grass everywhere he looked. Turning off the outside light, he padded back over to the wood burner and, swinging open the iron door he dropped another apple wood log into the embers.

Three bodies discovered in three days.

He sighed and poured himself a single malt. Crashing down into his favourite wingback chair, he tipped his head back against the soft leather. With a fresh sip of whisky down the hatch, he closed his eyes and breathed out a deep sigh, grateful that another day was over. The gentle chorus of moorhens calling to each other out along the river drifted through the twilight. If he kept his eyes shut another second he'd be asleep, so he opened them wide and took a deep breath as he considered the madness that was once again unfurling all around him.

Three people murdered right under his nose, and crucifix calling cards left on their bodies. Were they a message for him? Was this about the last case? His mind raced with countless possibilities.

No, the items left on the dead were not about him. The Angel of Death was trying to leave messages for other people, for the people he was getting revenge on. He rose from his chair and stepped over to his laptop. Opening it up, he navigated to Google and typed in *Angel of Death* and *mercy killers* into the search box. Unsurprisingly he found himself staring at a number of pages full of mostly American serial killers and references to the Bible. He flicked through page one, two, three, four... nothing. Not unless the killer really was on a psychopathic spree.

He sighed and slammed the laptop lid down.

*You're getting nowhere, Tom.*

He sipped the whisky and started pacing his room. He knew the key to the puzzle had something to do with fire, but whatever it was, he just couldn't find the answer.

*

Laura Innes kicked off her shoes and hung her coat up over the newel cap of her staircase. Another long day of stress was behind her, and she was ready for a cold drink, a warm dinner and then bed – in that order. Checking her answerphone she found a message from her boyfriend Vincent. She gave a heavy sigh as she listened to it.

*Hey Laura, it's Vinnie. Just wondering what's going on. You've been quiet lately. I've been thinking maybe we should move in together. There's more than enough room at my place and it seems crazy that we live so far apart. Anyway, give me a call when you get back.*

Or maybe not, she thought.

She deleted the message and wandered wearily to the kitchen where she found a cold bottle of lager in the fridge. Sod it, she said. Why not? She cracked it open and walked to the lounge, giving the answerphone another suspicious glance as she went.

Truth was, she wasn't sure she loved Vincent Goddard anymore. Yes, he had money, yes he was successful, but that was the problem. All he ever seemed to talk about was his property development company and how big he was going to expand it. He never listened to her problems, what was going through her mind. What *she* wanted out of life.

Yet the idea of breaking it off made her stomach flip upside down. Her life was unstable enough as it was without a gaping hole where her love life should be. She'd just got into Jacob's CID team and now they were up to their necks in what was shaping up to be one of the most notorious killing cases in the county's history.

If that wasn't bad enough, Marcus Bloody Kent was still leaning on her to report anything on Jacob that could be used to throw him out of the police force. She felt like she was being torn in a hundred directions and none of it was fair. All she wanted to do was work hard, follow the rules and be respected in the workplace.

She sank down into the chair, turned the TV on and sipped more lager.

Sod it, she thought again. Why not?

*

Anna Mazurek shook her head as she passed her eyes over Morgan's kitchen cupboards. "This is truly the most pathetic selection of food I have ever seen."

"It's good that you feel able to insult your senior officers so casually," he said with a smile.

"Just saying, sir."

"Less of the *sir*, for Christ's sake. It makes me feel like a bloody Rupert at the best of times, plus we're off duty."

"A bloody Rupert?"

"Sorry, Marines' slang for an officer."

"Ah, gotcha. It's just habit, anyway," she said. "You've asked me to call you Bill socially so many times I can't remember them all."

"Well, here's one more – call me Bill."

"In that case, what the hell are we having for dinner, Bill?"

He gave her a proud smile. "I thought I'd push the boat out."

"Oh yeah?"

He nodded. "If you look at the back of the cupboard next to the fridge, I'm pretty sure you'll find a can of macaroni and cheese."

She stopped dead and turned to him. "Are you taking the piss? I'm hungry!"

"Yes, Anna, as a matter of fact I *am* taking the piss."

He opened a drawer and pulled out a number of glossy paper menus. A cheeky smile spread across his face as he handed them to her. "This is where I store most of my food."

*

After dinner, they went back into the front room and Morgan crouched down as he went through his CDs. "If I'm not very much mistaken, I think you'll like this one."

She smiled as he manoeuvred away from the CD stack and over to his stereo, deliberately keeping the disc out of her sight so she wouldn't see it and spoil the surprise.

Dropping the disc into the stereo, he closed the lid and hit play. A second later, Albert King started singing *Born Under a Bad Sign.*

"Ah, you remembered," she said, remembering mentioning the song to him during the Witch-Hunt investigation.

"A classic all the way from 1967," he said wistfully. "I was three."

"And my dad would have been eight."

Morgan looked at her, smile fading. "I never did like maths. Shall we move on?"

She laughed, and realised she was enjoying herself for the first time in months. On occasion, she had looked at Morgan in a certain way but the age gap was too big, plus she knew it would be the end of their friendship and she would never want that. She would never tell him, but she saw him as a father figure and didn't want to do anything that would put that relationship in jeopardy.

"They don't make songs like this anymore."

Getting into the mood, Anna wiggled her packet of cigarettes at him. "May I?"

"Knock yourself out," he said, pulling one of his famous Robusto cigars from the pack on the arm of his chair. "You do realise that some people don't like smoking indoors, right?"

She rolled her eyes. "I had heard, but there's no accounting for taste."

Morgan laughed and looking up at a picture of him wearing the famous green beret, he thought back to his commando days. A long time ago, but most memories still as fresh as the day he made them. Braving the Tarzan assault course and the notorious endurance test during the depths of winter – the infamous thirty mile march with full fighting order on your back. Happy days, he thought with a genuine warmth.

His job as an inspector in the police was another universe compared with those days, but both presented testing challenges. During his time in the Marines, he had seen death and suffering while on tour in Afghanistan and Iraq that most people couldn't imagine but his policework had given him plenty of tough moments as well. Missing people, kidnaps, knifings, dumped bodies and terrible road accident injuries, all flashed through his mind like spectres at the oddest times.

Then he thought of Leanne. Being the wife of a commando was not easy, and neither was being the wife of a policeman. Perhaps, he thought quietly, she had put up with much more than any woman deserved to put up with. Maybe his way of life had driven her away.

He took another sip of the drink and lit the cigar. Lifting the bottle and reading the label, he laughed to himself and thought he must be getting close to his limit if he'd started going easy on his wife.

"Another drink, Anna?"

"I don't mind if I do, Bill."

"Good, because tomorrow I have to talk to God and between you, me and the gatepost I don't think he likes me very much."

*

Outside Morgan's rented home, Declan Taylor sat in the driver's seat of a stolen Fiat Ducato and watched his ex-wife through a pair of binoculars. She was sitting in the Welsh inspector's kitchen and the two of them were having a wicked little laugh over dinner.

Less than an hour ago a man in a small white van with *Little India* written on the side had pulled up and walked an armful of takeaway food bags up to the door. Morgan had opened the door and collected the meal. He looked like he might be a bit handy in a fight, did the burly Welsh bloke. He'd heard somewhere on the grapevine that he used to be a commando.

*Worth watching, Dex.*

But easily avoided if he stuck to the plan. Not even an ex Royal Marine would be able to help Anna Mazurek now – not with what he had in mind. When he made his move she wouldn't know what hit her. None of them would.

# CHAPTER 23

*Wednesday, 13ᵗʰ March*

C harlotte Ingram set up the wooden easel in her conservatory and made a cup of tea. She had woken only an hour or so ago but had already checked all her doors and windows were locked. Sarah and Hannah were both dead and so was a man named the Saint. She had an idea who that might be, and if she was right she had every reason to fear for her life. But what could she do?

She waited for the sun to move higher in the sky and give better natural light. She was keen to keep her mind occupied, but there was only one way to capture the right quality of light for her latest commission. Unpacking the metal tubes of Schmincke oil paint, she set them down on the easel tray and stared at the sketch she had already made of the breathtaking view from the top of Milk Hill.

With an elevation of just under one thousand feet, Wiltshire's highest point provided a sweeping panorama perfect for photographers and artists. She smiled when she looked at her sketch, made from the top of the hill a couple of weeks ago before any of this had happened.

Before this nightmare.

From the top she had been able to see the villages of East and West Kennett, divided by Overton Hill. When the sun breached the horizon and the first rays of light rippled across the rolling landscape, she had sketched Avebury's stone circle and made notes of its colours as it sparkled momentarily for a few moments before the sun went back in again. Inspired, she sat at her easel, slipped some earbuds into her ears and turned on her favourite piece of music as she started to mix her paints. He wasn't going to get her; she had a plan. Chris had family in Australia. They could start all over again in Queensland; somewhere remote where she would never be found.

With the sound of Schubert filling her world, she started to block out various sections ready for some finer detail work when she saw a shadow fall on the canvas and turned to see a man standing behind her. She gasped and staggered back from her chair, knocking both the chair and the easel over onto the tiled floor.

He gave a fiendish smirk. "Hello, Lotty."

She fumbled with the earbud wires, wrenching them from her ears. The soft comfort of Schubert was replaced with the sinister sound of his devilish chuckling.

"My *God*, it's you."

She watched his chest rise and fall like a wild animal's. "You thought I was dead, I suppose, or locked in a cage like some beast with the life pounded out of him."

She raised her palms. "Just stay away from me."

His face contorted into mock concern as he mimicked her. "*Just stay away from me…*"

"Please."

"You must have known I'd come for you."

She desperately scanned the garden for a sign of anyone who might be able to help her, a neighbour perhaps, but there was no one. And in here behind her double glazing, no one could hear her screams.

"I was young, I did as I was told."

He gave a bitter laugh. "Am I supposed to feel *sorry* for you?"

She subtly moved her hand to a side table. Thank god she had brought her mobile phone in here with her. It was obscured from his view by the easel, but the only problem was trying to use it without letting him see her. If she could just get her hand down to it, she might be able to dial 999 without his knowing about it. At least then they might hear them talking, or be able to trace the GPS signal or something.

He stepped closer, lifting two gloved hands in front of him as he moved.

"You stay away from me!"

"Or what?"

Before she could reply, he brought his fist up into her face and knocked her to the ground. She struggled up to her knees and tried to stand, but he lunged forwards, kicked her collapsed easel out of the way and knocked her to the ground a second time. She lashed out with her ankles, hooking his feet out from under him and sending him crashing to the floor.

He sprung up like a panther, lip curled back and rage in his eyes. Padding over to her, he hit her a third time and she saw stars. For a bleak, stomach-churning moment she thought she might lose consciousness but somehow she managed to cling on. She felt him grabbing her jacket and pulling her up to her feet, and then throwing her over his shoulder with no effort at all.

Her head was still spinning from the heavy blow, and she was still seeing stars as he padded across the room and along the corridor. In the kitchen she tried to fight back, but he slapped her hard across the face. When she opened her eyes, she saw now he had reached the front door and was taking her outside to a van parked on her drive. She wanted to fight back, but the truth was she was frightened the next punch might be enough to knock her out completely. She knew she had to keep conscious if she was to have a chance of knowing where he was taking her, a chance of surviving.

He blipped his locks and threw her in the back of the van. Tying her hands behind her back and covering her with a blanket, he mumbled under his breath. "Stay quiet. You move and you die."

She gave no response. Was this really happening? A moment ago she was preparing to paint a beautiful sunrise for a client and now this had happened. It had all been so fast she barely knew what to think.

She felt the cold metal of the van's floor as he squashed her legs up against one of the rear wheel arches. Still dizzy from the punches, she retched as the smell of petrol and grease from a steel scissor jack near her face drifted up into her nose. Lifting her head to try and look around and assess her new world, she caught her shoulder on the scissor jack and gouged a deep cut into her skin. She cried out in the darkness but her pain was muffled by the sound of the engine firing up.

Pulling away, the man stopped the mindless tune he had been humming and said, "Every past has a price, Lotty, and yours is very expensive indeed."

*

A few hours later, when Jacob and Anna walked into The Crowne Inn, a rapid hush descended on the cosy saloon bar leaving only the sound of the crackling fire. As they walked up to the bar, Jacob caught Sam's eye and gave her a polite smile. "Jim about?"

"He's in the cellar. What's this about?"

"Down in the cellar, eh?" Jacob called over the bar.

A voice called up from a trap door behind the bar. "Yes, but not for long."

They heard the ladder creaking as the big man emerged through the trap door and climbed back up into the bar. "We meet again, Chief Inspector."

Jacob frowned. "You weren't entirely honest with us before, were you Jim?"

Sam looked at her husband. "Jimmy?"

"What are you talking about?" he asked.

"You can save the big act," Anna said. "We know you've got form."

"Ah." He started to stack some clean glasses up behind the bar. "I was a young kid, stupid and high. I never knew what I was doing."

"Jimmy?" Sam asked.

"You assaulted a woman," Anna said.

Sam looked at him, confusion in her eyes. "My Jimmy would never do anything like that."

Jim Cowan gave his wife a sympathetic glance. He didn't have to say any words.

"Oh, Jimmy!"

"It was a *couple*, not just a woman," Jim protested. "He looked at me funny so I smacked him and then she joined in punching and scratching. Next thing you know the Old Bill's all over me and I'm in the drunk tank. Simple as that."

"You struck a woman."

"She hit me first. You make it sound like I go around beating up women. I don't."

Anna said, "And you're still claiming the CCTV out the front is a dummy?"

He nodded. "Check it out if you don't believe me. Like I said, we don't have any CCTV. It's a very quiet, rural area and there's never any trouble – not even a car window getting put in. Nothing."

Anna said, "Except for Sarah Bennett being abducted from your car park and murdered a few minutes' walk away?"

Before he could reply, Jacob spoke. "You refused to give an alibi when I asked you before, but I'm going to ask you again. Where were you between ten and twelve on Saturday night, Jimmy? Last time I ask before I take you down the nick."

The big man sighed. "All right, all right. I was up in Trowbridge. Me and a few mates have a bit of a casino going."

"An illegal casino?"

He gave a sad nod. "It's been going on for a few months now. A big, unlicensed operation. We've been dealing dope and speed from there, too. The boys in blue won't like it one little bit."

"Unlicensed? Illegal under the 2005 Gambling Act. My uniformed colleagues will be in touch, and the only way you get your alibi is giving us the names of everyone involved." Jacob smirked. "I'm guessing your buddies won't like that very much, but that's your problem."

"No, I don't think they will like it."

"You should have thought more carefully about what you were doing," Anna said.

A crestfallen Jimmy Cowan gave her a thoughtful look. "I was never much good at the thinking part."

"Don't be too hard on yourself," Jacob said. "And look at it this way, you might have implicated yourself in a number of indictable offenses and grassed on your mates, but you've been of great assistance to the police today."

"Thanks," he said sarcastically.

Jacob and Anna walked outside and crossed the car park to the Alvis. A light drizzle in the air softened the landscape and had covered the vintage powder blue convertible in a film of water. He looked east beyond the village and saw the stone circle where Sarah Bennett had been found on Sunday morning.

"What do you think?"

"I believe him," Anna said.

"Me too," said Jacob. "So long as his story works out."

"You're going to nick him for the illegal casino though, right?"

"A drug-dealing toerag who runs an illegal casino and beats women? Of course."

His phone rang. He saw from the caller ID that it was from the station so he climbed inside the shelter of the car to take the call.

"Jacob."

"It's Holloway, sir."

"Go ahead,"

"Not good news, I'm afraid. We just got a call from a man living in Marlborough. He say his wife's been kidnapped and he's officially reported her missing."

Jacob closed his eyes and let his head sink down until his chin was touching his chest.

*Not another one.*

Opening his eyes, he spoke into the phone with a calm and measured tone. "When?"

"Early this morning. She was snatched from her home while she was painting, following a break-in at her property."

"Painting?"

"He said she's a professional artist and she was working on a commission. He'd been away on business in Wales and got home to find the front door ajar. He found her easel knocked over in the conservatory and painting equipment all over the floor in a right mess but no sign of his wife."

Another sigh. "What's her name?"

"Charlotte Ingram, forty-two years old."

"OK, thanks Matt."

Anna slammed her door against a rush of cold air. "Sodding weather."

"Looks like he's struck again, Anna. A woman in Marlborough. Early forties again. Similar age to the other two."

"Maybe he has a thing for women of that age?" Anna said.

Jacob paused. "Or maybe they were friends at school?"

"We'd better get over there, boss."

As she buckled herself in, Jacob stamped on the accelerator pedal and swerved the car out onto the road.

*

Darkness. Her world was reduced to the black hood he had replaced the blanket with and the plastic cable ties pinning her wrists together and biting into her skin. She could tell from the sound of the engine and the motion of the van that they were driving again and somewhere above her she heard the sound of his tuneless whistling. When he spoke, she felt her skin crawl.

"They're all gone, you know."

"What? Who are you talking about?"

"All your little friends."

She felt her breathing quicken and began to feel light-headed. "I don't know what you mean."

But she did. She knew who he was and what he was doing and when she sobbed, the sound was redolent of a mourner breaking down at the funeral of a loved one.

"Stop crying. It's pathetic."

He spat the words through clenched teeth and she sensed the deep, hard rage in his words.

She decided to keep her mouth shut.

"It hardly matters now, anyway," he said in a casual sing-song way. "You'll be dead soon enough."

A wave of nausea washed over her when she heard not only the words but the way he said them.

As she struggled with the cable ties tearing into the soft flesh of her wrists, she knew, with no doubt, that he meant what he said.

# CHAPTER 24

I n Marlborough, a uniformed constable was standing sentry at the front door when Jacob and Anna climbed out of the car and walked up the garden path. Jacob gave him a quick nod and brushed past him as he caught Mia Francis's eye in the kitchen. She was wearing her usual white forensic suit and blue nitrile gloves and when she spoke her voice was low and measured. "Not good, I'm afraid."

Jacob took a deep breath and scanned the room. An expensively decorated room of hardwood floors, marble countertops and tile splashbacks was now a warzone with smashed glasses all over the sides, upturned plant pots on the windowsills and the contents of a previously laid table scattered across the floor. Casting his eyes through the archway into an expansive conservatory he saw more chaos – an easel and tubes of oil paint on the floor and a pair of white earbuds strewn on the floor, partly tangled around the leg of a wicker armchair in the corner.

"What happened here?"

"A fight, and a big one," Mia said.

"Any forensics?" Anna asked.

Mia nodded. "I've found a trace of blood and the whole place is covered in prints, unfortunately the prints belong to Mr and Mrs Ingram, which is what you would expect."

"And the blood?" Jacob asked.

"I'll run the sample when we get back to the lab."

"Fingers crossed then," said Anna.

Jacob stepped into the conservatory and looked at the destruction. He tried to imagine the scene. He saw Charlotte Ingram sitting at her easel, painting. She was listening to music as she worked. Had she heard her kidnapper break the front door open? It was hard to know. He crouched down on his hands and knees and peered under the chair. Finding an iPod, he reached out with his gloved hand and took hold of it.

He activated it and read the screen.

"Schubert viola arpeggione sonata," he muttered.

Anna looked over at him. "And?"

"And it's not a loud piece of music. She might have heard the door being opened and looked up to see her kidnapper. She might not. She might have been concentrating on her work." He got back up to his feet and found Mia talking to one of her CSI officers. "Where's the husband?"

"In the sitting room," she replied. "He's with PC Harper nursing a cup of tea."

Jacob thanked her. "And let me know if you find anything else, Mia. I need all the help I can get."

"Then I'm sorry to tell you we found nothing at the arson scene, either."

He blew out a deep breath. "All right, thanks."

They removed their gloves and forensic shoes as they walked down a long, narrow corridor on their way to the sitting room. Japanese silkscreen prints by Hokusai punctuated cream-coloured walls on either side, and the only furniture was an early Victorian console table covered in family photos neatly positioned around a viper's bowstring hemp.

When they reached the sitting room, Chris Ingram was huddled in the corner, his face ashen with worry and his hands wrapped around a cup of untouched tea.

Jacob looked at PC Harper. "Thanks. Could you wait outside in the hall?"

"Yes, sir.'

"Mr Ingram, I'm DCI Jacob and this is DS Mazurek."

With imploring eyes, he looked up at them and asked. "Any news?"

Jacob felt his anguish and took a moment out to let him calm down. He looked around the room and then sat down opposite him. The Old Vicarage was a solid testimony to the more substantial and impressive architecture of the past, with thick outer walls and deep, wooden windowsills beneath an intricate canopy of exposed oak beams. Tastefully decorated in a modern style, the room was finished off with an expensive open fireplace in which a sizeable blaze roared and crackled.

He lowered his voice. "I'm sorry to say we haven't been able to locate your wife yet, despite considerable efforts on our part. We've had dozens of officers going house to house and no one can remember seeing anything unusual happening. We even have a helicopter with thermal imaging and a canine unit."

Ingram flinched when he heard the word canine. "But you can't think she's dead?"

"There's nothing to suggest that at this time, sir, no." Jacob kept his voice low and level. "I know it's natural, but you mustn't let your mind wander into places like that. It won't do you or your wife any good."

"But what about this killer everyone's talking about," he muttered, hollow-eyed. "This *Angel of Death* the newspapers are writing about. What if her disappearance has got something to do with him?"

Jacob nodded. He understood. "Again, there's nothing to suggest that. None of his other victims were kidnapped first. At the moment, you have to hang on to that."

Ingram got up and started pacing up and down the length of the long living room, his slippers crushing the expensive white carpet as he trod back and forth. Running a panicked hand through his curly hair, he took off his glasses and rubbed his eyes. "I can't believe this is happening, to be honest. It's just like some sort of nightmare out of a horror film."

"Please," Anna said quietly. "Try and calm down."

He turned and faced them, replacing his glasses with a trembling hand. "I thought you made people wait twenty-four hours before taking action when someone went missing."

"Ordinarily, yes," Jacob said. "But with the recent murders in the area we can't take any chances. Can you tell me if your wife was acting unusual lately?"

"Well, I suppose in a *way*, she has been acting a little strange lately but it meant nothing until this nightmare."

Jacob's eyes fixed on him. "Like how?"

"She just seemed very bothered about this Angel of Death and his victims. We both watch the news and we know these things happen, but for some reason these things really got to her. She talked about it a lot, nervously."

"I see," Anna said. "Any idea why that might be?"

He shrugged. "Not at all. And there's just no way she would voluntarily vanish like this. She *must* have been taken and I just know it was him, the Angel of Death."

Jacob decided it would be best to get his mind on some concrete details and away from the terrible thoughts he was conjuring up. "Can you tell me what happened this morning?"

"I was in Cardiff yesterday for a business meeting. It went on late and I spent the night at a Travelodge. I had breakfast and then drove home. When I got back to the house the front door was ajar and I found all this mess. She was just… gone."

"What's your line of work, sir?" Anna asked.

"I'm a full-stack developer. It's my own business."

"Successful?"

"Very, and I love what I do."

"And what does this work entail?" Anna asked.

"It's software engineering, Sergeant. Being a full-stack engineer just means I can offer both front-end and back-end skills, it's more of a holistic approach and right now business is good."

Jacob nodded. "You work from home?"

"Sometimes, but not necessarily. A lot of my work involves driving out to small companies or other freelance businesses. That's what I was doing yesterday in Wales."

Jacob tapped his pen on his pad. "I presume you can give us the details of the people you met with yesterday?"

Ingram was aghast. "You can't think I did this?"

"It's just a formality," Jacob said calmly. "I wouldn't be doing my job if I didn't tie up all the loose ends. You want me to do this properly, don't you, Mr Ingram?"

Ingram calmed down and ran off a list of half a dozen names and numbers from his phone. Then he stared at them like a lost child searching for his mother. "Please, you will find her and bring her home?"

"I'll do everything in my power to find her, Mr Ingram." Jacob got to his feet and slipped his notebook in his pocket. "Thank you for your time, sir. Please be assured we're doing everything possible to find your wife and bring her safely home to you."

"Yes, of course you are… thanks."

Jacob didn't think he sounded very convinced, and he couldn't blame him. Neither was he.

Outside, Anna's phone rang as Jacob climbed back into the Alvis. He buckled up and started the engine and then Anna cut the call and climbed in beside him.

"That was Laura, boss. She says they got an IP address on your Shakespeare creep."

"Professor Seward?"

"Nope, a bloke named Oliver Booth. Some sort of art collector in Oxford."

Jacob gave a bitter laugh. "Not Ollie Booth?"

"You know him?"

He pushed back in his seat and drummed his fingers absent-mindedly on the steering wheel. "Me and Ollie Booth go back a long way."

"Oh yeah?" she asked. "Got form, has he?"

He nodded. "I know him from my time in Oxford. Laura is right when she says he collects art, but sadly Ollie Booth doesn't confine his acquisitions to the auction houses. A good chunk of his collection is stolen art."

"Ah."

"Exactly. He's a smooth, white collar crim who could charm the pants off anyone, but underneath he's a hard-nosed, dirty bastard and he's destroyed a lot of lives."

"And now it turns out he was knocking Sarah Bennett off behind her husband's back."

Jacob winced at the turn of phrase. "Looks that way. We're going to need to have a chat with him, and fast."

Anna buckled up her belt and relaxed on the soft leather chair. "By the way, I didn't know you were a fan of classical music. I thought you were a grease monkey in your spare time."

"Eh?"

"Back there you said the music Charlotte Ingram had on her iPod was a quiet piece."

"Schubert. Jess used to play it," he said, lowering his voice as he slid the key into the ignition. "She played the viola. That's how I knew."

# CHAPTER 25

S alisbury Cathedral dominated a large area in the city's south, its grounds bordering the River Avon as it wound its way to the east. Morgan had lived in the county for many years, but he had never visited it before and when he approached the medieval architectural masterpiece, he felt a sense of awe rising inside him. Staring up at the leaden sky, he followed the tallest spire in England as it twisted and stretched towards the heavens.

"All right, that's impressive."

Innes put her hands in her pockets and joined him, following the spire up into the clouds. When she brought her eyes back down to earth, she saw the Welshman was still captivated by it. "It's pretty amazing, isn't it?"

"I've seen it from all over town more times than I can remember," he said quietly. "But never from up this close. It's actually quite moving."

Out of nowhere, Innes said, "Do you believe in God, sir?"

He turned to her and frowned. "That's a bit heavy for a Wednesday afternoon, isn't it?"

"Just wondering," she said, shrugging. "I used to, but not since what happened to Mum."

"I know what you mean," he gave her a sympathetic smile and decided to get back to business. "Shall we go and have a chat with the Holy Joes, then?"

She laughed. "I'm right behind you. Where did he say he'd be?"

"Ah yes, the kindly Canon Chancellor. When we spoke this morning he told me he could be found in the Morning Chapel. Apparently that's across the other side."

They entered the building by the visitor entrance and made their way along the North Cloister Walk until they reached the South Main Transept. Crossing the nave, the immense scale of the cathedral struck Morgan once again. Pointed Gothic arches disappeared behind solid Purbeck marble columns. Beams of weak March sunlight streamed in through the stained glass windows and illuminated the triforium above their heads.

"It's even more amazing inside," Innes said.

"Not getting converted, are you?"

She gave him a look and they continued on their way past the Quire and along the North Quire Aisle to the Morning Chapel. Lingering outside in the nave for a moment longer, they stopped to take in the intricate fan vault ceiling high above them. Morgan had never paid too much attention in school and wasn't even sure if his classroom had touched on the subject of architecture, but he knew something special when he saw it. Now was one of those times.

He closed his eyes and considered the shape of the silence in this vast place. It was shattered by the sound of a deep, impressive organ playing the first few bars of Bach's St Matthew Passion. He knew this from his father who had sung in a choir during the family farm's richer days. The past wrapped around him as a slight musty smell drifted in the air – old hymn books and worn embroidered kneelers.

He remembered going to the chapel as a boy, up at the top of the village not half an hour's walk up-hill from his parents' farm. A small, neat space but with the same austere atmosphere and that familiar smell in the air. If he kept his eyes closed long enough he could hear the sound of the choir singing. *Calon Lân, Myfanwy, Guide Me, O Thou Great Redeemer.* It all seemed like so long ago.

"You're admiring the beauty of it, aren't you?"

Startled by a voice so near, they both swung around to see a tall, lean man standing right behind them. He was wearing a charcoal grey suit jacket over a black shirt and a bright white dog collar shone under a round chin sporting a mild shaving rash.

"I was, as a matter of fact," Morgan said.

"As an example of early English Gothic architecture it has few rivals. It differs in one important way from most other cathedrals of its time, so it's rather unique. The rib springs here start at the top of the lower arcade rather from floor to ceiling vault like most others." He looked at it in dreamy silence for a few moments. "Yes, it's so special."

Morgan and Innes caught each other's eye and suppressed a smile. "I've never been in here before."

"No?" The man offered a sad frown. "What a shame."

"We're looking for…"

"You've found him," he said, extending a hand to shake. "I'm Dr Guy Greenwood, the Canon Chancellor. I'm broadly in charge of public relations and visitor services."

They shook hands. "I'm DI Morgan and this is DC Innes. We're from Wiltshire CID investigating the murder of a homeless man found not far from here in the river."

"Yes, my assistant briefed me on the purpose of your visit. Shall we walk?"

They followed the Canon along the North Quire Aisle and past the Trinity Chapel. "I go around from time to time and make sure everything's in the right place for the visitors. We have an excellent team here but it does no harm to be prepared. You never know what will turn up."

"Therefore be ye also ready," Morgan said, fixing the man with his sharp, hazel eyes, "for in such an hour as ye think not the Son of man cometh."

Greenwood leaned his head back and cocked it to one side. "Matthew 24:44 – I'm impressed, Inspector. Are you a churchgoer?"

"Not anymore, sir."

The Canon offered a sage nod of understanding. "You'll find God again."

"Maybe, sir, but first I want to find the man who killed the Saint."

An unsettled pause as the final bars of Bach faded out in the vast space. "Yes, of course."

"If you don't mind my saying sir, you don't seem very upset about it."

He turned and faced Morgan. "My emotions are my affair, Inspector."

"I just thought with you being a religious man…"

"I have never used Church doctrine to condemn the actions of another, Mr Morgan. Sins are a crime of the soul, Inspector, dealt with by private confession and absolution."

"The arcane world of the church has always been a mystery to me, Mr Greenwood. Anyway, I know a lot of the homeless come in here from time to time. Did you know him?"

"We all knew the Saint, Inspector. He was a character. He even made the Bishop laugh once."

"The old one, sir, or the new one?"

"You *are* up to date with our affairs. The new one. Bishop Knightley."

"That's right, Peter Knightley. How long has he been here at the cathedral?"

"He started last year. He's coming up to his first anniversary as a matter of fact."

Innes asked, "And how long have you been here, sir?"

"Just a few months," he said quietly. "After many years away in Africa, God called me home to tend my own flock."

"I understand the Bishop wants to encourage the homeless to come into the cathedral?" Morgan asked.

"He's a Christian, Inspector."

Morgan nodded. "When was the last time you saw the Saint?"

"Last weekend. He came in to pray, as he so often did."

"And then?"

"And then he left. We'd like to offer them sanctuary all the time, Inspector, but it's simply not possible. After he prayed, he spoke with me for a few moments just outside the Chapter House and then went on his way."

"Do you know where he used to go?"

"They all have their own places where they like to go, where they find comfort. When the Saint wasn't at the shelters he spent much of his time down in the park near the train station."

"Queen Elizabeth Gardens?" Innes asked.

The Canon nodded.

"Where were you on Saturday night last weekend, Canon?"

He narrowed his eyes. "You suspect *me* of harming him?"

Morgan's voice was rich and comforting, the gentle lilt in his Welsh accent working hard to defuse the tension in the air. "It's protocol to ask, sir. It's not personal at all and I have no particular suspicions at this time. Please, just answer the question."

"What time?"

"From early evening onwards."

"I was in the cathedral until well after lunch – that's when I saw the Saint praying. After that I returned to my office and worked until six. Then I went home."

"And where is home, sir?"

"I live in Harnham, near the river."

"Not too far from where the Saint's body was found," Innes said.

"Now, look here just a minute…"

Morgan kept his gaze fixed on the man. "DC Innes makes a sound point, sir, based in fact."

"That doesn't mean I had anything to do with it. I'm offended."

"That's your right, sir. I'd like to thank you for your time as well."

They turned and walked down the South Quire Aisle, passing the Vestry and then turning left to walk back into the South Main Transept.

"Is he still watching us?" Innes said.

"Every step of the way," said Morgan darkly.

"So what now?"

"Now, we go and take a walk in Lizzie Gardens."

*

Jacob negotiated the ring road and drove up to Boars Hill. The tiny hamlet was home to many of Oxford's richest people and boasted some of the most luxurious properties in the entire county. Here, among these ancient oaks and leafy lanes, movers and shakers, investment bankers and rock stars shielded themselves from the real world with their millions.

Jacob pointed out the palatial home of another famous musician, but it failed to impress Anna Mazurek, sitting now on the partially collapsed passenger seat beside her boss.

"I'm not interested in the fragile egos of hypocritical rock stars," Anna said bluntly.

"Right."

"They need to get stuffed."

"Eh?"

She pushed down on the cream leather and frowned. "The seats."

"Ah, all in good time."

He glanced at the marked police car in his rear view mirror, full of uniforms ready for action if Booth decided to make a fuss or get nasty. Oliver Booth had no form for violence, but there was always a first time. If he thought he was looking at some serious time behind bars this might just be that time.

Anna glanced at yet more iron gates either side of the road; long private drives twisting out of sight. "Don't know why they don't call it Knobs Hill."

Jacob laughed at the comment, but his mind was already elsewhere. He indicated right and swung the heavy old car up to the very top of the hill. He changed up into third and the three litre engine growled under the bonnet. This was the most exclusive part of the little village with houses worth several million pounds each flashing by in a blur as they drove toward their destination.

"Doesn't it make you sick?" Anna said, almost to herself.

He glanced at her before turning back to the road. "What?"

"That a scumbag like Booth gets to live in a place like this."

He checked his mirror. "I've never really thought about it, to be honest. Anyway, he's on the level now, apparently."

"Come on! He's just an old lag who got all his money from stealing and trading art on the black market! He doesn't deserve this."

Jacob smiled. He liked Anna. She had spirit and wasn't afraid to speak her mind – he just hoped she knew where and when to keep her lips locked, especially if she had her eye on the greasy promotion pole. Senior officers knew when they had to keep their views to themselves.

"Come on, let's see what Ollie knows."

The house was an enormous white-painted art deco property built in the 1920s complete with a balcony running around its top floor. Set in two acres of private, peaceful woodland well away from the road it had the feel of a luxury spa retreat and Anna sighed as they pulled up on the sweeping gravel drive.

"Scumbag," she muttered.

They walked up the steps to the front door and rang the bell but there was no reply so they tried again.

Somewhere behind the house Jacob heard the gentle rumble of a single cylinder engine.

"What's that?" Anna asked.

"My money is on a ride-on mower."

"Already?"

"March is the start of the year as far as lawn care goes," he said.

"Judging by the state of your lawn, should you be offering advice?" she said.

"Can I help?"

A young man in a checked shirt, body warmer and muddy trousers skipped up some steps from the lawn to the patio area and walked toward the two of them. He was wearing heavy duty garden gloves and had grass cuttings smeared on his forehead.

Jacob showed his warrant card. "I'm DCI Jacob and this is…"

"Anna Mazurek," she said, stepping forward. "Detective Sergeant Anna Mazurek."

As the young man studied her warrant card, Jacob saw Anna scanning him in the way a lion looks at a gazelle.

"I take it you're not Oliver Booth?" Anna said.

"Me? You've got to be kidding!"

"This isn't Booth," Jacob said, turning to the man. "Where is he?"

"Out walking the dogs," he said. "He likes to take them out on the circular walk sometimes when the weather's good for it."

"And when might he be back?"

"Can I ask what this is all about?"

"It's a police matter between us and Mr Booth," Jacob said. "Do you know when he'll return from the walk?"

"Not too long now, I reckon. He's already been gone an hour. You can wait in the house if you like."

"That would be very kind, thank you."

The man opened the front door. "Just go through to your right. I won't come in because of my boots."

He pointed them through to a formal sitting room and told them to wait there. When he had left them, Anna sat down beside an empty fireplace while Jacob paced up and down the expansive cream plush pile. Pieces of expensive antique furniture were carefully placed and gave a sense of calm and order, and vases of fresh flowers filled the room with the scent of summer.

"Bloody scumbag," she said again. "I wonder how much of this furniture was stolen, too?"

"Now then, Sergeant."

Jacob paced to the far end of the room where two French doors gave a view of the impressive lawns to the south of the house. Here, he watched the gardener pad back down to the mower and fire the engine back up before driving it out of sight behind a large wooden summerhouse.

"Oliver Booth certainly has done very well for himself since going on the straight and narrow," he said, turning to study a large abstract oil painting hanging on the wall. "This is a Mondrian."

"Is that special?" Anna asked.

"It is if you think two million pounds in special."

She gasped. "Two million quid for that? It's four black lines and a red square."

Jacob pondered the artwork for another moment or two before turning on his heel.

"Can you hear dogs?"

"I can indeed."

He nudged his chin at the gardens beyond the window. "And talk of the devil, here's our man."

\*

The man sunk down into the seat of his van and watched the two detectives walking slowly from the cathedral's grounds. According to the radio, the police had found Hannah Wilson's body in Avebury Manor just as he had intended, and Charlotte Ingram was officially missing and presumed kidnapped from her own home just outside Marlborough. Things were heating up and the police were upping their game in pursuit of the killer.

He licked his dry lips as he tracked the police across the road. It looked like they might be heading into the park, and he knew what was waiting for them in there.

Or *who*, more like.

His mind raced as he tried to guess what they would tell the police and he thought back to his past and started to cry. Choking back the tears, he repeated the mantra he'd comforted himself with for twenty years. *You have to do it… it's the only way.*

It was fate, he told himself.

Purge the evil and make them pure again, for sinners deserve their fate.

*Fate.*

He spat the word out like it was poison. When it came down to it all, was there anything in this world that wasn't decided by fate?

They were talking to the homeless scumbags in the park about the Saint.

They were closing in, tightening the noose.

# CHAPTER 26

When Detective Inspector Bill Morgan walked into Queen Elizabeth Gardens and saw the small jumble of tents beneath the trees near the river, his heart sank. Locals called this place Lizzie Gardens and during the summer it was usually full of life as people enjoyed the park and its amenities, or just walked alongside the Avon as it made its way south through the county.

But during the winter it was a quieter, more solemn place. Often, the city's homeless would gather here, pitching their tents under the trees to shelter from the wind and rain and snow. The recent nerve agent attack on the city by Russian spies had cost over ten million pounds to decontaminate, but the park was overlooked, and many of those huddled here had wondered if they were at risk of the lethal poison.

For Morgan, the sight of those trying to keep warm in their tents was hard. He had never told anyone on the team, but his younger brother had run away from home when he was a teenager. He was brought up on a farm in Ceredigion in West Wales and life hadn't been easy. Money was hard to find and their father worked from dawn till dusk and often well after. There were arguments. Lots of them, and after one blazing row with his father, young Dafydd had left in the night.

They had searched for him on the farm, then further out in the towns of Aberaeron and Lampeter but found no trace of him. When local police tracked him as far as London they thought it was over, but they never got him home. If Morgan closed his eyes sometimes, he could still see the look on his mother's face when the sergeant told her he'd been found living rough but had moved on before they could reach him.

That night, Morgan decided two things. First, he wanted to be a policeman after he left the Marines and second, he'd do all he could for people without a home. He was a man of his word. He'd joined the police after leaving his life as a commando behind, and he'd given much of his time to volunteering at soup kitchens until the demands of detective inspector grew too heavy. He'd long since given up hope of ever seeing Dai again. Like his parents, he wondered if perhaps he was dead, but he could still help others like him.

Now, as he walked over to the tents in a city where the average house price was a third of a million pounds, he felt a wave of unease and disgust.

"Are you OK, sir?"

He glanced over at young Innes. He'd almost forgotten she was there, but seeing her bright, keen face under her umbrella brought him back to the land of the living.

"I'm fine."

"If you don't mind my asking, sir," she said tentatively, "you seemed very protective of Denny back at the Samaritans."

"Did I?"

She nodded. "Any particular reason?"

"Not that I can think of, Innes," he said. "But it doesn't hurt to show a little compassion to your fellow man, does it now?"

"No, sir."

"Especially those not as fortunate as yourself."

"Of course, sir."

He smiled inwardly. She was a smart cookie. She had sensed a connection between him and the homeless and she wanted to know more. That was natural, but Dai was family business, and that was the way he like to keep his world organised. Family and Others. Not even Jacob knew about Dai's sad story or the way it had impacted the modest Tŷ Coch farm on that gentle hill so far away.

"You're a good detective, Laura," he said, using her first name. "You keep doing what you're doing and you'll go a long way."

She blushed a little. "Thanks, sir, I appreciate that. By the way, you're not considering the Canon as a suspect in the Saint's death, are you?"

"Maybe. Harnham's upstream of where we found the body, and there are the crucifixes to consider."

"He didn't seem like a killer."

"Some of them are very good at hiding it." He drew in a sad, deep breath. "Righto, let's get this over with."

When they approached the small group of homeless people, their conversation hushed and everyone found something else to look at. Morgan's deep sympathy for their plight hadn't dulled his instincts or blinded him to the reality of the situation. Many of these people were drug addicts or drunks, and some were thieves, albeit mostly small-time. He knew most would be carrying knives and packets of drugs – cannabis resin, maybe some pills to take the edge off the nights.

Now, as he drew out his wallet, he manoeuvred so he was slightly in front of Innes. Just in case.

"I'm Bill Morgan," he said quietly, dropping the formal title. "I'm with the police but I'm not here to give you any trouble. I'm trying to find out what happened to the Saint. You've all heard by now, I'm sure."

Eyes darted from one to another before a short man with a scraggly beard stepped forward. He was wearing a blue cagoule with the hood tied up tight around his face. Water ran down the nylon in tiny rivulets and dripped onto the muddy grass. "We know."

Morgan nodded and put the wallet away. "It was a shitty thing and I want to catch the bastard who did it, but I don't think I can do that without your help."

Two of them turned their backs on him and went back into their tents. Morgan didn't take it personally, and focussed on the man with the beard. "Can you help me?"

He shrugged.

Morgan turned and watched the brown water as is tumbled down the Avon. The river was running high because of the weather. It was dirty and cold and not the sort of place to die in. "I'm worried the killer might have some sort of vendetta against homeless people."

The man snorted. "Then you've got your work cut out, ain't you?"

Morgan nodded.

"It's only a matter of time before you bastards move us on and we're all scared," he said. "After the poisonings, any one of us could be next. All you have to do is touch something with that stuff on it and it's over. We can't hide up in our houses like the rest of you."

"I know, I know…" his voice trailed away into the sound of a train blowing its horn as it left the nearby station. "Why did you call him the Saint?"

"He was always going on about the injustice of it all, about sin and vice and punishment. I think he felt guilty about something himself, as well. He talked about redemption a lot. That's why we called him the Saint," the man said. "He was always going on about how they'd all be punished. Them up in the big houses. Them in the cathedral. If you got any of them tossers out here on the streets they wouldn't survive three nights."

"Anything you can tell us might help us find his killer,"

The man hesitated and a woman wandered over to him and handed him a roll-up cigarette.

"I'm just trying to help."

"All right, look. There was talk that the Saint had bought a boat."

"A boat?"

"Nothing special, just a little thing big enough for one or two people to sleep in. He made some hints and talked about it from time to time but no one believed him. There's a lot of talk, you know? A lot of dreaming and fantasising. But maybe this time it was true. Maybe this time he was telling the truth and he really did have a boat."

"Did it have a name?"

"He said it was called Catherine, after his sister."

"I never even knew he had a sister," the woman said.

The man with the beard shrugged. "Doesn't matter one way or the other now, does it? But the boat was called Catherine, or so he said. He said he was going to sail to France on it, and get away forever. He talked about buying a villa down there. Said he was about to come into some money – big bucks, you know?"

The woman laughed. "The Saint didn't have enough money to buy a pair of socks, never mind a big house in France."

"Where was it moored?" Innes asked.

A look of grave confusion appeared on the man's face. "He kept it just outside of town, somewhere between the city and Harnham."

"Now, think carefully because this is important." Morgan lowered his voice to a confidential tone. "Who knew about this boat?"

"I can't help you there, chief," he said. "The Saint came and went as he pleased. There's no way of knowing who he told and who he never told."

"All right, thanks." Morgan put his hand in his pocket and pulled out a ten pound note. "Get something to warm yourself up."

*

Oliver Booth stormed into his front room and let his dogs loose. They ran over to the two detectives and started padding around them in circles and sniffing their legs. One of them growled.

"Easy, boy," Booth said. "It's no worse than the filth you've been sniffing out on the walk."

"Hello again, Ollie," Jacob said. "I'm sure you remember me, and this is DS Mazurek."

He threw the dog leads down on the sofa and unzipped his jacket. "Why are you in my house, Jacob?"

"Just wondered if you've been to any good plays lately."

"You what?"

"Specifically anything by Shakespeare."

Booth started to clam up. He took a step back and lifted his hand to scratch the back of his head. "I don't know what you're going on about. If you've come here to waste my time, I'll have my brief all over you like a cheap suit."

"You can drop the act, Ollie," Jacob said. "I know all about your little affair with Sarah Bennett. I know all about Iachimo and Imogen."

Booth turned and reached out for the mantelpiece, lowering his head down between his shoulders as if he was studying the carpet. "I never killed her."

"So you're aware of what happened to her?" Anna asked.

"Yes, I am. I read the papers and watch the news like everyone else."

Jacob looked around the room and sniffed. "Where were you on Saturday night, Ollie?"

The big man raised his head and spun around. Pointing a fat finger in Jacob's face he raised his voice and said, "You're not putting this on me! I told you I never killed her!"

The man looked as if he were about to explode, Anna thought. She considered calling in the uniforms who were waiting outside when Jacob straightened up to his full height and took a step closer to Booth, reaching for the handcuffs he kept in his pocket. "Settle down, Ollie."

"I never did it! I loved her."

"That's very touching," Anna said.

Booth fell silent for a few moments, thinking his story through. "She was a clever, brilliant woman, sergeant. We met at an auction. I'd never met anyone like her before. Her husband was as dull as dishwater. As boring as vanilla, she said. We hit it off, that's all."

"Ever tell her about your sordid past as an art thief and forger?" Jacob asked.

"There's no need to get personal, Mr Jacob. But as a matter of fact, I did. She said she didn't care so long as I was straight now. I am. She was going to leave Mr Vanilla and live with me."

Jacob kept his eyes fixed on Booth as he walked away from the mantelpiece and started to pad around in the plush carpet. "Your location on the night of her death, now."

"You can't think I'm this Angel of Death, surely?"

"You're stalling."

Booth deflated. "All right, all right. I was in London."

"Where and when?"

"Knocking off the Tate."

Jacob frowned. "I've not read about that."

"That's because they don't know about it yet," he said with a heavy sigh. "I had some inside help and stole that Mondrian. The one in the gallery is now one of my forgeries."

"Oliver Booth," Jacob said. "I'm arresting you on suspicion of breaking and entering and art theft. You do not have to say anything, but it may harm your defence if you do not mention when questioned something you later rely on in court."

"You should have stayed in retirement," Anna said.

Jacob fitted the cuffs to the big man. "Anything you do say may be given in evidence."

"What about my dogs?"

"Your brief can sort it out when you call him from the nick."

Leading him out to the car, Booth turned and said, "I bet this has made your day, Mr Jacob."

"Not really," he said. "Now I'm back to square one in my hunt for Sarah's killer."

*

The drunken man mumbled incoherently to himself as he made his way across the street and inside the cathedral grounds. Swaying and tottering with a system full of speed and booze, he stared up into the rain and saw the enormous spire as he drew closer to the famous cathedral. He'd been watching this place since the Saint disappeared in the night. Watching *him*. Now it was time to move things along. The Saint was dead and he knew why.

He walked faster, crossing the cathedral grounds and making his way to a large house. Knocking on the door, he warmed his hands as he waited for the door to open.

"You again."

"You got what I asked for, your Holiness?"

"You'd better come inside."

With a furtive glance over his shoulder, Denny Marks staggered inside the hallway and the door closed firmly behind him.

# CHAPTER 27

Morgan pushed on the accelerator pedal and changed up into fifth. For a wet and windy day in March the traffic wasn't doing anything unusual, and he and Innes settled down into the long line of cars snaking their way out of the city. When they finally broke free, the rain stopped and some sunshine cut through a break in the clouds, lighting up a soaked landscape as they made their way down to the river.

Sitting beside him, Laura Innes felt her iPhone ring in her pocket. She took it out and checked the screen hoping for some news concerning the case but instead saw a message from Vincent. She thought she had suppressed the sigh, but when Morgan glanced at her and asked her what was wrong, she realised she hadn't made a very good job of hiding her feelings.

"Everything okay, Laura?" he asked.

"It's nothing, sir. Just personal life crap."

"Personal life crap," he repeated with a smile. "So it's not just me then?"

"Definitely not."

"Anything I can help with?"

"It's nothing, really."

"You know you can ask if you need some help, right?"

She gave him a grateful smile and nodded her head. "Thanks, sir, but I can handle this." Then, her phone rang again. With relief, she saw it was back to business. "The boss, sir," she said. "Says he picked up Oliver Booth."

He turned and looked at her in shock. "Booth's the Angel of Death?"

"Nope, he arrested him for robbing the Tate in London. That was his alibi."

Morgan started chuckling. "Oh, dear, what a shame, how sad. Poor old Booth."

"I know. Having to confess to a robbery to avoid a murder charge…"

He slowed, signalled and turned onto a smaller road leading down to just west of where the River Nadder flowed into the Avon.

"Who says good things never happen to bad people?"

She smiled, but it quickly faded when she looked down at her phone a second time and saw Vinnie's message. Then, Morgan surprised her by cursing loudly, changing down and overtaking a car dawdling along the road. "Bloody road's a nightmare."

\*

By the time Morgan and Innes had found the *Catherine*, the sun was low and obscured by another bank of rainclouds moving in over the Downs. The temperature had dropped too, and down here by the water they both felt a dull dampness clinging to their bodies as they climbed onto the boat. A handful of other boats bobbed up and down gently on their moorings but other than that the world was silent except for the muted song of a moorhen somewhere in the reeds.

Standing on the compact aft deck of the modest cabin cruiser, Morgan imagined the Saint walking along the towpath in the dusk like some kind of spectre in his long woollen trench coat. He watched him now as he walked past Innes and looked furtively over his shoulders before stepping on board the boat and climbing down inside the cabin, seeking sanctuary from a bitter world.

He was almost real to him, in his long trench coat and hat.

"But what I don't understand is how he paid for it," Innes said.

Knocked from his thoughts, he looked over to the young detective, her copper-colored ringlets bouncing on her shoulders. She looked too young for the job, he thought out of nowhere. Too nice for a world like this. "Sorry?"

"How did he pay for it, sir?"

He raised his eyebrow and blew out a long breath. "The same way he paid for the Rolex and all the single malts, and with a bit of luck, I think we might just be about to find out."

And with that he pushed open the cabin door and headed down inside the boat.

*

From up here he could see the whole city. It seemed so peaceful, but every single one of those roofs was sheltering a web of lies, deceit and violence form the rest of the world. He knew their suffering. He felt it acutely. He knew guilt, too. He felt it coursing through his veins like some sort of blackened blood carrying evil from his heart to every part of his body.

He thought of the dead women. The dead man.

He had done this to them.

He thought of the missing woman.

He was responsible for this, too, and the fire.

From up here on the cathedral tower he felt like he could touch the face of God, but when he reached out with his hand there was nothing but the cold, chill air of a dying day. The pain rose inside him like acid.

*Oh, what a tangled web we weave, when first we practice to deceive.*

He knew in his heart that ultimately he had killed them all, and now his God would punish him as hard as any other sinner, but first, he had to bring this to an end. It was time for Denny Marks to meet his maker.

Gently rubbing the pectoral cross hanging around his neck and praying to be forgiven for what he was about to do, he turned and made his way back down the tower.

*

Inside the boat, the air was putrid and stale. A plate of rotten food was on the small fold-out table and a chipped mug of cold, sticky coffee sat beside it, just where the Saint had left it over a week ago. Morgan's job had brought him to many places like this, and he recognised the stench of abandonment and decay at once.

"All right, let's get this over with. Gloves on and look out for needles."

When he turned to look over his shoulder, Innes was standing behind him and holding her gloved hands up in front of his face. "One step ahead of you, sir."

"I'm sure you always will be, Laura," he gave a low sad laugh. "Now, somewhere in this boat is the answer to what the hell is going on here, and I want to find it, so get searching."

After systematically moving through the small boat and checking all the cupboards and drawers, Morgan resorted to looking inside the little compact boat oven but came up empty handed. "Maybe I was a tad too optimistic about the *Catherine*."

"I wouldn't speak too soon if I were you, sir. Don't do anything silly while your head's in that oven."

"Don't worry," he said with a laugh. "I won't."

"Good, because I think I might have something here."

Her voice was muffled and quiet and when he turned away from the oven he saw the young constable from a rather unflattering angle as she searched under one of the sleeping bunks. Getting to his feet he looked anywhere but at his young protégé. "What have you got then?"

"Not sure, but it looks like some sort of old tin hidden inside the mattress."

"Let's have a gander at it then."

He walked over to her as she crawled out from under the bed and clambered up to her feet. In her hands she held a rusted biscuit tin and the two detectives shared a glance. The small boat bobbed gently up and down on the river. Prising the lid open, the first thing they saw was two thick bundles of fifty pound notes.

"Bloody hell." Morgan ran the top of his blue nitrile-gloved thumb down the side of one of the bundles. "There must be five thousand quid in here."

"And yet he was living on the streets. Quite the mystery."

"I don't think he spent much time on the streets, at least not sleeping. When he wasn't in the shelters he was in here."

She peered forward on her tiptoes. "What's under the cash?"

"Looks like newspaper cuttings."

He set the tin down on the bed and pulled out a number of newspaper cuttings. "Well, what have we here?"

"Who's that?"

"If I'm not very much mistaken, it's the new Canon Chancellor of Salisbury Cathedral – Guy Greenwood."

Innes's eyebrows rose half an inch up her forehead. "There must be at least a dozen pictures of him in here."

"And all cut out of local newspapers by the looks of things."

"Not this one." She handed a black and white over to the inspector. "This one looks like an original."

"And taken some time ago judging by the look of the Canon – when he was a much younger man. What's this then?"

"Sir?"

"Looks like a passport." Nimble fingers pulled out the small maroon book. "It's out of date by a long way but we have a name."

"What is it?"

"Carl Daniel Buckland, born in Swindon in 1977."

Innes leaned forward and looked at the image of the man in the passport. "You think that's the Saint?"

"Hard to say. It might be stolen."

"But we have the name."

"And that means we can get hold of the dental records. Start praying they're a match."

"Talking of praying, sir – why would these papers about the Canon even be in here?"

"I don't know, but there must be an inch of papers in here and I don't know about you, but my office smells a lot better than this place. You bring any police tape?"

She pursed her lips and tucked her hand into her suit pocket. She pulled it out to reveal a fresh roll of blue and white boundary tape. "Voila."

"One of these days I'm going to catch you out."

She gave him a cheeky wink. "Don't count on it, sir."

"All right, let's put the tape up around the boat and get this biscuit tin back to HQ. I know we'll be working late, but speaking for myself, I could do with a hot cup of coffee and a sit down."

"That's because you're getting on, sir."

"Hey, I could beat you on a 10 K run any day."

"Is that a challenge?"

"What do you think?"

"Dangerous words, sir. Dangerous words."

He laughed. "Let's get the hell out of here. I think this little biscuit tin has the answer we're looking for and it's high time we found out what this is all about."

*

Charlotte Ingram was not unfit. She'd led a privileged life and she'd had the time and money to keep herself in good shape and eat well. She was strong and had stamina and she thought she might just have a chance of escaping from him if she kept her wits about her.

But her life had been darkened by the shadow of one afternoon. Just one insane mistake had ruined everything. She had struggled with it for a long time before reconciling herself to what had happened and what she could expect from fate for the part she had played in it.

Looking into the darkness of the van, she wondered where he was now; after another short drive, he'd left her alone in here hours ago. She'd tried to kick the side panel of the van but her legs were bound together and her hands were cuffed behind her with cable ties. She tried to scream but he'd stuck a gag down hard into her mouth with some duct tape. Besides, she couldn't hear a sound outside the van. Wherever he'd parked up, it must be isolated.

And inside somewhere, she considered. She couldn't hear the hum of distant traffic or the chatter of birds. No people talking and laughing, not even the sound of the wind on the side of the van. She was in a garage, or an abandoned factory, maybe. Her mind ran riot with terror.

*You deserve this.*

No. She fought it back. No, you don't.

*You deserve to die like this.*

She felt tears running down her cheeks and she started to snivel into the gag. Chris would be sitting at home now, worried senseless by it all. And what about her parents in Spain? Had they been told? Dad was nearly eighty, she thought. News like this would crush him out of existence.

*How does the hand of fate feel, now it is wrapped around your throat?*

She started to sob in the darkness.

*

In Exeter, the man lifted a glass of orange juice to his lips with nicotine-stained fingers and watched Sophie as she waited at the bar. Not a bad figure, he thought. Good-looking, too, *for her age*, he threw in with a smirk. Two deep at the bar, she waited patiently for her drinks. When they came, there were three of them – two glasses of wine and a beer.

They'd just finished a long lecture on criminal psychology delivered by a world-renowned expert and now they were hitting the bar. It looked like they needed it. He knew he would. After listening to an hour and half of gobbledegook he felt like doing the same, but he had to keep his mind sharp.

Now she turned and walked back to the table with her friends, three women and two men in expensive suits and haircuts. Handing drinks to those waiting, she took a sip and laughed in response to something one of the men had said. The tall one, with silver in his expensive hair. Did the copper back in Wiltshire know she was flirting like this?

The man with the silver in his hair said something else, to less effect, but reached out and touched her arm briefly. Sophie pulled away, subtle and polite. Perhaps Jacob had nothing to worry about after all. At least not in that department.

Seeing she was engrossed in the conversation he finished his drink and rose from the soft bench seat by the window. Walking around the room to ensure he never caught her eye, he left the large, busy bar and headed towards the stairs.

And her room.

# CHAPTER 28

I n the Old Watermill, Jacob stood in front of the little machine in his kitchen and waited patiently for the nozzles to fire the coffee into his cup. Normally a tea man with a preference for darjeeling, this evening seemed to call for something a little stronger. Apart from anything else, it would help warm him up, which was no small thing considering how cold the mill could get.

He stirred the warmed milk into his cup and carried it into his front room where he relaxed in his favourite armchair and thought about lighting the fire. His mother always made up a good fire, he recalled, but it was so much effort to clean the grate out he preferred to flick on the electric heater instead, which is what he did.

With a heavy heart, he turned to his side table and pulled a manila folder towards him. Inside was the life story of Charlotte Ingram from birth to kidnap and it was his job to go through it and search for anything that might lead to her recovery.

She was pretty. That was the first thing. Long blonde hair and bright blue eyes. She had a slim intelligent face and wore expensive, tasteful clothes. It wasn't a fatuous observation – in missing persons cases, looks could be important. The results from the blood sample Mia found in the kitchen were Charlotte's DNA, which was a let down, but he was still certain that someone had taken her, and that someone had to be the Angel of Death.

He sipped the coffee and studied her life. Charlotte Francesca Ingram, born in Southampton and raised in Wiltshire before moving to Oxford to go to university where she got a first. Oxford, again. And she was the same age as the other victims. He didn't believe in coincidences and knew this was an important link. All three of the female victims attended the University of Oxford at the same time, but different colleges. Tomorrow he'd have the team look more deeply into it.

He sipped more tea and went and back to the file.

After graduation, she excelled and moved to London to study at the Slade School of Fine Art. He raised an eyebrow. Did people still study that? He shrugged his shoulders – he had no idea what went on at universities and didn't care much either way. It had been like that since he dropped out of university in his second year. His mind wandered to those distant days but he was brought back with a jolt when someone knocked on his door.

He wished he'd drawn the curtains before sitting down with the coffee. At least that way he wouldn't have had to get up in order to hide from whoever was interrupting him. He reassured himself with the knowledge that they always go away after the third series of knocks, and returned his attention to the file.

Another series of knocks made two, and began to irritate him more, but he pushed on with his coffee and his file, not to be disturbed. When the third knock arrived, he put aside the file and coffee cup and rose from the chair. Whoever was at his door meant to see him, so he made his way from the sitting room and along the short corridor to the front door.

He swung the door open to see a tall, good-looking woman in motorcycle leathers climbing off a Ducati superbike. It could only be one person, and when she took off her helmet and shook her blonde hair free, his suspicions were confirmed. She looked even slimmer than usual in the leathers, which accentuated her figure. She turned and smiled at him.

"Just in time for coffee," he said.

"Coffee?" Anna Mazurek thrust her helmet into his arms. "After the day I've had, you've got to be kidding."

\*

She leaned into Jacob's fridge and sighed. "Is this all you've got?"

"What do you mean?"

"Beer," she said, lifting her head above the open fridge door until he could see her eyes.

"What about it?"

"Nothing," she said with huff, closing the door and handing him one of the bottles. "Just not a very good selection, that's all."

"It's not a bloody off licence."

She cracked the top off with the opener and slid it across the table. "You can say that again."

Jacob cracked his beer and took a swig, using the opportunity to hide the smile she had given him with her attitude. "Not bad though."

"It'll do."

He peered outside at her Ducati superbike. "I presume you're just having the one?"

She looked at the label and frowned. "I think that's a safe assumption."

They walked into the sitting room and crashed down on some seats, glad to take the weight off. After Jacob let out a long sigh, she put her beer bottle down on a coaster and said, "Come on, tell Auntie Anna all about it."

He tried to laugh. "The slower I am, the more people die. When I get something wrong, an innocent person dies and I have to live with that."

"We all have to." She paused a beat, unsure of how safe the ground was. "Tell me to bugger off if you think I'm prying, but it seems to me this is really about Jess again."

He turned to her sharply. "What do you mean?"

"These feelings of guilt you have when you can't save someone. I don't remember you being like this before the fire. That's all."

"Bugger off."

She sighed and set her beer down. "Fine. We don't have to talk about it, but please tell me you're still talking about it with the shrink."

"Lovelace?"

She nodded and fiddled with her beer bottle. "Uh-huh."

"I don't want to talk about that, either. I'm focussing on the case."

"We all are. What about Sophie?"

"No comment."

"I mean has she been able to help you?"

He slumped down further in the chair by the fire and let out another long, weary sigh. "I know you're trying to help but I have to focus on Avebury. He's still out there, Anna," he said, nodding his head at the window beside his chair. "And what bothers me is that any minute now that phone's going to ring with news of someone finding Charlotte Ingram's body... Lying dead in a ditch somewhere clutching one of those crosses."

Understanding spread over her face. "I know what you mean. I've been thinking the exact same thing since she went missing. But it's like you said – the other victims weren't kidnapped first, so we have to presume that for some crazy reason, this one's different. Maybe she's still alive."

He shook his head. "I wish I could share your optimism but everything my instinct is telling me says that she's already gone or he's going to kill her tonight."

He took a long drink from the bottle and pushed back in the leather wingback, his lean, chiselled jaw line flickering in the firelight. "I just feel so powerless. I can't help her and it's driving me insane."

Anna knew where this was coming from. They both did. Ever since his fiancée had died in the house fire, he had had to deal with some heavy-duty feelings of failure and inadequacy. He was there in the house that night, the intended victim of the fire, and if he had just been a little stronger, searched a bit longer in the smoke and flames, he might have been able to save her life. But he wasn't, and she had died as a result. She watched his lined face contort in the gentle light and saw how much it still tortured him.

"Any news on the other team's investigation?" she asked.

"Bill texted me and said he's got a good lead from the Saint's boat. Maybe even a name."

"There we are then." She picked up her bottle. "Let's see what tomorrow brings, eh?"

\*

Across the county in the HQ building, Innes could just see Morgan as he worked at his desk, obscured as he was behind a jumble of box files and Indian takeaway cartons. Everyone at the station knew about his military past and his demanding fitness regimen, but they also knew his other side, the half of him that threw caution to the wind and smoked fat cigars. As she walked over to the desk with two coffees in her hands, she had to accept that she found him an attractive and intriguing man, even if he was almost old enough to be her father.

"Your coffee, sir."

He looked up, startled. "Thanks, Laura – what time is it?"

She checked her watch. "Half ten."

He gave her a sympathetic look. "You go home. It's late, and I'm sure there's someone waiting for you."

"Well, actually, I think I finally found something that links the victims besides their age and the Oxford college angle."

He rubbed his tired eyes as he turned to look at her. "You've got my full attention, DC Innes. Go on."

"The names Sarah Taylor, Hannah Smith and Charlotte Johnson – that's Charlotte Ingram's maiden name – are all connected in one specific criminal case," she said. "It took a while to narrow it down, but…"

"Sir!"

Shocked by the raised voice, they both turned and watched Matt Holloway bound into the office. "It's the checks you asked me to do on the name Carl Buckland."

"And?"

"I think I've found something – A Carl Daniel Buckland who was born in Swindon in 1977 just happened to be a witness for the prosecution in a murder trial at Bristol Crown Court back in the late nineties."

Morgan's eyebrows rose half an inch. "Is that so?"

"It certainly is, sir."

Holloway looked over at a crestfallen Laura Innes. "What is it?"

Morgan gave a sympathetic smile. "I think Laura was about to unveil this particular secret, right Laura?"

She sighed. "Yes, I was. I finally found a link in the police records between the three female victims with reference to a murder investigation over twenty years ago. The name Buckland also comes up in the notes."

"But I think I got there first," Holloway said with a smile.

"I don't think so, hotshot," said Innes. "You get the silver medal on this one."

"Come on," Morgan said. "Let's keep things nice and cordial. What are the details of this murder, Matt?"

"Victim was a Julia Crawshaw. Her body was found floating in the Mill Pond at Figheldean in the summer of ninety-seven. A local man named Nathan Brett was arrested at the scene. Her boyfriend. He'd drowned her, by all accounts."

"Drowned, you say?"

Holloway couldn't resist a brief smile. "Yes, sir."

"I think we could be getting somewhere," Morgan said.

"What was the sentence?" Innes asked.

Holloway read on. "Mr Nathan Brett appeared in Swindon Court to confirm his identity and was then remanded in custody to appear in the Crown Court in Bristol. He pleaded not guilty to murder but after a fairly short trial he was found guilty and sentenced to twenty-two years inside."

Innes frowned. "A tad steep – was he particularly violent?"

"Nothing's mentioned."

"What about mental health issues?" Morgan asked.

He shook his head. "Again, nothing describing that here. And that's not all. As he was taken from the dock he screamed that he was an innocent man and that the whole thing had been a conspiracy to lock him up."

"Not unusual."

"But refusing to admit guilt in order to get parole is."

"Is that what he did?"

"Right across the whole of his sentence. He refused to show remorse or own up to the crime, even when told it would improve his chances of getting parole and shortening his sentence."

"Where is he now?"

"Released a few months ago."

"Bloody hell," Morgan said. "Where did he serve the sentence?"

"Woodhill in Buckinghamshire, sir. "Alongside developing an interest in the prison chapel where he studied theology, he also studied software engineering and coding and he took it all the way to the end. Eventually he wrote a PhD in it. Something about penetration software."

"Again," Morgan said. "I find myself on the verge of a joke, and yet circumstances forbid it."

Innes blushed.

"Anyway, this could be what we've been looking for. Good work, Matt, and you too, Laura."

"Thanks, sir. It wasn't easy because Buckland had been homeless for so long that there was no real paper trail to follow. That's when I decided to go right back to birth records and work my way forwards through his life. He dropped off the radar not long after the court case."

"We still need a positive ID on the corpse though," Innes said. "All we have right now is an out of date passport belonging to a man who was involved in a trial over twenty years ago. We still need to get a proper ID on the body, to ID that body as Carl Buckland."

"And there's no UK-wide national database of dental records," Morgan said, turning to Holloway. "So we'll have to contact one of his previous dentists and request his records. If they cut up rough we might be talking warrants, but I doubt they will, given the circumstances. As soon as we have confirmation that the Saint is the Carl Buckland who was one of the witnesses in the Crawshaw trial, then that changes everything."

"Doesn't it just?" Holloway said.

Morgan checked his watch. "It's nearly midnight and I'm ordering everyone to go home. First thing in the morning we get Dr Lyon on the dental records and I want HMP Woodhill contacted and all of Nathan Brett's files sent over for the boss. I want to know everything about him and some picture ID. If we really do have an ex-con loose on some sort of revenge killing spree, we're going to need to hunt him down in a hurry."

*

Sophie watched Theo Miles walk back from the bar with a drink in each hand. Sitting opposite her in the busy hotel bar, he placed the drink on her coaster and gave her a smile before sipping his beer. She had known Theo a long time, and learnt a lot from him, but she had always known his interest in her went well beyond work colleagues.

"That was quite a lecture," he said. "It didn't take Sherlock Holmes to know that Kit's keynote was going to be a sell-out. And he loves an audience."

"He has a brilliant mind," Sophie said.

"And a brilliant ego," he muttered. "You should have seen his face when the newspapers called him the English version of *Cracker*. He was unbearable for weeks."

"He's different now," she said. "His last case in Chicago hit him hard."

Theo paused a beat as they both recalled the Ferryman. "Like ours, then."

"Yes."

"We got him though."

"I'd rather not talk about it, Theo, if it's all the same to you."

He sipped his drink and blew out a breath. "Tell me, if you're free next…"

"Theo…"

She saw from his face that he understood.

"Is there someone else?" he asked.

She paused before answering, thinking back to the day she and Jacob had spent together at the Old Watermill after the Witch-Hunt murders. The truth was, she didn't know if there was someone else or not, but just remembering that time with him she knew she wanted there to be.

"There might be."

"Ah," he said. "You mean Heathcliff up in Wiltshire?"

"If you're talking about Tom Jacob, then yes, and stop being so pathetic."

He shrugged and took another sip of his beer. "Well, he is a bit broody."

"You've never even met him."

"I inferred it from his TV interviews."

She rolled her eyes. Typical Theo. "I'm going to bed."

"OK." He sounded deflated. "It *is* late, I suppose."

She slipped around the table and made her way up to her room. Sliding the keycard into the lock, she opened her door and stepped inside the hotel room. The smell of fresh sheets drifted in the air as she kicked off her shoes and sighed with relief. Walking to the window she watched the night-time cityscape for a few moments and then switched on the TV. Nothing new, so she decided to have a shower and then go to bed.

Taking off her clothes and wrapping a towel around her, she stopped to remove her contact lenses when she saw something that made her heart almost skip a beat. Nestling deeply in her pillow was a shiny silver coin. Scarcely believing her own eyes, she took a step back and gasped, pulling the towel up further around her as she moved.

*It couldn't be!*

Her breath quickened and she felt her heart beating harder in her chest. Panic reaction – dry mouth and trembling hands as the adrenaline coursed through her system. Leaning in closer, she realised with horror the coin had a tiny honeybee stamped into it.

Charon's obol.

*Him... in here?* She spun around and stared at the room, her flesh crawling with fear.

She started to feel dizzy now and her vision began to narrow into a tunnel. For one heart-stopping second she thought she had been drugged – drink spiked down in the bar? But then she pulled it together and realised she was having a panic attack.

She heard a noise in the bathroom. Breathing hard, she turned on her heel and stepped backwards from the bathroom door, but this meant walking deeper into the room and further away from the room's main door. The moment suddenly felt like a complex jigsaw puzzle in her mind. She contemplated the idea of the Ferryman in her bathroom, just waiting for her to return to her room and she felt sick.

And yet she had to walk right past the bathroom door to reach the exit.

*Solve the puzzle, Soph.*

Her terrified eyes crawled from the shadows of the room's entrance over to the phone beside the bed. One call to the front desk and maybe she could get someone to come up and…

Another noise in the bathroom.

She stepped back again, struggling to keep the panic attack away, to stay conscious. She knew she was no fainter, but she also knew that some people suffered from a condition called syncope where panic attacks induced unconsciousness. No, this wasn't going to happen to her. She had to hold it together.

Eyes crawled from the phone to the coin.

He had been in here, inside her private hotel room and left that coin on her pillow as a warning that he was coming for her. She just knew it. This was beyond a prank. The coin in the box sent to her house during the Witch-Hunt murders could be talked away, just, but not this. This was on another level. Two coins were no coincidence. Two perfect, ancient gold foil Greek coins stamped with a honeybee.

*I do this because I love you, honeybee.*

She needed help, and she realised she was thinking about Jacob. Not Theo Miles or Kit Bailey who were both downstairs, but the detective chief inspector who was seventy miles away. A ninety minute drive.

And right now, even the phone seemed too far away.

Another noise.

*Deal with this, Soph.*

She held her towel to her naked body and made her way slowly across the room, her bare feet pushing down silently in the soft hotel carpet.

Another noise, and she realised they were happening in frequent time intervals.

Approaching the other end of the room, she glanced over her shoulder at the coin in the pillow and then smacked the bathroom light on and slammed open the door.

Nothing.

When she walked inside and saw a faulty extraction fan making the noise, she could breathe again. Leaning up against the wall, she blew out a deep breath and closed her eyes. The noise had been nothing, but that only meant Alistair Keeley wasn't in her room now. Thinking back to the coin, she shuddered at the thought he *had* been in here.

And yet he had gone. If he meant her harm tonight, he would have done it here and now. She slowed her breathing and started to think straight again. She knew he was long gone. This was a mind game, and he wasn't going to win it. Should she call Jacob? No, it was too late and he would be asleep. She would do it in the morning. Feeling stronger now, she walked back into the main room and picked up the phone.

"Good evening, reception," a cheery voice said.

"Someone's been in my room," she said, a sense of rage now killing off her fear. "I want to change room right now."

*

Declan Taylor worked quickly but carefully. This was certainly the place he'd been looking for. Some called it the Cathedral and now he could see why. Staring up at its colossal size he felt dwarfed by its monumental scale and his mind buzzed with the possibilities such a location could offer. There could be nowhere better than here in which to play out the endgame he'd spent so long planning. Here, in this cold, isolated darkness, Anna Mazurek would finally understand the meaning of the word revenge.

When he laughed, his voice boomed and echoed eerily, bouncing from the frozen stone walls and receding into the surrounding darkness. In here, he could almost be a god, but then his hubris was tempered by a sharp, smacking sound somewhere behind him. He spun around, sweeping his torch over the vast, looming space in front of him but saw nothing.

*Get a hold of yourself, Dex.*

He slowed his breathing and felt his heart calm.

*Probably just some loose stones.*

With a devilish smile on his face, he made his way back to the Cathedral's entrance and considered his plan from every angle. It was flawless, wasn't it? He'd had a long time to hone it, carefully working out every last detail until there could be no possibility of error. He felt no guilt. She deserved everything that was coming to her. He'd loved her with his whole heart but she'd never loved him back. A loyal and honest love, unreciprocated. She never even changed her name when they got married. That had burned him, but he never spoke of it. She wasn't the kind to change her mind.

She owed him and now he would settle the account no matter what it took.

Here, in this dreadful place, his ex-wife would pay for what she had done to him, and pay hard.

# CHAPTER 29

*Thursday, 14ᵗʰ March*

As Jacob crossed the car park, his mind was buzzing with the news of a potential ID on the Saint and a substantial link between the victims. Evidence of a possible blackmail operation found on the Saint's boat had also stirred his mind. It looked like it might be the breakthrough they were all waiting for. If the Saint really was Carl Buckland, it wasn't crazy to speculate that the murders were centred on the murder trial at which he had given evidence against Nathan Brett, the defendant.

As he approached the main HQ building, he felt his phone buzzing in his suit pocket. Opening the heavy entrance door, he grabbed it and answered. "Sophie, hi. How's the course?"

The pause was one beat too long.

"Soph? What's the matter?"

"Oh God, I should have told you last night, I know."

"Told me what?" he asked.

"When I got back to my room last night in the conference centre, I found another coin."

Jacob's eyes narrowed as he tried to take in what she had just said. The words had hit him like an ice pick plunging into his chest and for a moment, he was almost unable to speak. "Wait, are you talking about the same sort of coin that was sent to you on New Year's Day?"

"Yes, exactly the same."

She sounded nervous and scared but this time there was little he could say to calm her. When she had received the first coin he was able to settle her down and reassure her it was the work of a crank, but he was too plugged into the real world to believe any crank would go this far. Stalking her all the way to a conference in Devon and breaking into a hotel room invited far too many risks for the casual crank. No, this had to be the work of Keeley.

The Ferryman.

"You think it's him, don't you?" she asked.

"I'm starting to, yes, but I know it's impossible."

"Is he still in prison?" Her voice was desperate.

"Yes, he's still inside," he said in a calm, measured tone.

"How do you know?"

"After the first coin was sent to you on New Year's Day I asked the Governor to inform me, officially, if Keeley is ever released and I've had no contact from him. I can assure you that Dr Alistair Keeley is safely locked up in solitary confinement where he has been since he arrived there straight after the trial."

"Then I don't understand. What's going on?"

"He must be working with someone else," he said. "It's the only way to explain what's happening. It's the only way he can be doing this."

"You mean he's orchestrating it all like some morbid play, all from the distance of his prison cell?"

"I know it sounds mad, but it's possible. I thought he worked alone, but clearly not."

"But who would be prepared to help a man like him?" she asked, incredulous. "He's one of the most dangerous and violent men in the country."

Jacob let a long sigh. "You'd be surprised."

"But what if this individual is as dangerous as Keeley?" she asked desperately. "What if he's prepared to kill to please him, or show him how dangerous he can be? Oh my *god*…" her voice trailed away.

"Just take it easy."

"He could be trying to impress him, some kind of copycat killer," she said hurriedly.

"Calm down, Soph. Are you still in the conference centre?"

"Yes."

"I want you to get out of there."

"I'm driving back to Wiltshire now."

"No, it's too dangerous. Whoever left the coin is obviously watching you. They might be waiting precisely for you to panic and take flight, to come back home. Is there someone there you trust?"

"Sure, Theo and Kit."

"Then ask one of them if you can stay at his place for a few days. I'm in the thick of it right now in this murder enquiry, right up to my neck. I can't help you if you come back here."

"I'll stay with Theo," she said reluctantly, thinking back to his charm offensive in the bar.

"Is there a problem?"

"No, I can handle Theo."

"Good. As soon as the case is over, I'll drive down and get you. In the meantime, call the local police and tell them who you are and what's happened. Get them to start an investigation into the break-in. They'll look for prints and go through hotel CCTV."

"What then?"

He sighed. "I'll liaise with Devon and Cornwall police and see if they can come up with any evidence to ID the man who put the coin in the room. I'm sorry, Soph."

"It was my career choice," she said evenly, more composed now she had talked to him. "Just leave it with me."

"Great. I'll see you in a few days. I could do with a seaside break."

She gave a weak laugh. "I can't wait."

"Tell me about it."

"Sounds like you've had a tough few days. Making any progress with the Angel of Death?"

"Maybe," he said. "We've got a briefing on developments right now. Wish me luck."

"In that case, good luck."

*

The briefing room in the heart of the headquarters building slowly filled with everyone who was on Operation Avebury. Approaching the middle of March and the weather had started to clear and warm up, allowing Jacob to crack open one of the windows close to where he was standing down in front of the enormous white board. Now, a gentle breeze of fresh air blew into the room as he rolled up his shirt sleeves and picked up a black marker pen.

"All right everyone, settle down please."

The chit-chat died down to a murmur and then eventually total hush filled the room. His head was still buzzing with Sophie's terrible revelation about the violation of her hotel room, but he had to focus on the case at hand. Charlotte Ingram was still missing and Sophie was, at least, safe right now.

"Thanks to everyone for being here bang on time this morning. As you'll all be aware, we were up against a wall on this one and starting to run out of ideas. The current situation is that we have three murders and a missing person – Charlotte Ingram. The official, public line is that there is no reason to connect her disappearance to the three deaths, but my instinct tells me that she was snatched by the man we are calling the Angel of Death. She may be still alive, and we have to presume she is, but time is running out."

"Bloody hell," someone said. "Four murders in a fortnight?"

Jacob ignored it. "Unfortunately, we have basically ruled out pretty everyone on our list of suspects, which had put us very much back at square one, and with a woman still missing this is not a strong place to be on the investigation. If she *is* still alive, then it can't be long until he kills her and *that* means we need to redouble our efforts to locate her and we're running out of time. However, it's not all doom and gloom because last night Bill Morgan, Matt Holloway and Laura Innes made a big step forward. Bill?"

Morgan got up and walked to the front.

"Thanks, boss. As some of you will know, yesterday we discovered intel pointing to an ID for the Saint – one Carl Buckland from Swindon. We uncovered this thanks to the discovery of his potential ownership of a boat moored on the River Avon. After walking up and down a lot of muddy towpaths this turned out to be true – a modest cabin cruiser called the *Catherine* was moored up on the north bank between Salisbury and Harnham."

A uniformed arm went up at the back. "I thought he was homeless?"

"Hence our interest in it, Norton." Morgan said. "As part of our search of the vessel, we found a passport belonging to an IC1 male of approximately the same age as the Saint. This is where we got our potential ID from. Last night I emailed Mia Francis and asked her to do some digging into dental records. She emailed me back around an hour ago to say that she had secured Mr Buckland's dental records and after sending them to Dr Richard Lyon up in Swindon we have been able to confirm a match. The Saint's real name is officially and formally Carl Buckland."

An excited murmur rippled around the room.

"Find anything else there?" Anna asked.

"That's where it gets interesting. First, we found five thousand pounds in fifty pound notes stuffed inside an old biscuit tin under what passed for a bed."

"Five grand?"

Morgan nodded.

"What the hell was he sleeping rough for if he had five grand in a sodding biscuit tin?" Anna said.

"He was saving it," Jacob said. "Saving it for a bigger purchase."

"That's what I thought when I saw it," Morgan said. "Some homeless people I spoke to told me the Saint intended to buy a place in France. It seemed like a joke to them, but now it's not so funny. And there's more. We also found a bag stuffed full of old newspaper articles, each one on Canon Guy Greenwood from Salisbury Cathedral. Some of the pictures in the articles had been drawn on, mostly on a theme of turning His Reverend Guy Greenwood into a devil."

"So Buckland clearly had some kind of problem with this man," Jacob said.

"For sure, but that's not the whole story. It took a long time to search with only his name and date of birth, but we also found out that Carl Buckland was one of several witnesses in a murder trial back in 1997."

A silence fell over the room.

"Don't tell me," Anna said. "Drowned?"

"You've got it in one," Morgan said. "Vic's name was Julia Crawshaw, and according to articles written at the time she was a big fan of wild swimming. Her boyfriend was seen murdering her by several witnesses."

Jacob's eyes fixed on his old friend. "Sarah and the other women were also witnesses in the trial?"

"You're one step ahead of me, boss. Before they were married, Sarah Bennett was Sarah Taylor, and Hannah Wilson was Hannah Smith. Charlotte Ingram's maiden name was Charlotte Johnson. All of these women testified alongside Carl Buckland that they had seen Nathan Brett kill Julia Crawshaw and dump her body in the mill pond. Brett was charged and convicted of her murder and sentenced to twenty-two years."

"And now Brett's out and looking for revenge," Anna said. "Bloody hell."

"Exactly," Morgan said. "He was released just before Christmas and there's been no sign of him since."

"Parole officer?"

"A woman in Bath who has totally dropped off the radar. Could be another of his victims."

Jacob ran a hand over his forehead. "If he's going around killing people for putting him inside, we need to know who else was involved in the trial."

"I'm going through the court transcripts and trial records now," Holloway said. "They're pretty heavy going but once I have a list of names of people Brett would have a grudge against, I'll start to track them down so we can warn them. We're just waiting for the prison files on Brett as we speak"

A dark silence descended over the briefing room.

Jacob's low, measured tones broke the hush. "All right, looks like we're getting some more pieces to the puzzle and we might finally have a prime suspect. Any more ideas?"

"The money in the boat has to be blackmail cash," Holloway said. "And my money's on the Canon being the victim."

"But why?" Anna asked. "Why would Carl Buckland, a witness for the prosecution be blackmailing the Canon Chancellor of Salisbury Cathedral?"

"You think he had something to do with the case?" asked Holloway.

"Could be anything," Morgan said. "Buckland might have seen him doing something naughty that has nothing at all to do with the case."

Jacob nodded. "All right, we need some picture ID of Brett right away. He's obviously using a fake name and the only way to get to him is if we find out what he looks like. Are you searching the police database for his mugshot?"

Morgan turned to his boss, enjoying his moment of glory. "Indeed we are, sir. Young Innes is on it right now – waiting for a message from the records department. Any word, Laura?"

She was already looking at her phone. "Just came through now, sir." A smile appeared on her face as she excitedly waved her phone in the air. "We've got him."

Jacob and Morgan exchanged a glance. "You've got a positive ID on Brett?"

"Yes, sir," she said, handing Jacob the phone. "And it turns out we've already talked to him."

Jacob raised his eyebrows as his heart quickened in his chest. "I'm officially interested but I've never seen this man before in my life. Who is he, Bill?"

Morgan looked at the phone. "Bloody hell, this is Preston Rossiter, the cab driver. Preston Bloody Rossiter is Nathan Brett, the Angel of Death."

The room burst to life as everyone started talking to each other.

"Right," Jacob said. "Not a word to the press and I want that man in custody within the hour. If she's still alive, we might just be able to save Charlotte Ingram after all."

*

When Charlotte woke, she knew she'd spent another night in the van. Was he trying to starve her to death in here? Maybe that was his plan. Perhaps this maniac wasn't going to drown her like he drowned all his other victims, after all. She heard a door slamming somewhere outside, and then the rear doors of the van opened up. The light was dim but still made her squint after so long in the dark, and then she saw his silhouette.

He dumped a bag into the back of the van and slammed it shut again. She noticed the corner of the bag had fallen into the door jamb and stopped it closing completely. She hesitated, waiting until his footsteps had receded away and she heard the other door close again. She felt her heart beating in her chest. Was it just another trap? Was he waiting for her, playing mind games with her?

She saw her chance and wasted no time in gently pushing the rear door wide open with her shoes. Crunching her stomach muscles, she was able to hoist herself up until her head was at the right angle to look down beyond her feet and through the open door.

She squinted in the semi-darkness. Creamy dust motes drifted on broken shafts of light, streaming in from a boarded-up window above a steel workbench. The smell of creosote and tarred twine wafted up to her nostrils and made her feel slightly nauseous again.

It was a garage, then, just as she had speculated. The real question was where, but that didn't matter right now. All that mattered now was getting the hell out of this place and finding the nearest safe place to call the police. This crazy son of a bitch had to be taken into custody as fast as possible, even though she knew it would mean big problems for her and the others.

She squirmed back and forth, shifting from side to side until she had wriggled down the length of the van and her legs were hanging over the back door.

A noise.

She held her breath and shut her eyes, desperately praying he hadn't returned already. When she heard the noise a second time she realised it was the sound of someone slamming a car door somewhere outside the garage. Maybe someone who could help her, she thought.

Or maybe him, or one of his friends.

Continuing to shimmy over the edge of the van, she eventually reached the rubber seal running around the open door and tumbled out onto a cold, concrete floor. She landed with a heavy smack on her backside and nearly cracked the back of her skull on the rear bumper, but at least she was out.

She glanced around in a bid to see anything that might identify her location, but it was a normal garage like any one of dozens she had seen through her life. Rolling onto her front, her face scraped against the concrete floor as she brought her knees up under her stomach and then finally hauled her body up until she was kneeling on the floor. With one last push of effort she was able to heave herself to her feet.

"Going somewhere?"

She turned and saw the man. He was nothing more than a silhouette in the hallway, the bright kitchen light shining behind him. In his hand, he was holding what looked like a long boning knife.

Gagged, she was unable to respond, even if it just meant begging.

"Thing is, we haven't even started yet."

He laughed, and stepped towards her. Raising the knife in the air, he made a big act of slashing it in front of her face and making her scream into the gag and pull her head back from the cold steel. Then he stepped forward and grabbed hold of her hair.

"No knives for you, Lotty," he said calmly. "You have to drown, just like all the others, only I had a lot of business to attend to. But don't worry. I just need to stop off at my other place and grab something and then we're good to go."

She sobbed with fear and humiliation as he easily hoisted her over his shoulder and threw her into the back of the van. He leaned in and gave her a hefty slap across the face. "Try it again and it all ends in here."

Then he slammed the door, this time making sure it was properly locked and secured.

She had failed, and there was nothing more she could do to save herself.

Her only chance was if the police found her before he completed his promise and killed her. She heard the van's diesel engine firing up. She had been using the rear wheel-arch cover as a makeshift pillow but now vibrations from the engine's revs rattled and drilled into her ear and she was forced to wriggle further into the centre.

She felt motion, and then rolled back as the vehicle surged forwards. Light streamed in from the windscreen up in the cab and the radio suddenly burst to life. A tinny noise filled the inside of the van, and then the man cursed and twiddled the dial. She heard him ranging through various stations until the sounds of Verdi filled the van's interior.

*It'll all be over soon enough.*

She remembered his words with a shudder. He had delivered them in as creepy and menacing a tone as he could muster, but the truly frightening thing was that she knew he meant it. This was no show, no performance he was putting on to upset and punish her. This was the real deal, and the punishment would be brutal and final.

# CHAPTER 30

With clouds gathering over the Downs, Jacob cruised the 1962 Alvis south to Salisbury. Sophie and the obol were still in his thoughts, but this Theo Miles character had stepped in and helped her. For now, he could put his worries aside.

He changed up and raced along the main road, desperate to reach Rossiter before he had a chance to kill Charlotte Ingram. But then, perhaps it was already too late. Then his mind drifted back to Theo Miles. How much did she know about this man? She had told him that he was a trusted colleague, but hadn't she also said that he had interviewed Keeley on several occasions before and after the trial? He knew him, he had studied his mind. Maybe he had grown a little too close to his subject.

And he was in the conference centre when the coin was left on her pillow.

*Get a grip, Tom*, he muttered. *You're being paranoid.*

He pushed it from his mind and settled back into the old leather seat. Secretly enjoying the deep, classic roar of the vintage engine, he changed down and took a shallow bend. He knew he really should buy himself a newer car, but the truth was he'd grown used to the old thing, rusty coachwork and all. He enjoyed the act of restoring it to its former glory, and saw it running parallel to his own recovery following the fire.

He had the funds to go out and buy a new Jaguar or Mercedes any time he wanted, but this was about more than that. This wasn't about picking something shiny and writing a cheque to flatter his own ego. This was about character and hard work and building something new for himself. He knew himself well enough to know that he couldn't move on until the job was done. The car would be restored, and so would he. He increased speed again, happily breaking the limit by a long way and checking his mirror to make sure Mia Francis and the CSI team were still keeping up with him.

They were, and beside him, Anna Mazurek was scrolling through her messages but finding nothing new. She slipped the phone in her pocket and sighed.

"Problems?" he asked.

"Yes and no. Rossiter's involved, there's no doubt in my mind about that. But when Bill and Laura met him, they didn't get the impression he was the type who could kill in such a violent way – or kill at all, for that matter."

"We know he's Brett, Anna. We have his mugshot on file and we know he studied computer science and theology in prison, hence the crucifixes. We have a professional duty to pick him up and interview him. See what we can get out of him." He turned and glanced at her quickly, before returning his gaze to the road. "What's on your mind?"

She took a deep breath and sighed. "I'm still not convinced, but it's just a hunch."

"Never disregard instinct." Jacob slowed and indicated to take a turn. "If it's true that we only use ten percent of our minds, you have to wonder what the other ninety percent is doing."

"Or the other ninety-nine percent in Kent's case."

He laughed. "You might think that, but I couldn't possibly comment."

"But what if I'm right and it's not Rossiter?"

"How so?"

"I mean, we know Rossiter is really Nathan Brett, but who says it's Brett going around killing everyone? Just because Brett is out doesn't mean he's the Angel of Death. What then?"

"Then we're back out on the streets asking questions," he said. "Because that means the killer is still out there somewhere and he's already taken three lives – and don't forget about Charlotte Ingram and the missing parole officer."

She sighed again and shook her head. "There are some serious crazies in the world."

"And the only thing between them and the public is us."

Turning to him as he changed up into fourth after another bend, she said, "Why style himself as the Angel of Death though?"

"That's what Rossiter can tell us."

"Maybe."

"I'm wrong all the time," Jacob said with an honest smile. "I'm no superman, Anna. They only exist on the pages of romance novels. I'm just human, and this time maybe *you're* right. And if you are then great – if this doesn't teach you to listen to your heart then I don't know what will. But in the meantime we follow procedure and pick up Rossiter."

"Nathan Brett."

"Yeah, him."

Jacob pulled up outside Rossiter's house and killed the engine just as Mia pulled up behind them. Looking at the house, he saw several downstairs lights were on, lighting the dull day, and they could see someone moving around inside. "All right, looks like it's showtime."

They walked up the path and rang the bell. Minutes later, Rossiter came to the door, sore eyes blinking in the light of the hallway. "Yes?"

"I'm DCI Jacob and this is DS Mazurek."

"Not you lot again." He said with a sigh. "As I already told your colleagues, I'll sue if you keep harassing me like this. First you bother me at my place of work and now here at my home."

"Preston Rossiter, I am arresting you on suspicion of murder. You do not have to say anything but it may harm your defence if you do not mention when questioned something you later rely on in court," Anna stepped forward and pulled some cuffs from her belt as Jacob continued telling him his arrest caution. "Anything you do say may be given in evidence."

"This is insane!"

"Take it easy, sir."

"I'll personally name you in the lawsuit for this, Jacob. This is defamation of character! My neighbours are watching this."

Mia Francis and her team were in their forensic suits now and marching up the path.

"You better have a…"

Jacob waved the search warrant in his face. "Signed by a magistrate just for you, sir."

Rossiter stared at them with cold eyes as Jacob turned to Mia Francis and her team who were standing behind him and spoke in a low, professional tone. "All right, search the whole place."

Rossiter bristled as Anna pulled him away from the front door. "You'll not find what you're looking for in here."

"Just let them get on with their job," Jacob said, and pulled him away to the Alvis. "We're going for a ride down to the station. Be good and I won't throw obstruction in, as well."

They moved Rossiter down the path and Jacob helped him down inside the old car. Slamming the door on him, he turned to Anna. "Let him sit in there for a few minutes to soften him up and pray Mia finds Charlotte alive and well."

"If she's in the house, sir."

After a quarter of an hour, Mia stepped out of the front door and walked towards them.

"Any luck?" Jacob asked.

"No sign of Ingram or a body in any of the rooms, sorry, but we did find this. She sighed and held up a clear evidence bag. "A well-thumbed Bible, some duct tape and a pair of leather gloves. All found upstairs behind the hot water tank."

"Not a very original place to hide something," Anna said.

Rossiter visibly slumped in the back seat.

"Mr Rossiter?"

"I don't know what to say, except I've never seen them before."

Jacob peered into the bag and then handed it back to Mia. "I want the full range of tests on these."

Mia took the bag. "Already ordered it."

"I knew it in my heart, Mia," Jacob said with a crooked smile.

"And keep looking for Charlotte Ingram."

When he turned to Rossiter, the smile faded into a grim frown. "You're coming with us."

*

Jacob pulled up a chair beside Anna and sat down. They were sitting in Bourne Hill Police Station in Salisbury city centre and facing them was the bleak, ashen face of Preston Rossiter and his solicitor Sheridan Murray. They had spent hours waiting for him to arrive from London and the day was getting on. Now, the well-dressed brief laced long, pale fingers together and sighed as he offered the two detectives a neutral stare. Then, he spoke one word.

"Well?"

Jacob ignored the question and studied Rossiter. He looked scared, and this bothered him. A man who could brutally murder people and leave calling cards behind to taunt the police wouldn't be scared in a police interview room. He'd interviewed them before, countless times. They were calm, cocky. Arrogant and rude.

"Your client has been arrested for murder, Mr Murray," Anna said. "An official CSI search of his home produced several rolls of duct tape and some gloves."

"And was there any duct tape used in the commission of the Angel of Death's murders?"

Anna opened her mouth to speak. "Well…"

"No," he said flatly. "I've followed the news and read your reports. My client is not guilty of these crimes. He has protested to me his total innocence in the matter of these terrible killings and has concerns that the evidence found in his property may have been planted there either by the police or the real killer."

Jacob relaxed in his chair. "Except your client isn't who he says he is."

Murray shot a suspicious glance at Rossiter. "What are they talking about? This is nonsense."

"No, it's not," Rossiter said, crushed by the weight of all the lies. "It's true."

The lawyer stared at him, wide-eyed. "What did you say?"

Jacob said, "Your client has been positively identified as Nathan Brett, a man who has just spent over twenty years in prison for drowning a young woman in 1997. Isn't that true, Mr Brett?"

The blood drained from Rossiter's face and his hands began to tremble. "What?"

"You heard me."

"That's the most insane nonsense I've ever heard in my life!" Rossiter protested. "I'm not Nathan Brett! My real name is Edmund Bell!"

A look of confusion covered Anna's face like a shadow.

Jacob's expression mirrored her. "What did you just say?"

"Edmund Bell," Rossiter said, deflating in his chair. "I was Nathan Brett's defence lawyer at his trial."

"You were his defence lawyer?"

"Yes, and I lost the case. He always said he'd get his revenge on me, and I guess this was it."

"If you're telling the truth, and looking at what he did to everyone else who crossed him," Jacob said darkly, "I'd say you got off lightly."

"I am telling the truth!"

Anna pulled out the prison files. "Then explain this."

Rossiter and Murray stared at the file and saw his face in the mugshot.

"I'm sorry but there's been some sort of mistake," Rossiter said. "Someone must have hacked this or something. I'm not Nathan Brett and those things you found in my house aren't mine. I've never seen them before."

"We have your taxi following Carl Buckland around on the night he died," Jacob said. "Why would that be?"

He sighed, aware of everyone waiting for an answer. "I got suspicious of all the times he asked me to drive him out to the middle of nowhere. I'd noticed that when he came back he always had plenty of cash on him – big notes, fifties, often – and I wanted to find out what was going on. That's why I was following him, and I found the boat with the cash in it but lost my nerve and left it where it was."

"Why should we believe any of this?" Anna said. "Especially the stuff about Nathan Brett?"

"It's true," he said meekly. "Long after the Nathan Brett trial I was disbarred for dishonesty and taking bribes and that's why I changed my name and ended up driving cabs. It was a difficult time in my life. I let a lot of people that I cared about down really hard. I was part of my father's law firm, Bell, Barber & Pagett. My parents had spent a fortune lining up all the ducks to get me a good career. I went to Marlborough School and then Wadham College, Oxford to read law before starting work with my father."

Jacob shook his head. "Coddled from cradle to grave, sadly your dishonest nature changed all that and now you're picking up drunks from the local chippy at throwing-out time."

"Or throwing up time, as we used to call it."

"Very good, Anna," Jacob said. "Very good."

"Have you finished insulting my client?" Murray said. "It's very late and we'd both like to get back to our homes." He picked up his folders and fixed his eyes on Jacob. "If you're looking for the Angel of Death then you've got the wrong man."

As the solicitor's words tumbled from his lips, Jacob felt his world fall away.

\*

As the sun slowly crept toward the western horizon, the man felt deeply that God was on his side. He knew he must be because he had achieved so much in so little time, but there was so much more to do. His revenge wasn't over yet. Simple and pure, only now he was the Angel of Death deciding who lived and who died. Looking down at Charlotte Ingram as he dragged her into the silent cathedral, he felt a wave of power wash over him. "Time to cleanse your soul, sinner."

"Please, no!" she called out. "Why have you brought me here?"

"You know why, Lotty."

Gripping her by the back of her neck, he forced her head under the surface of the famous font. A fiendish smile crawled over his face as he watched her struggling and kicking out. But she was no match for him, and seconds later she fell limp. It was sooner than he had expected, and he considered the possibility that she was trying to fool him so he held her under for another sixty seconds just to make sure.

*Nearly done*, he thought, dragging her dead body out of the font and watching her tumble to the cold stone floor. When he saw the shape of her face in the blue light, his head told him what had happened but his heart refused to believe it. Was God's work nearly done? Moving away, his cautious footfall was amplified by the immense size of the cathedral all around him. Seeing another man approaching along the dark nave, he stepped back into the shadows.

The man reached the dead woman and fell to his knees beside her. He started to sob with the dead woman's hand in his own, he didn't notice the shadows moving behind him until the last moment.

Turning, he gasped and saw the face of his tormentor. "My God!" he called out. "You would take a life in this most holy of places? This is wickedness beyond description."

"As wicked as what you did to me, all those years ago?"

# CHAPTER 31

Jacob frowned and turned to Anna. "All right, get me the governor of Woodhill Prison in a hurry."

"But we've already got his mugshot from the police database, sir," Anna said.

"No, we haven't," Jacob said bluntly. "Don't you see what he's done? We know Nathan Brett has sodding degrees in theology and IT, including hacking. I want to talk to a real human being and I want to see the original paper files on the prisoner. He's out there somewhere and we still have a missing woman. Talking with the governor is the best way to expedite the process."

"But none of this has anything to do with my client," Murray said.

"We don't know that," said Anna.

Jacob sighed. "No, we don't."

"I've told you the whole truth," Rossiter said. "What more do you want?"

"I want to know more about Nathan Brett."

"I can tell you no more than what's in his file on the police database."

Jacob clenched his jaw. "We've already established that the file has been compromised, including the insertion of your image over his, presumably to punish you for your part in the trial."

"Presumably," Rossiter said.

Murray sniffed and leaned back in his seat. "Where is this going, Chief Inspector? We are not here to assist you in your enquiry."

Jacob ignored him and kept his eyes fixed on Rossiter. "Could you describe him?"

"Not really."

"Helpful."

His lawyer frowned. "It was over twenty years ago, Chief Inspector!"

Rossiter scrunched his eyes shut as he tried to recall the man. "He was average height and size, with brown hair and a narrow, lean face."

"Could be anyone," Anna said.

"Could you ID him from a picture?"

"Maybe."

Holloway knocked and entered the room. "That was Mia Francis, sir. The items found in Mr Rossiter's house are clean of prints which suggests they were deliberately hidden there to implicate him."

"As we said," Murray said smugly.

"Bloody hell," Anna said. "This is some rabbit hole."

Murray sighed. "And what about my client?"

"Until I can rule him out formally, he's staying right here at the station," Jacob said. "He could be implicated in any number of ways so one way or the other, he's spending the night in the cells."

As they got up from their chairs to leave and stepped out into the corridor, Innes called out as she approached them. "That was the Dean at the cathedral, sir. He says he's overheard raised voices in the cathedral. He's concerned because the Canon was meeting Simon Marshall from the Samaritans there this evening, and he thinks something terrible has happened."

Jacob felt his heart quicken. "All right, thanks Laura."

Still flanked on either side by uniformed constables, Rossiter stopped walking and turned. "Did you say Simon Marshall?"

Jacob turned his eyes to the prisoner. "Yes, why?"

"That was the name of one of the prosecutors in Julia Crawshaw's murder trial."

Jacob and Anna shared an anxious glance.

"Are you sure about that?" Jacob asked. "I haven't come across his name in the court files yet."

"He wasn't on the original team," Rossiter said. "They brought him in at the end to turn the heat up because he had such a brutal reputation. You'll definitely find references to him if you keep searching,"

"And you're totally sure about this?" Anna asked.

He nodded. "Yes, and he didn't pull any punches either. Thanks to austerity there's usually just a single counsel today but back in those days there was more than one prosecutor in a Crown Court trial and he was absolutely ruthless during his questioning. In my opinion he was the main contributing factor to the jury finding him guilty of murder."

"That's right," Jacob said. "I remember now. On the night of the arson attack at his converted barn, he told me he used to be a barrister in a previous life."

"Brett vowed revenge against him in a big way," Rossiter said.

"Sir," Holloway said turning the corner. "The Dean's just called a second time. He reported raised voices and men fighting inside the cathedral!"

"Bloody hell," Jacob said. "We need to get over there right now. Marshall's in danger! He's the final victim, Anna! It was the Canon all along! He wasn't working in African churches for the last twenty years at all. It was a cover story. He was in prison serving time for Julia Crawshaw's murder."

"So we won't be needing the Governor of Woodhill, then?" Anna said.

"I don't think so – looks like we just got a break." Jacob turned to the custody sergeant. "How far are we from the cathedral, Mike?"

"Fifteen minute walk or five minute drive."

"Thanks." Jacob grabbed his car keys. "Get some uniforms together and send them up to the cathedral as fast as you can."

\*

Jacob and Anna raced across town in the Alvis. Ahead of them, like a beacon, the cathedral's mighty spire rose above the city, its arc-light illumination cutting a bright line in the drizzly twilight. As he stamped on the throttle, visions of a dead Charlotte Ingram rose in his mind like ghosts.

"I hope we're not too late, Anna."

"Boss?"

"For Charlotte."

She lowered her voice. "Don't get your hopes up, boss."

"I know, I know…"

He changed down into second and the engine roared in response. Taking a corner at speed, the tyres squealed on the wet tarmac as he spun the wheel around and speeded up for the straight.

"You think Rossiter is telling the truth, boss?"

"Probably. Another one of my screw ups. Looks like you were right after all."

"Maybe," she said quietly. "One way or another, looks like Rossiter's walking. And that Murray's a proper bastard, isn't he?"

"Just doing his job."

"I can't believe the Law Society let people like that stay on the rolls."

Jacob squinted at the rainy street, listening carefully to her words. "What did you say?"

"I said how is it a bastard like Murray can stay on the rolls – why?"

Swerving to a halt a few moments later in Choristers Square he shrugged. "Nothing." Emerging from the car into a dark, rainy evening, the floodlit spire of the cathedral stretched up into the sky above them. They ran along the path towards the Dean. He was standing out of the rain under the voussoir stones above the east entrance, wringing his hands.

"Thank goodness you're here! They're fighting! I don't know what's happening."

Jacob held him by his shoulders and manoeuvred him out of the way. "You need to move away from the cathedral, sir."

"Yes, quite."

"Where are they?"

The Dean pointed around to the south. "That way."

"Thanks," Anna said.

Beside her, Jacob stared up into the drizzle at the awe-inspiring spire stretching up to an unseen heaven.

Murray.

Stay on the rolls.

Law Society.

He felt a shock of realisation hit him like a knife in the chest. Turning to his sergeant with wide eyes, he said, "How can I have been such a fool, Anna?"

"Boss?"

"We need to get in there, right now!"

Jacob and Anna burst inside. Well after visiting hours, the vast cathedral was as quiet as the grave. They walked around the colossal medieval structure, passing the Chapter House and walking along the cloister garth and past the plumber before entering the building by the south transept.

Jacob's heels clipped on the flagstones as he paced down the aisle. As they reached the nave, Anna scanned the cavernous space and took a step forward, but Jacob grabbed her arm and stopped her. "Wait."

"What is it?" she asked, turning.

"Look."

He jutted his chin down at the old flagstone tiled floor. "Water."

She saw now what he had seen – a trail of water running in a long, thin streak all the way along the length of the nave. Here and there among the messy line of water were the unmistakable shapes of footprints.

"Looks like someone's been dragging something," Jacob said. "A body, maybe."

"And it's coming from the font." Her words were uttered quietly, but they echoed in the vast space, nonetheless.

They followed the trail from the impressive, green patinated bronze font all the way up the nave to the sanctuary at the east end of the cathedral.

"And it's going up there," Jacob said. "To the High Altar."

Making their way into the beautiful chapel, they saw the back of a woman's head. She was sitting on one of the hundreds of wooden chairs at the front, silent and still, right at the end of the water trail in a chilling parody of worship.

"Hello?" Anna said respectfully.

No response.

Anna turned to Jacob and he saw they were thinking the same thing.

Dead.

Deeper in the Trinity Chapel now, and a deep, radiant Egyptian blue lit the entire scene as the weak March sunset light outside illuminated the famous east window, an elaborate stained-glass masterpiece.

Jacob raised his hands to his head and turned his face to heaven. As he stared up into the intricate chapel vault he felt his failure to save her life gnaw at his soul. He lowered his head, his chin touching his chest as he muttered a silent curse. "I failed her."

Seeing the dead woman's terrified, sightless eyes staring up into the blue light made Anna shiver with disgust and fear. "Who the hell would do something like this?"

"We know who," Jacob said. "And he's in here somewhere."

He turned away from the dead body and raised his voice until it boomed in the solemn, empty space all around them. "We know you're in here! You can't get away! We have the entire cathedral surrounded with police officers."

A noise.

They turned and ran back into the main part of the cathedral, passing through the retrochoir. A man screamed, and something metal crashed onto the stone floor.

"That way!"

Jacob and Anna burst into the sanctuary. Guy Greenwood was standing with his feet wide apart and a six inch boning knife in his hand. Moonlight filtered by the stained glass above his head coloured his face a blood red. Beside him, Marshall was pushed up against the wall of the tower, his chest rising and falling rapidly with hurried, panicked breaths.

Jacob took a step forward, palms out to indicate no harm. "Drop the knife, Greenwood!"

"But I…"

Marshall's terrified eyes swivelled between the Canon and Jacob.

"Now!" Jacob repeated.

The blade clattered to the tiled floor.

"Now kick it over here."

The wind howled outside as Greenwood obeyed the detective.

Anna moved a step closer. "Guy Greenwood, I'm arresting you on suspicion of murder…"

Jacob raised a hand to stop her. "He's not the killer," he said coolly. Turning away from the Canon, he fixed his eyes on the cowering figure of Simon Marshall as he clung to the wall in fear. "Is he, Nathan?"

# CHAPTER 32

Anna Mazurek stared back at her boss with confusion etched deep on her face. "Boss?"

"Guy Greenwood isn't Nathan Brett." Jacob spoke to Anna, but never once took his eyes away from the good Samaritan. "Marshall is. He's the killer. Simon Marshall is Nathan Brett."

The Canon shared Anna's bewilderment. "You thought I would take a life in the chapel, of all places?"

Jacob searched the Canon's face for any signs of deception but saw only a deep anguish. "And you're no angel, so keep your mouth shut."

Greenwood began to sob uncontrollably. "God, what did I unleash all those years ago?"

Brett saw his chance and seized it, pulling a small switchblade knife from his pocket and sliding behind the Canon in one fluid movement. He raised the knife to his neck and pushed the button on the handle to extend the blade.

"Don't come any closer, Jacob."

Greenwood kicked and grunted in rage, but quickly settled down when Brett pushed the blade of the switchblade knife deeper into the flesh of his throat.

"Keep still!" Brett's yell echoed in the vast cathedral.

Greenwood struggled again, desperately trying to free himself from Brett's iron grip, but Brett tightened his hold on him and sneered with contempt. "I'm tempted to run this blade across your throat right now and let you bleed out like the pig you are."

"Then why don't you?" Greenwood said.

"Because I have something much grander planned for you *Canon*."

Without warning, Brett began dragging Greenwood away from Jacob and Anna and out of the sanctuary. "Come after me and I'll kill him in a heartbeat."

"This is madness, Nathan," Jacob said calmly. "The cathedral is surrounded by police officers and there's nowhere you can go. Let the Canon go and drop the knife."

"He must pay for what he did!"

And then they were gone, fading into the shadows of the rood screen. A second later they heard footsteps scurrying away, receding into some dark corner of the gigantic building and then the sound of a heavy door slamming somewhere in the centre of the nave, just beyond the choir stalls.

Jacob and Anna glanced at one another. "I need you to go outside and make sure every escape route away from this building is blocked," he said. "And then call the fire service and alert them to a possible jumper."

"What about you?" she asked. "You're not going up there after him alone?"

"Just do as I ask, Anna."

She gave it consideration, but relented. "Consider it done, boss."

He watched her run into the darkness of the nave and then sprinted over to the door Brett had used to make his escape with the hostage.

Opening it, his worst fears were confirmed when he saw a stone spiral staircase leading up towards the triforium. Staring upwards, something told him this wasn't Brett's final destination. The tall detective sprinted up the circular stone steps, clinging onto the guiderail to stop himself slipping over as he climbed the medieval tower.

At the top of the staircase, he saw Brett dragging the Canon around a narrow walkway which ran around the inside of the cathedral. Already high above the nave, Greenwood was white and sweat was beading on his forehead as the deranged killer hauled him further away from the safety of the law.

"Stay where you are!" Jacob yelled, but Brett ignored him and dragged his victim into the shadows of another narrow corridor.

Jacob gave chase, running along the narrow corridor with barely enough room to fit his broad shoulders in. Another circular staircase was ahead of him, and hearing Greenwood's mangled screams, he speeded up and broke into a sprint. The corridor changed now, from modern breeze blocks to the old, cream-coloured stone cut by masons hundreds of years ago.

Up ahead of him he heard the sound of another heavy door slamming against stonework. He reached the door and opened it to find a second, narrower staircase. A small sign on the wall advised tourists they were en route to the famous spire. Jacob continued after them, reaching the top to find a third door, partly open and blowing in the wind.

Bursting out of the old wooden door, he found himself on a narrow balcony at the top of the tower and the base of the famous spire. A metal bar had been fitted in front of the original carved stone balustrade to add another degree of protection from the deadly fall, but he still felt uneasy as the wind blew a sheet of rain in his face. Looking down at least two hundred feet, he felt a wave of nausea wash over him.

At the end of the balcony, Brett was cornered like an animal in the maelstrom, rain lashing wildly at his face and his hair streaking down over his forehead as he turned his tortured face towards him. When he saw Jacob take a step closer to him, a glimmer of hope flashed in the eyes of the pale-faced Canon.

"Get back!" Brett screamed.

"It's over Nathan" Jacob said. "You can't go anywhere. Like I just said, there are police officers surrounding the cathedral and those sirens you can hear are even more backup."

"And I said get back or I'll kill him right now!"

Jacob took a step back, stalling for time. In the distance, he heard the rain-muffled sound of more emergency vehicle sirens.

\*

Anna burst out of the cathedral to find a world of pouring rain and flashing blue lights. Scanning the chaos she saw DI Kate Atwell from Bourne Hill and at least a dozen uniformed officers. Beside her was the surreal sight of both the Dean and Peter Knightley, the Bishop of Salisbury.

Again, the Dean wrung his hands for a moment, ashen with the terror of what he had just witnessed in a place he had previously considered sacred and safe. Behind them, a Mercedes fire engine equipped with a ladder platform pulled up onto the cathedral grounds and parked beside the police cars.

Anna ran over to Atwell. "Thank God – you already called them, ma'am."

"As soon as we heard this was going down at the cathedral I thought it might be a sensible precaution." She turned to the constables and ordered them to seal off any possible way out of cathedral grounds. "Now then, what's going on in there?"

"Not sure, ma'am – it's bloody mayhem."

"Has Jacob apprehended Greenwood?"

"Greenwood isn't the killer."

Atwell furrowed her brow. "Greenwood isn't Nathan Brett?"

Anna shook her head and tried to slow her breathing. "No, Simon Marshall is Nathan Brett. Simon Marshall is the Angel of Death."

"That's not what I was told by my guvnor," she said. "How the hell did he work that out?"

"I have no idea," Anna said, shrugging. "I'm sure he'll explain everything when this is all over."

"If he makes it, the crazy sod – look!"

Anna followed her pointing arm up to the base of the spire and saw Jacob standing a few feet away from Brett and the Canon over two hundred and twenty feet above the ground. They were protected by a metal rail, but any fall would be brutally fatal.

Atwell sighed and shook her head. "Christ almighty, what's he playing at?"

"He's doing his job, ma'am."

"He's going to get himself killed!" She turned to DC Alex Wilson. "Get up there in a hurry, Wilson. He's going to need some backup!"

Wilson gave the spire an anxious glance. "Yes ma'am."

"He specifically told me to make sure no one else goes up there!" Anna said.

"I'm not happy with that," said Atwell.

"He's the SIO!"

"Not down here, not right now. He's in danger."

"At least let me go, ma'am," Anna said.

"That's not your call, Sergeant."

Before Anna could reply, Mark Roland, the Fire Crew Manager walked over to them. When he spoke his words were as calm and measured as ever. "I've ordered the engine forward with a man ready to go up the ladder and another team are inflating an air cushion in case he jumps."

"Thanks, Mark," Kate Atwell said.

"But there are problems," he said. "First, the ladder only extends to twenty-three metres, second is that we have no way of knowing which side of the spire they're going to fall from, and third, because of the design of the cathedral, anyone falling off that spire hasn't got a direct drop to the air cushion but a lot of very hard roofing to hit on the way down. Still, we're setting it up beneath their current location and that's all we can do."

Anna watched the fire engine drive further forward now, and pull up as close as possible to the ancient building while the second team inflated the enormous air cushion. With the rain getting heavier and the blue lights strobing up against the side of the cathedral, she stared up into the night and prayed Jacob was all right.

*

Jacob took another step closer to the two men. His heart pounded in chest like a drum as he assessed the situation and worked out the best way forward. He knew what Sophie would say – this was all about Brett's psychology. He struggled to remember what she had said about what was motivating the Angel of Death – revenge killings, not spree killings – but when he thought about her his mind flooded with images of the obol she had told him about.

Someone stalking her.

Someone breaking into the hotel room and violating her personal space.

Someone terrifying her.

Cold rain whipped at his face and brought him back with a sharp jolt. He had to shake her from his mind if he was to save the Canon's life and bring Brett into custody for the murders.

"It's over, Nathan."

Brett glanced down at the ground hundreds of feet below. He was still holding the knife to Greenwood's throat. "You get away from me, you hear?"

Jacob raised his palms in a calming gesture. "We don't want any more bloodshed. Enough people have been killed this week already."

Nathan Brett's mouth twisted into a sneer. "No, they haven't. Not nearly enough."

"Let him go!"

"He'll go down fast," he said calmly. "Two seconds at the most. Hitting the ground from this height will mean instant death, so no limbo of comatose paraplegia for you, unlike my beloved Julia."

"Your beloved Julia?" Jacob said.

Sophie was right. This was about revenge.

"I'm innocent, Jacob! I never killed Julia!"

"All right, I'm listening to you."

"These bastards killed her to keep her quiet and then they framed me for the crime."

Greenwood was ashen, clinging to the rails with terror on his face. He shuffled back so his back was to the wall.

In his fevered imagination, he had imagined Brett killing himself, but now he realised with horror that he really was going to dump him off the edge of the tower like a bag of sand.

"Just come away from the edge of the tower, Nathan," Jacob said calmly. "And let him go. It's all over now."

"Get back Jacob!" he said firmly. "Come any closer and he goes over the side."

Jacob came to a sudden stop and raised his palms. "Just take it easy, Nathan. I just want to talk – nothing more."

"Yeah, right."

"It's true. You don't want to see any more bloodshed today any more than I do."

"You don't know what I want."

Jacob lowered his voice. "I know you don't want to kill anymore." He took another slow step toward Nathan. "I know you're pumped up with adrenaline, but just think about what's going on here very carefully."

Nathan squeezed the Canon closer to his body and moved back a step closer to the edge. "I know what's going on here, Chief Inspector. You think you're going to take me in for the murders and you're wrong. I'll put myself over the side and take this bastard over with me, if you don't take a step back."

Jacob swallowed hard and stepped back again. "You don't want to do that."

A deranged, desperate laugh emanated from Nathan's mouth. "But I will if I have to."

Jacob saw he was sweating profusely. It was cold, and they were still out in the driving rain so Jacob knew it was fear – pure, unbridled fear. He'd faced people like this before. Cornered animals who lashed out erratically because they thought they had no other choice.

Jacob decided to rush him. Wiping the rain from his eyes, he took another step toward the two men.

*

Hundreds of feet below and in the warmth and safety of his car, Declan Taylor watched his ex-wife as she stood in a group of police officers huddled under umbrellas outside in the cathedral grounds. He had stalked her on social media during his time in prison, but there was nothing like the real thing. It was dark and there was some drizzle in the air, but he could see her well enough in the neon flash of the emergency lights. It seemed like she hadn't aged at all, and seeing her face brought back strong memories of good times.

And bad times.

Without realising it, his lip had curled up as he stared at her. Now she was pointing up at the enormous tower and other officers were nodding and talking to her. She looked tired but in control. Professional. Slimmer than before. And not at all like she had missed him for one second.

He raised his phone and started to snap pictures of her, zooming in for some close-ups of her face just for good measure. If she wasn't sorry about what had happened, she soon would be.

# CHAPTER 33

"Get back!" Brett said. "I just told you to get back and you're not listening to me! Get away from me or I'll slash his throat right open."

Greenwood's eyes widened like saucers. "For God's sake, do as his says!"

Jacob noticed that Brett's hands were trembling but whether that was fear or the cold he had no idea. Hearing a noise to his right, he turned and saw DI Alex Wilson making the final few steps and finally reaching the door. "Stay where you are!"

The young man's chest heaved up and down with the effort of the climb. "Thank God you're still alive, sir."

"Who's that?" Brett snapped.

"It's just one of my colleagues. He's not coming out here."

"He'd better not, Jacob!"

Jacob shook his head calmly. "It's just me and you now."

"And me," Greenwood said, grimly looking over the side.

Brett pushed the knife in, piercing his skin with the top of the blade. "You keep it shut!"

Jacob raised his hands, palms out. "Just take it easy, Nathan. You don't want any more blood on your hands."

"Like hell I don't!" he snarled. "This bastard ruined my life. He's the worst, Jacob! The very worst!"

"Tell me what he did," Jacob said. "Just calm down and tell me. I'm listening."

"Why don't you tell him?" Brett said, shaking him roughly by the collar. "Eh?"

Greenwood said nothing.

"Then let me," Brett continued, raising his voice above the howling wind as it drove the rain across the balcony. "When the good Canon Greenwood here studied his doctorate in theology at All Souls College in Oxford, he also worked in the exam department. To fund a nasty drug habit, he got in the habit of stealing exam papers from the various colleges and selling them to students desperate to pass their exams with firsts."

"Is this true?" Jacob asked.

Greenwood was silent, eyes closed and mumbling a prayer.

"Sarah, Hannah and Charlotte decided they might like to get first class degrees the easy way and bought some of the stolen papers so they could cheat their way through the exams, only my Julia found out what they'd done. She was a student there, too, at one of the colleges and word got around. She decided to go to the police about it. So his Holiness here, fearing for his reputation and his career, cooked up a little plot to silence Julia with the help of local scumbag Carl Buckland."

Jacob pushed the rain out of his eyes and blinked at him. "Whatever he did, it doesn't give you the right to punish him now!"

"Not legally, maybe." His voice was cold and hard. "But morally I have every right. Can you imagine being framed for a murder you never committed and sent to prison for the best part of your life for it?"

Jacob's breathing slowed. "No," he said quietly. "No I can't."

"I don't have to imagine, Jacob, because thanks to this bastard I know for a fact."

Jacob said nothing, but watched now as a second engine from the fire service pulled off the road and mounted the kerb before driving up on the grass on the other side of the cathedral. Looked like they were trying to cover both sides of the spire, but they had to hurry.

"Buckland killed my Julia and then they all conspired to put me inside, providing false testimony. That was enough for the jury to find me guilty of my own girlfriend's murder!"

"False testimony?"

"They lied in court, Jacob!"

"Perjury?"

Brett nodded, pushed the knife deeper into the other man's flesh. "They colluded and lied to have me sent down for nearly a quarter of a century, just to silence Julia and save themselves."

He was crying now, his red eyes bursting with fear and rage as the rain lashed at his face and wet hair streaked down from his head, sticking to his face in black stripes.

Jacob felt his anguish, and even some rage on his behalf. "The jury found you guilty fair and square, Nathan."

"The jury believed their lies," Brett yelled. "And that bastard Marshall who prosecuted me like I was the devil incarnate!"

"Simon Marshall, the prosecutor?"

"The whole team were bastards, but Marshall was the worst. Persecutor, more like. He did everything he could to lock me up. Good job he died while I was in prison or I'd have killed him, too, and the bastard judge."

"That's why you used his name?"

"Why not? They gave me a sentence of twenty-two years without parole. I should never have been in the courtroom, Jacob!"

"But the law says you killed Julia Crawshaw."

"The law is wrong. I never harmed a human being in my life until I drowned Carl Buckland in the river, and I tell you it felt *good!* It felt right, too – him and the other three. Avenging poor Julia's life in the fairest way."

"So you moved here after prison to get your revenge?"

"No, not at all. Prison broke me. When I got out I wanted to put it all behind me. I changed my name, using the bastard prosecutor's for a laugh, and then devoted myself to helping the homeless, but then one day I saw the man they called the Saint. Only I knew his real name.

I recognised him as Carl Buckland, one of the witnesses who had given false testimony at my trial. He was always too out of his head to recognise me, so I followed him one night on one of his little pilgrimages up here to come and pray."

Jacob felt the pieces of the puzzle slotting into place. "Only he wasn't praying, was he?"

"No, he was blackmailing this bastard for stealing the exam papers and persuading him to kill Julia to save his own skin. See, poor old Carl got into drugs after the murder in a big way and ended up a proper down and out. He wound up here in Salisbury and then one day he saw how high up the greasy pole theology student Guy Greenwood had climbed."

"And he blackmailed me," Greenwood said.

"But if this story is true, he was guilty of murder," Jacob said. "Why not blackmail him back?"

Greenwood laughed. "I tried that. You know what he said? He told me he had nothing to lose and I should go ahead and do it. He said he would rather be in prison with three hot meals a day and a warm bed than sleeping rough. But I, on the other hand, had rather more to lose."

"Then you must have been very relieved when Carl Buckland died," Jacob said.

"Not at all. When he died, his down and out mate Denny Marks found his boat and worked out why he was blackmailing me. Then he started doing the same thing. I'm glad this has happened tonight, Chief Inspector. I'd started to consider killing Mr Marks to stop the blackmail.

Perhaps what little of what is left of my soul has been saved."

"I doubt it." Brett pushed the knife and made Greenwood cry out and mutter a hasty prayer. "And if you're interested, he stole from the cathedral's funds to pay him, as well."

"Where is Denny?" Jacob asked, concerned.

"He took my money and went back down to Devon."

"I'll be checking he's all right with my colleagues, Greenwood."

"As you wish."

"But why all this, Nathan? Why the crucifixes? Why the Angel of Death?"

"It was a message to them. Canon Greenwood's PhD was on the Angel of Death in biblical scripture."

"How did you know that?"

"Over twenty years in prison is a lot of time, Mr Jacob."

"And that's why you left the crosses? To scare them?"

"Partly, but I also wanted to frame this bastard for the crimes. I want to live, Jacob! They stole my life. I wanted to get my revenge on them and then fly away and live whatever life I have left. When I confronted Buckland that night he spilled all the beans and told me everything they had planned to silence Julia and frame me. I'd already decided to get my revenge on them, but it was good to hear it from his lips. I killed him and left the first cross."

"So what was the plan?" Jacob said. "Frame Greenwood as the killer and then make it look like he killed himself by jumping off this tower, all so you'd get away with it?"

Brett smiled, a grotesque devilish smirk. "And live off the wicked old bastard's money as well, not a bad plan, eh? I was going to go to the south of France and buy a nice little place in the hills. Living high on the hog off of this bastard's money and knowing they'd all got the punishment they deserved. Then you came along."

"Any police officer would have done the same, Nathan. You might not have been a killer when they sent you to prison back in ninety-seven, but you sure as hell are now."

Brett shook his head. "When you lose the only person you've loved, the only person you'll ever love... the rest of your life is like walking on a tightrope and you could go over the edge at any time."

"I know, Nathan, but you have to end this now."

"I lost her forever, Jacob." Brett's wild eyes danced all over Jacob, almost imploring him to understand, to say that he got it, and that he forgave him his sins. Instead the policeman said nothing. "I got to the river that day expecting to propose to her and instead I found her body floating in the water. Her legs all tangled up in the reeds. Her blank eyes staring back at me. She wasn't dead. She was in a coma induced by the drowning. She died a few hours later. I threw up, you know. I felt sick and I didn't know what to do. That's when Buckland screamed at me and ran off to call you bastards."

"I'm not responsible for any of that," he said, his voice rising now. "And what happened to you was wrong. Wicked and wrong, Nathan, but so is what you've done this week. You've killed four people and that's murder."

"I haven't killed four people." His voice was strangely serene now. "I've killed five people."

"Your parole officer?"

Brett nodded and twisted Greenwood around, pushing the Canon over towards the balustrade, pivoting on his right leg as he hauled the other man up over the old masonry. "And soon it will be six."

Jacob stalled for time. "Wait! Why frame Rossiter?"

"To buy me time," he said. "And it worked, too."

Jacob searched the man's anguished face for a glimpse of humanity, anything he could reason with but found nothing but hatred and fear. "You don't need to do this, Nathan!"

"Like hell I don't! Did you know this bastard also tried to burn me alive this week in my own home?"

"The barn fire?" Jacob asked.

"The barn fire," Brett said. "The Canon here saw me talking to Denny one night and recognised me. When he read about the crucifixes he put to and two together and tried to kill me before I got to him."

"Is this true?" Jacob asked.

Greenwood sobbed more. "I pray that God can forgive me."

"He might," Brett said. "But I sure as hell won't."

"No!"

Jacob lunged forward and grabbed Greenwood's right arm as he went over the edge. The Canon's body slammed against the intricate stonework with a hefty smack and he howled with terror when he looked down and saw the drop beneath him.

DI Alex Wilson burst out of the door and charged towards Brett who was now climbing up one of the smaller stone pinnacles at the end of the balcony.

"Get down, man!" Wilson yelled.

Brett released one of his hands from the pinnacle and waved it at the young detective. "Stay away from me! I'm warning you! I won't go back to prison!"

Wilson froze on the spot and looked back at Jacob, but he was still struggling to haul Greenwood back over the balustrade.

Wind drove another sheet of rain over the side of the cathedral, lashing Brett as he clung desperately to the stone pinnacle. As Jacob pulled Greenwood back over to safety, he saw a look in Brett's eyes and knew at once it was over.

Brett muttered a silent prayer and a second later, he closed his eyes and gently released his grip on the masonry.

"No!" Jacob yelled, reaching out to grab him, but he was too late.

He fell in perfect silence, and the next thing they heard was the dull thud of his body bouncing on the lead roof and then the terrible gunshot crack as he smacked into the stone paving running around the cathedral.

"Oh, Christ!" Wilson said. He looked down and realised the firemen still hadn't inflated the air cushion to block Brett's fall.

Jacob slammed his fist into the stone balustrade and cursed into the night. "Damn it all to hell!"

"What about me?" Greenwood said.

Jacob took hold of his arm. "You're coming with me. If half of what he said is true, then you're facing some serious charges relating to theft and conspiracy to murder."

"You can't detain me!" he said. "I haven't broken any law. I'm the victim! I've been blackmailed and bullied and nearly thrown off this roof!"

"If I'm not very much mistaken sir," Wilson said, turning to look at the Canon with disgust. "Along with the exam paper theft and conspiracy to murder, Mr Brett alleged the Canon here had stolen cathedral funds to pay Mr Buckland's and Mr Marks's blackmail demands."

Jacob gave the young man a look of admiration. "So he did, Wilson, so he did."

Turning to the bishop, Jacob said, "Guy Greenwood, I am arresting you on suspicion of conspiracy to murder and of theft. You do not have to say anything, but it may harm your defence if you do not mention when questioned something you later rely on in court. Anything you do say may be given in evidence."

"You can't do this to me!" Greenwood squealed.

Jacob swept the rain from his eyes once again and raised his voice as he addressed Wilson. "Take him away."

# CHAPTER 34

Safely on the ground, Jacob watched Wilson guide Greenwood up into the back of the police van. The Canon had calmed considerably since his outburst at the top of the tower and now he slumped down against the seat with a deep frown forming on his lined face.

Jacob closed and locked the cage and then slammed the outer door hard enough to make the vehicle rock on its suspension. Glancing across the enormous grounds he saw Mia Francis and her CSI team setting up a forensics tent around Nathan Brett's smashed body. She had arrived a few moments ago along with the rest of the team from HQ. As she worked in the floodlights, directing her team here and there, he gave a silent thanks that he was surrounded by such a professional team and then turned to Anna.

"That was one sick bastard," Anna said.

Jacob was quiet a long time, then he said, "Did he deserve to die, though?"

"Not like *that*," she said instantly.

"They drove him to this," he said, nudging his chin at the police van carrying Greenwood. "They created a monster, Anna. He was an innocent man dreaming of a life with his girlfriend and then they took everything from him. They murdered her and framed him for the crime to cover up the theft of exam papers and save a few careers."

He paused and blew out a slow breath, shaking his head. "And because of the law – the law we enforce and protect – he spent nearly a quarter of a century behind bars. Think about that."

"It wasn't our fault," she said firmly. "The evidence was solid enough for an arrest and a charge. After that it was in the hands of the court."

"And bastards like Greenwood."

"They'll get theirs, boss."

He shook his head again. "Will they? He's a Canon working for the sodding Bishop of Salisbury for pity's sake. He'll have more connections than a switchboard."

They watched the police van containing Greenwood pull out of the cathedral grounds and join the gentle traffic trundling through the city.

"You want a drink?" she asked.

"I really don't," he said. "I want to go home and forget all about today. Is that okay?"

"Of course it's okay, she said. "I'm no stranger to drinking alone. I have my blues records and there's always Inspector Morgan if I get really desperate."

"Bill's great company," he said, defending his old friend. "His anecdotes are the funniest on earth."

"I know," she said. "I'm only joking."

He looked at her, held her gaze for a few seconds. "He's too old for you, Anna."

Now she looked into his eyes and played dumb. "I have absolutely no idea what you could mean."

"Sure."

"Anyway, I'm with Gaz."

"And how is that going?"

"It's not. Not really." She turned and looked at him, narrowing her eyes. "Wait a minute, guv, how the hell did you know Simon Marshall was really Nathan Brett?"

"On the night of the arson attack, Marshall told me he was a barrister and that he'd left the Law Society a long time ago, I didn't think about it at the time but they're not in the Law Society are they? The professional association for barristers is the General Council of the Bar. The real Simon Marshall, the prosecutor at Brett's trial was a barrister, and no barrister would make that mistake so I knew he'd lied to me. That meant he couldn't have been a prosecutor in the trial. He was using the prosecutor's name as part of his sick revenge fantasy."

"Well, let's just say — wait, I'm getting a call."

She reached into her pocket and looked at her phone. What she saw made her gasp.

"What the hell is it?" Jacob asked.

"Look." She held the phone up and showed him a picture of her standing talking to DI Kate Atwell and Mark Roland a few moments ago. "It's from Declan, my ex."

Jacob instantly turned and scanned the area from where the picture was taken but there was no sign of him. "Wherever he is, he's not there anymore."

"Of course not." She laughed bitterly. "He's not stupid, guv. He'll be long gone by now."

"Is there a message?" he asked.

She bit her lip, gave a solemn nod and handed him the phone. "Scroll down."

When he read it, he felt a wave of protective anger rise inside him.

*Not long now, Ania.*

"Ania, it's the Polish version of my name. He knows only my closest family call me that."

He handed her the phone and gave her shoulder a reassuring squeeze. "Don't worry about this, Anna, OK? No one threatens a member of my team and he's not going to get away with it. First thing in the morning we'll trace the call and put a search out for him."

"The phone will be a burner and we won't find him."

"What he's doing is against the law, and you know it. This is stalking and harassment and the Protection from Harassment Act includes threatening emails just like this. Try and stay calm."

"Calm, guv? I'm bloody livid. If I ever catch up with the bastard he'll wish he'd never been born."

Her words were drowned out by the sound of an unmarked police car pulling up beside them. Morgan climbed out and slammed the door. He ran over to them, eyes wide with excitement. "Dispatch just told me it was Marshall from the Samaritans!"

"You're kidding?" Anna said.

He ignored her. "You get the bastard?"

Jacob put his hands in his pockets and looked down at the grass. "He killed himself."

"Bloody hell!"

"He was innocent, Bill. Innocent of Julia Crawshaw's murder. Greenwood and the others set him up for the crime to cover up a theft."

Morgan ran a hand through his hair and then flicked the rainwater from his hand on to the grass. "Christ almighty, that's awful."

"Listen, I want an early night," Jacob said. "There's something going on with Sophie and now this Declan business. I need some sleep."

"Declan business?" Morgan asked.

Anna explained, and then Morgan offered to drive her back to her place. "I'll even look under the beds," he said with a wink. "Come on, Anna."

*

Jacob drove home in silence. He was feeling angry and frustrated. The case had spun out of control again and six people had died. Five murders and a suicide. In the soft light of the Alvis's instrument panel, mellowed by the gentle sweeping action of the windscreen wipers, he found himself feeling quiet sympathy for Nathan Brett.

He changed down and took the final turnoff leading to his house.

The man had been innocent and his entire life destroyed by the selfish and murderous actions of monsters. And yet in dealing out his brutal revenge he too had become one of those monsters. Was murder ever justified, he considered. Did Brett have the moral right to do what he had done? He blinked in the gloom and pulled onto the gravelled drive of the Old Watermill.

Switching the engine off, he thought he saw a shadow moving along the other side of the riverbank just beyond the old granary building in the front garden.

*Get a grip, Tom.*

It was nothing, just the movement of a willow tree blowing in the wind, but whoever had left that coin on Sophie's pillow at the conference centre had spooked him. Luckily, she was safe now thanks to Dr Theo Miles, but the break-in of her hotel room would require investigation given her history to Alistair Keeley. He would call Devon and Cornwall Police first thing in the morning and make sure it was being taken seriously.

And then there was Declan Taylor to think about.

Dex the Ex, as Anna sometimes call him.

A very different sort of beast from the Ferryman, Taylor was a violent thug with a short temper and after tonight's performance with the stalking and photo outside the cathedral he had escalated his harassment of Anna. That too would require sorting out.

He sighed and climbed out of the car.

Pushing the key into the back door of the Old Watermill, he had never needed his bed more than right now.

# EPILOGUE

*Friday, 15<sup>th</sup> March*

I n the darkness of his cell, Dr Alistair Keeley studied the calculations one more time. The hard surface made it slightly easier to work out. Removing one variable from the equation, and assuming an impact velocity of twelve metres per second from a seven metre drop, he should survive the fall but with severely broken legs. It was risky, but not as dangerous as screwing up the amount of headache tablets required to look like a convincing suicide.

Plus he wouldn't be conscious, and he couldn't have that.

No, this was the only way and he had to get it right or he'd be in the Underworld long before his time.

When he heard the key in the heavy metal door, he glanced at his watch and smiled.

"Bang on time."

One of the two prison guards cleared this throat, the other twirled a set of keys around on a dull steel chain. "Step outside the cell, Keeley."

He obeyed and they fitted handcuffs on him.

"You've got one hour."

If there was one thing Alistair Keeley knew about the world it was how long he was allowed to spend outside of his cell every day. Twenty-three hours per day inside the four walls of his cell, and one hour outside of the four walls of his cell. A highly-intelligent man with what the prison psychiatrist had described as a dangerously high IQ, it hadn't take him long to calculate this meant a little under ninety-six percent of his life would be spent in his tiny cell.

Or that was the theory.

He walked down the corridor to the phone bank and with his hands still cuffed together, he lifted the greasy, yellow plastic receiver from the cradle and made his call.

"I'm here." The voice was gravelly and agitated.

"You left the coin exactly as I told you to?"

"Yes."

He felt a wave of exhalation ripple through his body. "Good, you did well. Where is she now?"

"In Devon. She stayed with one of the blokes from the conference."

"No Jacob to the rescue?"

"No sign of him. So this is it, I'm finished with this now."

Keeley frowned hard and lowered his voice. "You're finished when I say you are, and you know what I'm capable of if you don't do as you're told, understand?"

The man backed down. "Yes."

"Good. Anyway, not long now until Dr Anderson travels to the Underworld."

A long pause. "What does that mean? I'm not doing it, if that's what you think."

"I never asked you to. Besides, only I know how to send her across the river."

"But how? You're in solitary confinement in a maximum security prison."

The Ferryman closed his eyes and cracked his neck, both sides. Sighing with relief, he put the phone down into the cradle and turned to go back to the darkness. The words were quiet on his lips, for his ears only and not for the guards.

"Just leave that to me."

Printed in Great Britain
by Amazon